THE 13TH PAN BOOK OF HORROR STORIES

Herbert van Thal has compiled a number of anthologies which include some of the writings of James Agate, Ernest Newman and Hilaire Belloc as well as a volume on Victorian Travellers. He has also resuscitated the works of many neglected Victorian writers. In 1971 his autobiography, *The Tops of the Mulberry Trees*, was published, as well as *The Music Lovers' Companion* (with Gervase Hughes). He has just completed a 'biographical anthology' of Walter Savage Landor and is preparing a biography of Caroline of Ansbach, Queen Consort of George II.

Also available in this series

THE PAN BOOK OF HORROR STORIES (Vols 1–12)

THE 13TH
PAN BOOK OF
HORROR STORIES

Edited by
HERBERT VAN THAL

UNABRIDGED

PAN BOOKS LTD : LONDON

This collection first published 1972 by Pan Books Ltd,
33 Tothill Street, London, SW1.

ISBN 0 330 23331 9

2nd Printing 1973

© Pan Books Ltd 1972

Printed in Great Britain by
Richard Clay (The Chaucer Press), Ltd,
Bungay, Suffolk

CONTENTS

ACKNOWLEDGEMENTS

The Editor wishes to acknowledge the following permissions to quote from copyright material:

Norman Kaufman and his agent, London Management Limited of 235/241 Regent Street, London, W1A 2JT, for FLAME and AWAKE, SLEEPING TIGRESS.

David Farrer and his agent, Toby Eady of 27 Chesham Place, London, SW1, for THE REVENGE.

L. Micallef and his agent, London Management Limited, for AGGROPHOBIA.

Carl Thomson and his agent, Toby Eady, for THE SWANS.

David Case and his publishers, Macdonald and Company Limited of St Giles House, 49/50 Poland Street, London, W1A 2LG, for THE DEAD END from 'The Cell and Other Tales of Horror'.

Alan Hillery c/o Pan Books Limited of 33 Tothill Street, London, SW1, for THE MAN WHOSE NOSE WAS TOO BIG.

Harry Turner and his agent, London Management Limited, for THE TWINS.

Dulcie Gray and her agent, London Management Limited, for THE WINDOW WATCHER.

Cecily Ware and London Management Limited, for SPINALONGA by John Ware.

THE 13TH PAN BOOK OF HORROR STORIES

THE MAN WHOSE NOSE WAS TOO BIG

Alan Hillery

The street lights spewed their muffled glow into the London fog as the taxi threaded its way through the traffic and lurched to a halt by the pavement. Outside the pillared entrance to the Cardinal Club, a commissionaire emerged from the evening gloom and, pulling open the car door, offered his hand to extricate me from the horsehair interior. I gratefully accepted and, after paying the driver, allowed myself to be ushered into the cloistered interior of the city's most exclusive club. Upon passing through the foyer, a hand took my cloak and hat and I was shown to a corner of the main room, where stood a small table flanked by two imposing winged arm-chairs. Seating myself in one of them I pulled from my pocket the telegram I had received that morning, and read it for the tenth time.

'Meet me 8 PM – Cardinal Club – Gorman'

The Gorman in question was Sir Miles Gorman, a British diplomat, recently returned from Mombalasa, the largest of the colonies held by Britain in Africa, and the lifelong friend and companion of the late General Randolph Locie, British High Commissioner of the Mombalasian territories.

Locie had died some two months previously and, due to the fact that his death had occurred while on duty, it had received scant attention from the British Press. Indeed, my own paper, the *Metropolitan Evening Standard*, had missed it altogether, and had been forced to confine itself to covering the arrival and subsequent burial of the body in St John's Cemetery, Islington.

The events had been normal in every way, save for two unusual factors; first, nobody in England had been able to ascertain the cause of death, and second, the body had arrived in London in a sealed, lined coffin, with strict instructions that it was to remain unopened. Consequently, no one but the doctors in the Cape Town hospital in which he died had viewed the General's last remains.

These circumstances did not escape comment, but had not caused anyone to probe too deeply, as death is a private thing and none of my Press colleagues, myself included, had felt inclined to trouble the next of kin with questions which may have proved distressing. In any event, when a corpse is transported long distances for burial, it is common practice for it to be in a sealed casket, to prevent decay of the body tissues, and, in addition, it was widely known that some months prior to his death, Locie had been involved in a motor accident; it was thus presumed that death had resulted from injuries sustained at that time, and the unopened coffin was attributed to the fact that the heat of Africa had necessitated immediate embalming, with the resultant need to keep the body from exposure to air.

Thus the questions had remained unanswered and, as the days passed into weeks, the death of General Randolph Locie gave way to more pressing news, and the subject was forgotten.

But not by me.

Call it intuition if you like, or just a newsman's 'nose' for a story, but in my own mind I was far from convinced that everything had been as it appeared. To begin with, almost eight months had elapsed between the date of the alleged car accident and the General's death, eight months, during which time he had been back at his work apparently fully recovered. Also, a veiled rumour had it that he had spent some time in a mental institution during those eight months, but again had returned to work with no obvious ill effects.

The pieces of the puzzle just didn't fit, there was something missing, a common link to join the unrelated incidents. My suspicions were further aroused when I began making enquiries: people in the Foreign Office who could have helped always seemed to be 'unavailable', doctors in the South African hospital 'did not wish to discuss the matter', even the family found it 'too upsetting to talk about'.

Frustration welled up inside me; all my senses told me that I was on the threshold of an outstanding story, and yet there seemed to be nobody willing to open the door. I was almost ready to abandon my attempts when Sir Miles Gorman arrived in London.

Gorman had spent the greater part of his sixty years in the diplomatic service, the latter twenty-three of these in the British Embassy in Mombalasa. During this time he and Locie had become close friends and constant companions, and I felt that he, if anyone, would hold the key that could unlock the mysteries of my story.

My initial overtures were greeted with the same guarded suspicion that I had come to know so well. I never managed to get beyond his secretary. He always seemed to be 'out of town' or 'in conference' or 'indisposed'. I was now convinced beyond doubt that Locie's death had not been from natural causes, and yet I seemed unable to find anyone who would help me.

I appeared to be fighting for a lost cause, when one morning a telegram arrived at my office; it was from Sir Miles Gorman, and it was this telegram that I now held in my hand, as I sat in the winged arm-chair in the main room of the Cardinal Club.

My thoughts were interrupted by the arrival of two large whisky and sodas, accompanied by a tall, elderly man with thinning grey hair, beetling eyebrows and a large waxed moustache. He was wearing a black dinner suit, white shirt and bow tie, and immaculate black patent leather shoes.

As I rose to greet him, I knew instinctively that this was Sir Miles and that, at last, my search for the truth was at an end. He shook me warmly by the hand, and lowered himself with a tired, almost relieved, sigh into the chair opposite me.

'Well, young man', he began, 'you're prompt, I'll say that for you, eight o'clock I said, and eight it is; now what is it that's so important?'

'It's about General Randolph Locie,' I said, looking him directly in the eye. 'There are certain aspects of his illness and death which are, to say the least, suspicious; you were his close friend during the last years of his life and if, as I believe, all was not as it appeared, you would be the most likely person to know what really happened.'

He stiffened momentarily at my words, and a troubled look came into his eyes.

'And what,' he said defensively, 'leads you to assume that the General's unfortunate death was in any way unnatural? Surely you newspaper people received full reports from Cape Town?'

'Reports yes,' I replied, 'details no; it may interest you to learn, Sir Miles, that not one newspaper in this country was able to find the exact cause of death.'

'Brain damage,' he said quickly, 'damage to the lower cells of the brain; you must have known that he was involved in a motor accident – he died from his injuries.'

'Eight months afterwards?' I queried. 'Eight months during which time he was back at the Embassy, obviously fully recovered. Come, Sir Miles, I know it to be true that within days of the accident he was addressing tribal councils, and making a tour of the territories.'

He made no reply, but passed his hand wearily over his brow.

'Also,' I continued, 'I understand that later the General received treatment in a hospital, and still managed to recover sufficiently to take up his duties again, before he died. I ask you, Sir, can you in all honesty expect any clear-thinking individual to believe that despite the circumstances, Locie's death was a normal one?'

Gorman sat silently contemplating his now-empty glass; it was as though some private feud was taking place behind the hard, blue eyes. Almost as if the forces of good and evil were fighting their last battle within his mind.

When at last he spoke, it was in a voice which trembled with emotion.

'You're right, of course,' he nodded, 'I guessed what was wrong when you began hounding me, I knew the longer I eluded you the more your suspicions would be aroused, in any case, someone should know, it's too much to have inside one – to know and be unable to tell,' his voice took on a new gravity. 'Young man, you are about to hear a story so strange, so horrible, so unbelievable that it defies human comprehension, a story of such suffering that the mind of man baulks at its understanding, the story of the last months in the life of General Randolph Locie.'

I felt my heartbeat quicken in anticipation as, with newly charged glass and glowing cigar, Sir Miles Gorman began his tale.

'It began almost eleven months ago, it was a Saturday evening, and Locie and myself had enjoyed dinner at the home of one of the junior embassy officials. After dining, we retired to the veranda for coffee, where we fell to discussing the various affairs affecting the corner of the world which was our responsibility.

'As happens on such occasions, the wine and conversation which flowed, erased time from our minds, and it was not until the small hours of Sunday morning that we finally took leave of our host, and made ready for our journey home.

'Locie, who had drunk rather more than he should, was clearly in no fit state to drive himself, and so I offered to take him home in my own car, before going on to my residence. The General, however, was quite adamant about his capabilities, and insisted that he should drive himself. As a compromise, therefore, we agreed that he should go on ahead, whilst I brought up the rear, to be on hand should any obstacles appear on the road, as was quite usual in that rather desolate corner of Africa.'

Sir Miles paused, and sipped his whisky before continuing.

'We had travelled some twenty miles without seeing a sign of life, when suddenly, for a reason which eludes me to this day, Locie's car swerved violently, left the road, and came to rest with the bonnet nestled against a tree. I can only presume that some animal had wandered onto the road, or else the excess of wine had caused him to lose control.'

'So there was an accident,' I interjected, 'at least that part of the story was true.'

'Oh yes,' he nodded, 'he crashed his car certainly, and for a time it looked fairly serious. When I got to him, he was slumped over the wheel, unconscious, obviously having struck his forehead. Anyway, I carried him to my car, and as the nearest hospital was almost one hundred miles away, I took him to a small medical station in a nearby village, you know the sort of thing, two or three beds and one doctor, mainly there to keep down disease among the natives.

'The doctor examined him and found no broken bones but as he was still deeply unconscious, we decided it would be safer to leave him there until he came round. As I could be of no further assistance, I made my way home and fell into a fitful sleep.

'My work took me out of the district for the next few days, and so I was unable to check on his condition and it was not until the following Friday that I returned to my office in the Embassy. You can imagine, therefore, that I was more than somewhat surprised to find Locie back at his desk, with nothing more to show for his mishap than a small lump on the head.'

'A remarkable recovery,' I murmured.

Sir Miles nodded in agreement.

'Indeed yes, it appears that the concussion had lasted only two days, and as there were no other injuries, the doctor, after a further day's observation, felt fit to allow his patient to leave, and within a week all traces of the accident had disappeared, and the matter was forgotten.'

Gorman paused as further supplies of whisky were laid before us; he took a sip, and continued.

'It was about three weeks later that Locie first began to complain of severe headaches, the source of the pain being located just behind the left eye.

'At first he took little heed of this, reasoning that overwork was the cause, but as time went by, they became progressively worse, until eventually when in the throes of such an attack his screams of agony could be heard throughout the Embassy corridors. As though this condition were not sufficiently bad, he began to faint away at his work, and on these occasions medical help was necessary to restore him.

'Obviously, this state of affairs could not continue, and so he was ordered to rest at home, with daily visits from his doctor.'

'It appears his brain must have received some damage in the accident,' I said, 'something which had not been apparent at the time.'

'This was the assumption upon which the doctor worked,' replied Sir Miles, 'but as I visited him each day, it became obvious that his state of health was deteriorating rapidly. He was losing weight too quickly, he took on a grey, pallid complexion, and the pains in his head, once spasmodic, were now with him continually, until such time that no amount of sedation from his doctor could bring relief.'

'He must have suffered terribly,' I murmured, almost to myself.

'He did indeed,' replied Sir Miles, gravely, 'but the suffering he experienced at this time was nothing compared to that which lay in store for him.'

'So what happened next?'

'Well, it became increasingly apparent that his condition was becoming ever more grave, so it was decided to move him to a hospital in Cape Town.'

'The mental hospital, you mean?'

He shook his head.

'Not at this stage, no, the purpose was to carry out an exploratory operation on his brain, in an endeavour to locate the supposed damage suffered in the accident. Anyway, he was taken to the hospital, and held under observation for a few days, while various tests were carried out in an attempt to avert surgery.

'Needless to say these all proved negative, and the only recourse left to the doctors, was to open the skull, and examine the brain first-hand.

'I sought permission from the surgeon to observe the operation, and in view of my position and close friendship with Locie, this was granted.

'Upon the appointed day I seated myself in the observation chamber adjacent to the operating theatre, and watched with bated breath as the inert form of my friend was wheeled in, and laid on the table.

'It was as though I looked upon a stranger – the eyes, once so clear and bright, were dark hollows sunk deep into the head, the frail body, wasted almost beyond recognition, with shiny grey skin stretched tautly over the framework of bones, whilst his head, shaved clean for the forthcoming operation, gleamed beneath the lights.

'With deft fingers, the surgeon traced a faint line across the head, about five inches above the eyes, and as I watched in horror, he took a saw, and as though he were a carpenter saw-ing wood, he laid it gently across the line, and holding the head steady with one hand, forced the saw down, causing the sharp teeth to bite deep into the skull.

'That sound, young man, will live with me until the end of my days, and yet even this was not sufficient to prepare me for what was to follow.

'For one hour the surgeon probed and examined the now exposed brain, and found nothing, everything was normal, nothing appeared out of place.

'With a resigned gesture he turned to me, and as he did so, the silence of the room was shattered by a piercing scream. All eyes turned to a young nurse, whose trembling hand was point-ing to the bloody splodge which was Locie's head.

' "There's something there," she whispered, "it moved! It moved!"

'In a flash, the surgeon was bending over Locie, feverishly searching for the object which the nurse had seen, and I felt my stomach turn as he withdrew his hand, holding in the forceps what at first appeared to be a writhing clot of blood. He shook it gently, and six waving legs became apparent, six hairy legs, attached to a small bloated body – it was a spider!'

I recoiled in horror at his words.

'A spider?' I gasped, 'in his head?'

Sir Miles nodded.

'Yes, a spider, it seems that during his stay at the medical station, and while he was still suffering from concussion, the spider, in its search for warmth during the cold African night, had crawled onto his face, and up his nose, there burrowing deep into the delicate membranes. Locie, of course being unconscious, felt nothing. The pain he subsequently suffered being due to the spider slowly eating its way into his head.'

'And he died?'

'On the contrary, once the source of trouble had been removed, he made a rapid recovery, and within a few months, although he was still weak, was able to return to work.'

'And then?'

'All seemed to be well at first, he gradually put on weight and was able to enjoy much of his old life. The worst seemed to be over; he never knew the truth of course, that would have been too much for him. Anyway, he seemed to be fully recovered, when suddenly within the space of a week, the pains returned threefold, the skin again took on the grey sheen, and this time, worst of all, he went blind, and had a complete mental breakdown.'

I felt my skin crawl.

'Good God!' I said quietly, 'not another spider?'

Sir Miles looked at me for a long time before he answered, and when he did, it was in a voice drawn with tension.

'No, young man,' he said, 'not another spider.'

'Then in heaven's name what?'

He ignored my question, and continued the story. 'As I said, Locie's mind snapped, and there was no alternative but to remove him to an asylum. At first, I visited him regularly, but it was hopeless, his sightless eyes saw nothing, his deranged mind was unable to function. Gradually, the man was reduced to a vegetable, and it became clear that the end was close.

'The doctor who had performed the original operation was called in, and he agreed that Locie's only chance of survival lay in a further operation, his opinion being that the spider must have caused irreparable damage to the brain during its stay in Locie's head. Damage which may have been overlooked amid the shock which had been present at the first operation.

'A date was set, and once again I watched numbly as my colleague was laid upon the slab beneath the harsh glare of the lamps.

'Once more I heard the sickening crunch as the steel teeth of the saw bit into the head.

'His macabre preliminaries completed, the surgeon laid aside the saw, and prised open the skull. Suddenly he recoiled with a cry of disgust.

'There, completely embedded in the frontal lobe of Locie's brain, was a moving, crawling, festering mass of tiny legs and bodies, spiders scuttled everywhere, some running two by two as if performing some ghastly dance, some with eggs upon their backs, fleeing from the glare into some darkened crevice inside the wretched General's head.

'The surgeon hurredly flicked away several blood spattered specimens which had succeeded in crawling on to his hand and arm, and reeled back from the table.'

'You mean,' I asked in horror, 'all these spiders had gained entry through the nose?'

He shook his head. 'No,' he replied, 'the truth of the matter is that the original spider had belonged to a species which had a particularly short gestation period, and what no one could have known was that it was a female, and had found time to lay her eggs whilst living in Locie's brain. These eggs had hatched in the warmth, and it was this that led to the second batch being born into his brain cells, which in turn they devoured in their effort to stay alive.'

'And the General?'

'Mercifully he died without regaining consciousness. Of course the true story was never told; after all, who would have believed it?'

The following morning I took the bus to Islington, and my steps led me to St John's cemetery. I had little difficulty in locating my goal, and soon I was standing beside the grave of

General Randolph Locie. I let my thoughts wander to the occupant of the coffin lying beneath my feet, what suffering the wretched being must have felt, what anguish, what pain, what agony, before death ran down the final curtain on the entire ghastly charade.

As I stood there, lost in my thoughts, something moved, and I watched in fascinated horror as two small, bloated spiders emerged from the wet earth of the grave, and crawling away were lost in the grass.

I felt my senses reel, as I leaned against the headstone for support, and, bending quietly over the cold damp slab, I was violently sick.

FLAME !

Norman Kaufman

I like to burn children.

I *like* to burn them.

There you are, I've said it: now be fair, you weren't really THAT shocked. There's too much hypocrisy in this world already, and if people took my tip and aired their secret thoughts once in a while, there'd be a lot less of these mental conflicts and restraints and repressions that, believe me, are collectively responsible for so much breakdown in health that you see all about you day by day –

But forgive me, I digress: let me enlarge on what I was saying at the start.

Because I really do enjoy burning them and that's gospel truth. And I'm not mad either. I certainly don't *FEEL* mad; and as for looks, well, I suppose you could say I'm one of the great nondescript. I'm taller than average and I'm very thin, and I've only got this one suit, which is now a very shiny blue, and two shirts, both white, or nearly white. My hair is sort of dark brown, my eyes are the same, my skin is kind of sallow. There you are, just plain ordinary-looking: no madness, no twitching, no froth at the corner of my mouth.

But let me put you in the picture: let me tell you what happened this very morning.

There I was, sitting on the top deck of this bus, smoking peacefully, not a care in the world; and then a young woman came upstairs and sat in front of me; and blow me down if she didn't have a young child in her arms – well, I say child, but perhaps baby would be the better word, for it was no more than eight or nine months old. Of course, the woman *HAS* to bring the little tot upstairs on the bus, because it's more than flesh and blood can stand to go without a smoke for ten minutes, regardless of the baby's health. (Pardon the attempt at sarcasm, but these things do annoy me, especially when I can't do a thing about it.)

But there it is: she sat down, slung the baby over her left shoulder and proceeded to light up one of her tipped fags. The infant's legs dangled over the mother's chest and its head nestled between her shoulder and her neck. And right about then, I felt the first spark of – well, of elation, I suppose you could call it. It's the feeling I always get when such an opportunity presents itself.

The baby gazed unwinkingly at me – God knows what goes on in these tiny infantile minds! – but I knew in my heart that this was too good an opening to miss. The upper deck was barely populated, I was on the back seat, there was no one else in my field of vision – except of course, my intended source of entertainment.

I gave the woman a moment or two to settle into the smoking-and-staring-out-of-the-window routine. And then I moved, swiftly. Perhaps some inkling of my objective pene-trated the baby's subconscious, for I swear it opened its tiny mouth to yell out.

And that was precisely the moment I chose to stub my cigarette on its little pink tongue.

Well well!

If you could only have been there! Never before and never since have I heard such a scream: a thin wail of pure un-earthly terror and uncomprehending agony that flayed at my nerves as I quickly dropped my cigarette to the floor and ex-tinguished it under my shoe.

The young woman slewed round in sudden shock; other heads turned round farther up the platform; and I sat there, looking for all the world like a man who had been enjoying the comparative peace of a bus ride when a little brat had abruptly and inexplicably begun shrieking its head off.

By the time the uproar had subsided somewhat, and the young woman had ascertained the source and cause of injury, yours truly had alighted from the bus, losing myself quickly in the throngs that congested the Saturday marketplace. From there I set out into the country: I love my week-end walks, away from the stink and the smoke of city life. And it gives me time to think of — how can I put it? — of refinements to my little pastime. I wonder if it's at all feasible for me to smoke my cigarette until it's just a stub of, say, a half-inch in length; and then, if I can manage to find similar circumstances to those on the bus this morning, instead of just touching the tip of the butt to the child's tongue, I can *leave it in the mouth* — it's certainly worth thinking about.

This looks a nice quiet spot for a lie-down. A bit of a rest, I think, and then back to the lodgings for tea ...

I'm Timmy and I'm seven and this is Phil and he's seven as well and we're here in the woods about a mile past the market centre. We've found this old bloke lying here asleep. Well, we think he's old anyway, he must be about thirty-one or thirty-nine or forty-seven or something, and he's dead thin and he's got brown hair and his face is all pale like I am when I've been sick after eating too much toffee and then Mummy smacks me.

Me and Phil are having a game what we've tried to play before but somebody always stops us. We've tied this old bloke up so he can't get away and we've put some sticky-tape over his mouth so he can't say anything to anyone and Phil's daddy is a policeman and Phil's found some very old handcuffs and we've put them on this bloke's hands and we've lost the key but I suppose we'll find it somewhere but we don't need it yet anyway.

It's a good job we put them handcuffs on first and that sticky-tape, because he's waking up now and he's making all sorts of grunts and things through the tape, but me and Phil are going to have our game first and then we'll let him go. I got some matches out of the kitchen this morning and I hope Mummy doesn't find out 'cos she won't half bash me if she does. Anyway we've got pokers as well from our houses, and I don't think anyone'll miss them 'cos we've got electric fires now and so has Phil's house as well.

We've lit the matches and we're making a little fire here and we're putting the ends of the pokers in the fire and we're waiting till they've got a red tip, you know, sort of glowing and hot. It doesn't half take a long time to get hot though. But Phil says he's waiting till his poker is *WHITE* at the end and not red, like he's seen on the pictures on the telly.

Now I think mine's hot enough anyway, so I'm putting it on this bloke's legs and face and arms, like this and like this. And Phil's doing it now as well, and his poker's really *WHITE* at the end...

Oh this is really funny, me and Phil are laughing like anything: this bloke's making all *SORTS* of daft noises, and he's rolling about all over the floor, but he can't get up because we tied his legs together as well. His eyes are all wide open and staring, and he's kind of – well, it's like all wet coming from under the sticky-tape, all spit and sick and things. Ooh, look at his eyes, Phil!

Wonder what happens if I put my poker in one of his eyes. Like this.

What a funny smell.

He's stopped moving now. He's just lying there now. So me and Phil can just go on with the game without having to mess about. It's a smashing game this. Smashing.

Me and Phil, we like burning grown-ups.

We *like* burning them.

THE TWINS

Harry Turner

Hans and Carl Van Droog were identical twins. Nature had endowed them so exactly alike that even the doctor who had brought them into the world couldn't distinguish between them. Both were dwarfs of unusually hideous appearance, their backs surmounted by humps of twisted bone. Their gargoyle features and slavering lips were grotesquely accentuated by tiny eyes that peeped from between ridges of coarse, mottled flesh. As children, their appearance on the street caused dogs to bark and women to cross themselves. No vestige of human kindness ever touched them; they were deserted as babes, shunned as adults and stared at like beasts.

Being so totally ostracized it was natural perhaps for them to turn in on each other, establishing an intense rapport that was rare, even for exact twins.

They grew to repulsive adulthood in the cobbled streets of Amsterdam, their education derived from the charity of local nuns, pious Catholics who taught them to read and thank God for his merciful blessings.

No foster mother, however well intentioned, could bear them under her roof for more than a few weeks. With mumbled excuses they would turn Hans and Carl out on to the streets again to rummage for scraps between the gabled merchants' palaces along the Herengracht Canal.

On their thirteenth birthday, passably literate and immensely strong for their size, they ventured across the city to the open fields north of the Amstel.

It was here they first saw the travelling fair from Antwerp in Belgium. The blaring music of the barrel organs and the gaudily painted caravans exercised a powerful influence over the two brothers. They watched in awe as the sideshows unfolded, with jugglers, musicians, fire-eaters and sword-swallowers.

The owner of the fair, Jon Werper, spotted the twins almost immediately, and recognizing their commercial potential, decided to approach them directly. He was the first human being, apart from the nuns, who had addressed them without fear or obvious revulsion.

Even the succession of foster mothers had treated them like lame animals.

Werper was a large, genial Belgian, with a showman's gift for rhetoric. Spellbound, the twins heard him commend their size, their shape and, God be praised, even their looks. Within a week they were working for him, erecting tents, carrying leather buckets, cleaning the brass on his caravan wheels.

He fed them well and lodged them in a spare trailer alongside the horses. After a month he suggested that they take part in one of his sideshows. It would be worth their while, better wages than for just cleaning and carrying. Reluctant at first, they finally agreed when he threw down a small pouch bulging with guilders – one month's pay in advance!

They were an immediate success. Crowds flocked to the fair and watched the twins as they did cartwheels and other gymnastic tricks learnt in the Amsterdam backstreets. It was gruelling work, no less arduous than skivvying, but they took to it with resolution.

One evening when the crowds had gone and Jon Werper was asleep, the brothers crept from beneath the straw of their trailer and spied on him through a crack in the door of his caravan. Around Werper's waist was a stout belt with brass studs, attached to this was a huge pouch containing the day's takings. Carl looked at Hans and their two pairs of tiny eyes blazed with sudden excitement.

Carl eased the caravan door open and they squeezed inside, hands clasped together like babes in the wood. Werper grunted in his sleep and half turned towards them. In an instant, and as silently as wraiths, the twins fell upon his huge body. Hans seized his arms and Carl pressed his stunted, horny thumbs deep into Werper's windpipe.

He died with scarcely a gurgle and after stripping him of his money belt they set light to his caravan and fled.

The authorities cared very little for travelling fairs and so their investigation during the subsequent hullaballoo was brief and cursory. An unfortunate accident it seemed, that had not only destroyed the person of genial Jon Werper but also frightened away his two prize performers, the pathetic brothers Van Droog.

Carl and Hans laid low for several weeks, living on nuts and vegetable husks, sharing everything as always, exactly fifty-fifty. Their short experience in Werper's fairground had been enough, however, to determine them on a career which would repay some of the insults and sneers heaped on them by their more fortunate fellow-citizens. Their decision to travel Europe as a two-man novelty act, was commercially sound. So hideous were they as they wrestled nude, or executed intricate balancing tricks that word of their performance spread like wildfire.

By their eighteenth birthday they owned a fine caravan, two black Belgian dray-horses and a wardrobe of rich costumes to clothe their twisted bodies. They recruited other acts, bearded ladies, fire-eaters, Indian jugglers, snake charmers and even a troupe of musicians. They grew rich, were careful to pay their performers well, and always kept their own act as the star attraction, which indeed it was.

Love came to the brothers Van Droog shortly after their twentieth birthday. They had just completed a successful tour of Northern France and were moving homewards through Holland.

Passing by a little village, their caravan came across another small fair. It was a shabby affair, with mangy dogs jumping hoops and a rickety, pock-marked barrel-organ. The brothers stopped to watch, grinning patronizingly at the feebleness of it all.

Suddenly, from behind the barrel-organ, stepped a young

gipsy girl of twenty or so. She was a ravishing beauty, with raven hair and smooth round breasts that bounced as she walked. Ignoring Carl and Hans she seized a tambourine and flung herself into a wild dance, skirts flaring, legs flashing. A few village onlookers applauded wildly and threw coins while Carl and Hans exchanged glances. Carl leaned forward and pointed his ape-hand at the girl.

'You dance for us,' he cried, 'and we shall pay you well.'

'Yes,' echoed Hans excitedly, 'join us and you shall have clothes and wines and a fine caravan.'

The gipsy girl surveyed the grisly pair with sudden interest. She was poor and hungry and the sight of these rich caravans with their big black horses and coloured pennants made her pulse beat even faster. Before she could answer, however, a burly Negro with a shining bald head sprang down from the barrel-organ.

'She cannot accept your offer,' he cried harshly. 'She owes many guilders. She must work for me to pay all her debts. Now be off – you pair of foul devils.'

The brothers eyed the menacing figure of the Negro. Although quite old he was built like an ox, with bulging shoulders and a drum of a chest.

'How much does she owe?' asked Carl, 'how many guilders?'

The Negro scowled, and the girl shrank from him. 'She is not for sale. She works for me. Be off with you or I'll break your ugly heads.'

Carl and Hans glanced at each other, there were still a few villagers watching the scene and any precipitate action would certainly be remembered, and even reported to the authorities. Hans cupped his paw to his mouth and whispered a snatch of words to his brother. Carl nodded and turned to the Negro.

'You may keep the girl, blackamoor,' he said viciously, 'we have no need of her.'

At this the girl fell to her knees and crossed herself. The Negro grinned, showing huge white teeth.

'On your way, twisted ones,' he cried triumphantly, 'and may the devil take you.'

Ten miles away and an hour later, as darkness gathered in the forest, Carl and Hans pitched camp and lit wood-fires. Their fellow performers huddled together and drank warm broth while one of the musicians strummed a mandolin. One by one the performers retired to their caravans until the camp was silent. The brothers waited another hour until they were satisfied that their compatriots were fast asleep before setting off on foot along the track which led back to the village. It was a longish haul, but the brothers scampered along like monkeys, chattering and laughing excitedly. On the village outskirts they threw themselves flat and wormed their way towards the Negro's camp. A fire crackled, throwing flames high into the dark sky. The brothers could see it clearly from the safe shelter of a dense bush. The gipsy girl was pushing logs onto the fire and as she leant forward the flickering light showed up her wobbling breasts.

Carl and Hans whimpered and licked their lips. The Negro was asleep a few yards from the girl, his big chest moving up and down, his arms spreadeagled. Carl touched his brother's shoulder and they sprang forward together, leaping clear over the blazing campfire. The gipsy girl gave a cry of fear and then Carl's hand clamped over her mouth. Hans crouched low and drew a long dagger from his belt. The Negro, disturbed by the girl's cry, rolled sideways and began to kneel up. Hans took a pace forward and plunged the dagger, hilt-deep into his throat.

The Negro jack-knifed, blood spouting from the severed jugular, and fell dead as a stone at Hans' little feet.

Seizing a hand each, the brothers dragged the startled girl into the forest and back onto the narrow, dusty track. When she realised that they were not intent on murdering her, she felt less afraid. Supported on either side by their hideous but powerful arms, she skimmed over the rough ground like a young gazelle. Once safely at their caravan Hans and Carl made a soft bed for the girl in an empty trailer and gave her wine and fruit. She ate and drank hungrily, sitting cross-legged among the silk cushions while the brothers squatted a yard away, watching her in fascination.

She was a sharp, quick-witted girl and she quickly realized that the brothers' interest in her could be turned to her advantage. She smiled coquettishly at the repulsive pair, deliberately revealing her thighs and leaning forward to allow them a glimpse of her breasts. Eventually she feigned tiredness and lay back into the cushions. Hans and Carl crept silently to their caravans to dream their special dreams.

The next morning they cut the sword-swallower's head off while he was asleep, told their fellow-performers that he had fled with the day's takings, and set the gipsy girl up in his caravan. From that moment onwards she was treated like a princess. The brothers filled her caravan with perfume and silken drapes, they bought her a new horse and decorated the animal with plumes of ostrich feathers and silver bells.

She ate at the brothers' table and they insisted on giving her only the choicest cuts, the finest wines. She danced for them and shared top-billing at the fair. Something about the combination, a beautiful gipsy girl and two vile trolls, seemed to exercise a huge fascination for the crowds. They flocked to see the show and often followed it on foot to the next village to see it for a second time.

The months went by and the brothers displayed no sign of losing interest in the gipsy girl. She knew by now that they both nursed a raging lust for her but were afraid to show it openly.

Indeed, anything, which in their view might offend her, was treated with the utmost severity. When the east wind blew they purchased a mountain of blankets just to keep her warm. When her horse grew lame they flogged the poor beast to death with staves and fed his carcass to the dogs.

In early spring, nearly a year after she had joined them, a curious and unexpected incident took place. She called them both into her caravan late at night and bade them sit down. As always in her presence they were subdued and anxious to satisfy her smallest whim. She dropped her silken robe and stood in front of them quite naked.

'Come, my little ones,' she said impatiently. 'I am ready now.'

First Hans, and then Carl, ventured to reach out and touch her proud body. Swiftly she pulled them both down beside her and helped them struggle out of their clothes.

A child was born to the gipsy girl during the autumn that followed. A fine child with raven hair and strong, straight limbs. Carl and Hans were delirious with pleasure. Proudly they stooped over the crib, cooing and gurgling at the splendid infant. The gipsy girl, meanwhile, surveyed them with a cool and cynical eye.

Their generosity had grown now to a level of wanton recklessness. Her body was clothed in robes from Paris and the Orient, jewels and gold pendants decorated her throat. Her caravan was drawn by four white Arab stallions, a black servant fanned her as she lounged on embroidered cushions. No luxury was overlooked, no treasure too costly for her to possess.

The child grew and was doted over by the twins. They even purchased tiny rings to decorate his chubby fingers.

One bright September morning, on the child's first birthday, Carl and Hans brought their caravans into the ancient city of Orléans. Business had been very brisk and the brothers and their ravishing gipsy girl were now famous throughout Europe.

The brothers left their servants to erect the tents and set off alone to scour the Orléans markets for further treasures. By mid-afternoon huge storm clouds had gathered and a raw wind lashed the city. Carl and Hans abandoned their shopping expedition early, anxious to return to the gipsy girl and their child before the storm broke. As they rode into the camp the rain started, a mighty deluge that whipped the canvas tents into a frenzy and turned the fields into a swirling quagmire. Hastily they tied their horses and scampered towards the shelter of the caravans.

As Carl mounted the first step he suddenly froze and put a gnarled finger to his lips. Hans stopped at his brother's signal and they both remained like statues – listening.

The gipsy girl's voice came filtering through the half-open window – it sounded shrill and urgent.

Carl sprang silently to the top step and pressed his eye to a crack in the door. What he saw made his body convulse like a severed worm.

The gipsy girl was in the arms of a tall, bronzed man, who was covering her upturned face with hungry, wanton kisses. Her arms encircled his body, pressing him closer in a frenzy of passion.

Suddenly she arched against him and laughed. 'Oh, those fools,' she said, nuzzling his throat. 'Those two repulsive swine. How I despise them.'

The man kissed her again and joined in her laughter.

'My pretty one,' he said, 'how long before we take flight and leave those gargoyles for ever? I can't bear the thought of them drooling over you.'

'Soon,' she said tossing her mane of hair. 'Soon. When I have treasures enough to buy us a passage to Spain and a fine house with servants.'

The man embraced her again. 'My clever one,' he said. 'And the child – they really believe it's *theirs*?'

'Yes, yes,' cried the girl, shaking with laughter. 'They really believe it's *theirs*. Why, those two monstrous fools couldn't sire a toad!'

The man picked up a flagon of wine and drank deeply. 'He is my son,' he said proudly, pointing to the crib. 'My own son, Rodriguez. What have you suffered, my sweet angels – but it won't be for much longer.'

The girl stroked the man's cheek. He was a gipsy like herself, tall and swarthy with dark curls and a proud moustache.

'I would suffer anything for you,' she whispered. 'When I knew I had your child growing in me I *knew* I had to think of some clever plan – some pretty trick to deceive them both.'

The man kissed her forehead.

'It was a stroke of genius,' he said. 'But I must fly now before they return.'

Outside the caravan step Carl and Hans clung to each other. Silent tears of rage rolled down their cheeks. Hans drew his dagger but Carl stayed him with a gesture. Quietly they retraced their steps and tip-toed to their caravan.

The next morning the storm had passed but the camp was a hive of activity. Many of the tents had been damaged and there was much work to be done, freeing the caravan wheels from the mud.

The latest and most elaborate addition to the fair was a house of horror which the brothers had brought from Holland. Gawping villagers paid to go inside a dark labyrinth of passages and hear hideous groans and have artificial spiders brush against their faces. A new refinement had been the dismembered corpse. Customers were invited to plunge their fingers into a rotting tomato – the eye – run their hands over some dank sheep offal – the entrails – and touch a mat of goat hair – the dead man's head. As all this took place in total darkness the general effect was suitably spine-chilling.

As the sun warmed the damp fields, the gipsy girl relaxed on a pile of Turkish carpets, watching the frenzied activity and eating grapes. At noon she found herself dozing off but was awakened by Carl's hand gently touching her cheek. He had a curious expression on his hideous face and beckoned for her to follow him. Hans was waiting at the house of horror and greeted her courteously.

'Our *latest* sideshow,' he said blandly. 'Carl and I would like to show it to you.'

The gipsy girl felt an uneasy prickle at the nape of her neck. It was rare for them to involve her in acts or sideshows other than her own.

'I don't feel like it,' she said, holding back.

The brothers took her arms, one on each side.

'Come,' they said in unison. 'We want to show you.'

Inside the wooden house it was as black as night and Carl closed the door behind them.

'You must pretend,' he said, 'that we are going to let you touch a freshly killed corpse. Tell us how *real* you think it is.'

'Yes,' said Hans, 'we should like to hear your *opinion*.'

With a numb, spiralling dread the gipsy girl allowed herself to be projected into a damp, airless room. Carl pushed her towards a dim black shape.

'It's only a table,' he said, giggling softly. 'Just feel it! Go on, touch it!'

Slowly the girl reached out her hand – and then withdrew it. Carl took her wrist firmly and pushed it back again – this time her fingers closed round a soft pulpy object.

'It's a tomato,' giggled Hans, 'supposed to be the dead man's eye.'

Carl moved her arm quickly to the left and it came into contact with a mass of wet, slippery pipes.

'His guts,' explained Hans. 'Sheep offal. Clever, isn't it, my dear?'

The girl tried to twist away but Carl held her in a vice-like grip.

'Now his hair,' said Hans gleefully, 'still warm with blood.'

The girl's hand was plunged into a warm hair mass – and she screamed.

'Only a goatskin,' said Carl, tightening his grip.

By now the girl was trembling helplessly, possessed by a terror that seemed to melt the very marrow of her bones.

'This way, my dear,' cooed Hans, propelling her sideways.

Suddenly they were in a small candlelit chamber, furnished sparsely with chairs and a low table. The flickering light threw grotesque shadows against the wooden walls. Hans closed the door and grinned wolfishly at the gipsy girl.

'Realistic enough for you, my dear?' he said, a thread a saliva hanging from his lip.

She tried to mouth a reply but none came. It was all too hideous, too horrible.

'You've killed him,' she suddenly blurted. 'The only man I've ever loved. You loathsome degenerates. You've killed him.'

Carl and Hans exchanged quick glances.

'Killed your lover?' said Carl. 'My dear girl, what are you talking about?'

'In there,' screamed the girl, 'that was a *real* eye, *real* blood, *real* hair, you've killed him, you've killed him.'

And with this she slid to the floor sobbing and moaning. For some minutes she remained on her knees, shoulders heaving, breath rasping, and then Carl rapped on the table.

'Get up,' he ordered, 'you've got a visitor.'

Slowly she lifted her head, and her heart missed a beat. Standing against the wall, his dark hair tumbling over his forehead, was her lover. He looked bewildered, but very much alive.

With a little cry the gipsy girl flung herself into his arms.

'Jesu be praised,' she sobbed, clinging to him.

The man kissed her and held her close.

'I had a message that you were ill,' he said, 'God knows how they found me.'

Carl and Hans stood motionless, eyeing the lovers with a cruel detachment. Suddenly Carl seized a small casket from the table and held it out.

'For you,' he said simply, 'a wedding present from Hans and I. *Open it.*'

The gipsy girl took the casket with trembling hands and lifted the hinged lid. Her lover stood close and looked over her shoulder.

Inside on a small velvet cushion was their child's head, freshly severed; the eyes had been torn from the sockets and the scalp was a pulpy mass where the hair had been neatly sliced away in one complete piece.

THE SWANS

Carl Thomson

It was autumn again.

Summer still lingered in the heat of the sun, but autumn had unmistakably arrived. The yellow and pale-green leaves of the fragile silver birches shimmered in the cool breeze. The tall beech trees looked elegant in their new-season finery of gold and orange.

We strolled noisily through the rusty carpet of fallen leaves – our hands buried in the pockets of our overcoats, our eyes enchanted by the glorious colours of the countryside. The air was musty with the decay and the subtle scent of late-season flowers that intoxicated us with a drunken sleepiness. We did not speak. The heavy mood of the afternoon cast a spell upon us: a spell of silence that we had no inclination to break. We waded through glades of bracken that snapped and crackled under our persuasive progress. A pair of pheasants clattered into the air and flapped out of sight behind a bank of holly bushes, resplendent with red waxen berries. We were startled by their sudden flight and she automatically grabbed my arm. Then we laughed aloud at our momentary fear – but still we didn't speak. We continued our walk, hand-in-hand, adrift in pleasurable thoughts. She, of her love for me? Me, of my love for the countryside.

We scrambled over a bank and stumbled along the uneven surface of the lane. Loose stones rattled under our shoes and ran ahead, sparking off each other. A large flock of lapwings wheeled into the air, warned of a possible danger by our noisy journey along the lane. Their plaintive cries saddened us and we were sorry to have disturbed them. A green woodpecker laughed hysterically as it flew to an old fir-tree deeper in the wood. We laughed too. It didn't matter that we hadn't understood the joke.

As we drew near the village, the sun faded and a light drizzle began to fall. We turned up the collars of our coats and walked more hurriedly. We hadn't gone very far when the drizzle became a shower and the shower a heavy rain.

A few metres from the lane I saw a small wooden shack – partially hidden by a luxuriant growth of ivy. The door was open and hanging precariously from the top hinge, the window-frame was missing. Nevertheless, it looked like a sanctuary from the fury of the elements.

We ran to it, and under the protection of its leaking roof, we took off our overcoats and shook the rain from them. As our eyes became accustomed to the gloom, we saw the water trickling down the walls and dripping from the ceiling. We crammed ourselves into the one, cobwebbed corner that was dry. We wove together into a passionate embrace, confiding ourselves to each other.

There was an especial sweetness about her lips that afternoon. I was tantalized by the smoothness of her damp cheeks and fascinated by the drops of rain on her eye-lashes. I kissed her long black hair. The scent of her body sent thrills of excitement through me. I tasted the bitterness of bruised rose petals from the crushed flower in her hair. I felt the flutter of her eye-lashes on my neck. I held her tighter in my arms and fell in love.

A small spider descended on a silken thread and began to spin a web between her cool damp hair and my flushed cheek. Its busy little feet tickled me and I jerked my head back in surprise. She stared with disbelief at the cruelty of my sudden movement. Then she saw the spider and giggled. She raised a slender finger and enticed the gentle creature on to it. I felt the coolness of her hand against my face and was reminded of my love for her. She was absorbed watching the spider run along the back of her hand. I tilted up her face and made her look at me. As she raised her head I saw a tear sparkle in the corner of one of her eyes. I leaned forward and softly caressed her lips with mine – then I asked her to marry me. She lowered her eyes and an enigmatic smile curled on her mouth. I knew then

that she would deny me. I kissed her bowed head and my
hands fell to my sides. She raised a hand above our heads.
From it hung the spider, spinning round and round on its
silver thread. She lowered it to the dusty floor and we watched
it scamper to the dark safety of a broken flower-pot. I took her
hand and we stepped out into the sweet-smelling, newly-
refreshed countryside.

The rain had stopped. We walked silently, listening to the
insistent dripping from the trees. The sodden leaves clung to
our shoes and the mud made our feet heavy.

As we approached the first cottages to the village, we became aware of a faint whistling noise. We stopped to listen
and turned towards the sound. The whistling grew louder and
then – through the gathering darkness of the evening – a flock
of Whooper swans flew over, one after the other. Their graceful necks were outstretched, their large wings beating in
unison. The air, forced between their pinions, whistled a
haunting music. We were enthralled at the power and majesty
of these beautiful swans as they flew over – heading south for
the winter. We stared upwards, long after they had passed
from view behind the trees of the wood.

She sighed deeply. I turned to her in surprise. Tears were
running down her cheeks. I put my arm around her and drew
her to me.

Her voice was unsteady as she spoke. 'Darling. It has been
the most perfect day of my life. And I shall never forget it, as
long as I live.'

I looked down at her pale white face, framed by the long,
black tresses of her hair and I knew that she had to be mine –
mine for all time. I turned my head away and drew her closer
to my side. I felt her nestle her head against my shoulder. As
we walked through the sleepy centre of the village, I could see
the image of her face hanging before me in the dusk of the
evening. That face was for ever engraved on my mind.

We did not speak.

I unlatched the cottage door and we entered the warmth of my hidden retreat. I piled an armful of logs on the glowing coals of the parlour fire and coaxed the embers into vivid, crackling flames. I sat back on my heels watching the spectrum of colours and listened to the hiss of the damp wood. I watched – fascinated by the little jets of steam that burst forth from suffocating cavities.

A sharp retort. The vicious bite from a fleeing spark jerked me from my musing and I fell back onto the carpet. Again I was startled – this time by a peal of merry laughter. I leaned my head against the seat of an arm-chair and looked up into the smiling face of my mistress. She held toward me a cup of steaming tea. I took it from her and she knelt at my side. I put the cup on the floor and leaned forward to pull her down into my arms. She laughed again and held her arms above her head, out of my reach. As she did so, the cup that she was holding tipped and a cascade of scalding tea poured over my reaching arm.

The last thing that I remember clearly was the expression of her face – her lips parted with horror, her eyes very large and round.

I remember launching myself at her and wrapping my arms about her. I remember us falling – me on top of her. I remember, though now it is beginning to get rather misty, holding her by her shoulders and shaking her roughly up and down. I seem to remember her head banging on the polished brass fender around the fire, but I cannot be sure. The last thing that I can recollect was the pain from the hot tea that was spilled over my bare arms.

Maybe it was several days – it seemed like a vacant eternity – or could it have been only a few hours? I shall never know.

The fire is dead. It is funny that that should be the first thing I notice. The fire is cold and grey. There is no heat coming from it at all. The room is cold. I am cold. I am kneeling. I am hunched forward on my elbows in a position of deep obeisance. I stare vacantly at the fire. That dead, grey dust holds my attention. I am unable to turn my eyes away. As I watch, the dark-grey, charred image of a twig disintegrates.

There is no sound as it crumbles into powder. A wave of icy fear covers my body. Involuntarily, I close my eyes. I am aware of the heavy throb of my blood pounding in my head.

A sudden attack of cramp in my right leg makes me thrust out the leg and I spin around in an effort to ease the muscle. As I turn and fall backwards, I bump into something cold behind me. In a reflex action, I roll over in the opposite way, the cramp in my leg almost making me cry out with agony. Then I cry out. A loud, disembodied scream. A scream that sounds as if it is coming from a great distance and from another person. But I know that it is coming from me.

Her head is bent and lying on her shoulder. Her hair is covering the upper part of her face. Beneath this black veil I can see the gaping hole of her mouth and the startling whiteness of her bared teeth. There is a black line running from the corner of her mouth, down the side of her cheek onto the naked whiteness of her ear. This black line fascinates me. What can it be? It is so straight. I wonder why she doesn't move. Why is she sleeping with her body contorted in such an awkward manner? Gingerly I reach out my hand and touch her marble cheek. I touch the straight black line with an inquisitive finger. A piece of it flakes away under my finger-nail. I withdraw my hand sharply. Again I feel a stab of fear and my scalp prickles. I'm sure that my hair is standing up on the nape of my neck.

Why is she so cold? But even as I wonder, I know that she is dead and that I have killed her.

The hot coffee warmed me and I became alive again. I picked up the mug from the kitchen table and wandered through into the sitting-room. I stood in the middle of the room staring listlessly at the roaring fire, and before it, on the carpet, the undisturbed body of my late mistress. I cupped the mug of coffee between my hands and its warmth pleased me. I stared for several minutes until my eyes went out of focus and I had a blurred image of the room. Then a feeling of irritation crept over me. An itching, nagging irritation. I scratched my head with a nervous finger. I felt the sharp sting of pain as my finger-nail ripped away the skin and the hair-oil seared the wound.

'Damn! It's her!' I had to get rid of her. I had to be able to sit in front of my fire without her lying there in the way. 'Damn her!' I returned to the kitchen and put the empty mug in the sink. From the shelf above the table, I took a carving-knife and returned to the sitting-room. I went over to the fire and picked up a small log. I placed it upright on the hearth. The carving-knife, easily, split the log in two. I threw the two halves of wood onto the static fire. I stepped over her body and sat on the floor with my back resting against the arm-chair. I put my fingers about her ankle and pulled it to me. I caressed that perfect ankle. It was a masterpiece – the sublime creation. I loved that ankle. I loved that leg. It was the most beautiful leg that I had ever seen. It was mine and I loved it. I bent and kissed it gently but the coldness offended my lips and I began to shake uncontrollably.

The carving-knife cut through her flesh very easily but wouldn't cut the bone. I tried very hard. I sawed backwards and forwards, leaning heavily on the knife, but all to no avail. Perspiration ran down my brow and I wiped it away impatiently with the sleeve of my shirt.

The head surprised me. After the frustration I had experienced with the leg, the neck was easy.

Should I keep the head? I wasn't sure.

It wasn't as pretty as I remembered it from before. The open mouth and blank staring eyes bothered me. The thin, drawn-back lips weren't very passionate now. I reached behind me and pulled a cushion from the seat of the arm-chair. I stabbed the material with the knife and feathers were everywhere – flying like snow-flakes. I giggled with amusement. It was so unexpected. I laughed aloud as I threw handfuls at the fire and was delighted at the hungry eagerness of the flames as they devoured the feathers. I laughed with the angry crackles and snapping of the red flames as they consumed those fleecy petals. My eye-brows were singed and my hair too, but I refused to move.

The fire died to a subtle, glowering glimmer and once more, I became aware of her body. I was resentful of her presence between me and the fire.

I grabbed her head and thrust it into the cushion-cover.

I laughed and held it high above my head. I chanted as I swung the bundle from side to side, like a pendulum.

'I love you, I love you not! I love you, I love you not!'

Then, unaccountably, my joy was overwhelmed by an up-surge of misery. I felt the grip of loneliness and a blanket of deep desolation descend over me. Defiantly I held that bundle high and swung it to and fro. Defiantly I shouted, 'I love You, I love You Not! I love You, I love You Not!' But a cloud-burst of tears blinded my eyes and I could hear the haunting whistling from the wing-beats of the Whooper swans – the most perfect day of her life.

THE REVENGE

David Farrer

Yesterday had been Maurice's fiftieth birthday. He had celebrated it mildly with French acquaintances in Rabat. He had many acquaintances, but little use for friends, who tended to ask embarrassing questions. Now as he drove his Citroen back towards Tangier, he was in a contented mood. Morocco was not a bad country to live in. There was an ample supply of willing women, and if he felt like it, boys for the asking. He had a flourishing export-import business and could live in comfort, even affluence. It was a pity of course that it was unsafe to return to England; the weight of the past, scarcely noticeable in this country where a degree of shadiness, at least among the European residents, was the rule rather than the exception, might still, even after twenty-five years, fall heavily upon him if he tried to go home.

And it hadn't really been his fault, or at least not more his than it had been Edward's. They had been in full partnership. All right, they had gambled with clients' money but, given time, those suckers would have been repaid in full. It had been amazing luck that he had had a friend in the office of the Director of Public Prosecutions, who had tipped him off. There had been not a moment to lose, certainly no time to warn Edward, who was on a fishing holiday in the West of Scotland. So he had simply cut and run, leaving Edward to take the rap. Too bad that he'd got three years, but in practice that meant only two, for he was quite sure that Edward would earn full remission for good conduct. At twenty-three, there would have been plenty of time to make a fresh start – and in England too, which was barred to him. He wondered idly how Edward had made out – poor, middle-class, strait-laced Edward who had for a time, he supposed, fallen under his fatal spell. Married, most likely, with at least two kids, probably living somewhere on the fringe of suburbia. He must have lived down the scandal long ago. People like Edward did. Did he still bear him a grudge. Probably not, Edward was too decent.

Maurice pulled up before a filling station for more petrol. The road had been paralleling the coast, the almost inactive Atlantic breakers rustling the wide expanse of sandy beach. It was very peaceful; life should be good. Was it the climacteric of reaching his half-century that had aroused these memories of his twenties which were so much better placed in oblivion? Idly he glanced at a signpost a few yards from the filling station. It indicated Aba Risa at a distance of thirty kilo-metres. The village contained a famous Muslim shrine which he had often meant to visit. He looked at his watch; it was only half past four, plenty of time to make the detour and reach Tangier in time for dinner, or he could if necessary stop off at Arcila where that reprobate Englishman kept a surprisingly good restaurant. He over-tipped the good-looking Berber garage attendant and swung the Citroen on to the side road.

Half an hour later – it was impossible on Moroccan side roads to travel at more than twenty miles an hour – he was confronted with a fork in the road, with no indication of whether the right or left road led to Aba Risa. On the whole, as far as Maurice could see, the left looked slightly less boulder-strewn, and he chose it. Soon he was regretting the choice, the road narrowed to a track on which it was impossible to reverse without plunging into a dense cactus hedge. Apart from a few mouldy inquisitive goats and a distant camel, there was no sign of life. Hot now, and irritated, he accelerated; there was a grinding crash, and his car lurched to a halt.

Maurice was an excellent driver, and a hopeless mechanic. Even if he had known what particular disaster had occurred to the Citroen, he would have been incapable of doing anything about it. Cursing himself for his idiotic detour, he pulled a brandy flask from the car's side pocket, gulped from it, lit a cigarette, and strove to consider his situation. It became all too clear to him that he had only two alternatives. Either he must

walk at least fifteen kilometres back to the main Tangier-
Rabat road, or he must sit where he was in the unlikely hope
that another motorist with a knowledge of mechanics would be
so ill-advised as to venture along this nightmare road. The first
alternative he dreaded. He was a big man, but sex and alcohol,
while not yet denying him his share of fleshy good looks, had
undermined his physique. He could not remember when he
had last walked an uninterrupted mile. Yet the second alternative – probably to spend the whole night where he was –
seemed with every gulp of brandy even more unappetising.
Might not even the goats turn savage after dark?

Maurice dragged himself, swearing, from the Citroen, and
steadied himself for the start of the long march. And then,
sweet music, he heard in the distance the unmistakable noise of
an approaching vehicle. Soon, round a bend in the track,
appeared the silhouette of a sturdy Land-Rover, which
stopped fifty yards from him. The driver got out – a man, it
seemed to Maurice through the fumes of brandy – of about his
own age, dressed Berber fashion, in the traditional burnous.
He approached and, in impeccable English, asked: 'Can I
help?'

'Thank God you've appeared. I thought I'd be marooned
here for the night.'

'You've got to know this road.'

'Road!'

'Well – yes, I agree.'

'I'm a hopeless mechanic anyway, I'm afraid.'

The burnous examined the car briefly. 'There's nothing you
could have done anyway,' he said, 'the back axle's gone.'

'Where do we go from here?' Maurice's voice was petulant
as he hated being put into an inferior position.

'If you feel up to it, we'll just have to push the car into the
ditch, so that I can get by.'

'Leaving me?'

'Leaving you,' he spoke gently but with authority, 'I hope,
to be my guest for the night, till we can get a mechanic out in
the morning.'

A sense of relief came to Maurice as jointly they heaved the Citroen into the cactus hedge, left it there, the cynosure perhaps of many a goat's eyes. A good Samaritan in the nick of time. 'I can't be grateful enough to you,' he said, as they returned to the Land-Rover.

'You *are* Maurice Ashtead, aren't you?'

Maurice stopped in his tracks. 'How on earth did you know?'

'You're quite well known in these parts: the export-import man from Tangier. And anyway twenty-five years is not long enough sometimes to forget a face.'

'What do you mean?'

'I'm not surprised that in this rather uncouth disguise you don't remember me. I happen to find it comfortable for the climate. The name is Edward Finlay.'

'Edward Finlay?'

'Formerly of Ashtead & Finley, Stockbrokers.'

For a moment Maurice was silenced. Then, although he had never felt any real regret, he found himself saying, 'I'm sorry.'

'After twenty-five years? Sorrow doesn't last that long. Anyway, forget it, and be my overnight guest.'

Silently they got into the Land-Rover, edged past the Citroen, and proceeded.

Some fifteen kilometres and half an hour later, while the sun sank rapidly into the Atlantic Ocean, there appeared in the arid plain a small wooded knoll. Edward gestured towards it. 'My small and modest domain.'

Still half in a state of shock, Maurice asked, 'What do you do here?'

'Farm, in a somewhat dilatory way, oranges, a bit of maize. It's a sort of tiny oasis, a fresh-water spring. Olives too, one can't help it, all those olive trees. I'm also, in a very half-hearted and amateurish way, writing a book which will never be published.'

Maurice was silent. They passed through the wooden gates. One the left he noticed what looked like a small guest-house. Would he, he wondered, be sleeping there? Then they came to a low-slung, commodious bungalow, in front of which was a pool in the centre of the circular drive. Edward got out, opened the door for Maurice, and clapped his hands. 'Welcome to the Château Finlay,' he said. The front door was opened by one of the most strikingly good-looking, fair-skinned Berber youths he had ever seen. 'This is Ahmed,' Edward said. Ahmed bowed. 'Ahmed will show you your quarters. You'll want a bath, and Ahmed will bring you a change of clothes when you're ready.'

'That's very good of him.'

'We usually dine about eight; Ahmed will show you where.'

So his guess had been right. Edward *had* married. He couldn't imagine him just having a mistress.

As he led Maurice to his room and started to run his bath, Ahmed's attitude was so demure as to be provocative; and Maurice needed little provocation. These native boys were just as seductive to him as any woman. Still, he told himself, as he soaked in his bath, he must be careful. Edward's attitude to him was almost too good to be true – and after all the damned thing was still a *crime* in Morocco. He must be wary of a trap. Could Edward really have forgiven him? Would he have forgiven Edward? Was Edward deliberately throwing Ahmed at his head?

Guided by the still-demure Ahmed, he found Edward mixing a martini in the open-ended, terraced sitting-room, furnished sparely, with low chairs and tables, and, on the walls, paintings by Moroccan artists he had recently seen in Tangier.

'I hope Ahmed did his duty by you.'

'Beautifully.'

'A martini, or would you prefer Scotch?'

'No, martini, thanks.'

'My wife Amina will be with us for dinner.'

'I didn't know you'd married.'

'It took me a long time to persuade her to abandon the veil, but now she's getting accustomed to the occasional English visitor.'

'What made you settle here?'

'Simple. A visit to Tangier after it was all over, and a week-end in Tetuan where I met Amina.'

'Can you afford just to be an occasional farmer?'

'Fortunately a very forgiving aunt died.'

'Lucky you. Do you never go back to England?'

'Occasionally; I *can*, you see.'

'Edward,' Maurice found himself saying it again, 'I'm sorry.'

'Maurice, if anything I suppose *I* should be sorry for *you*. But let's have a toast,' he raised his martini, 'to the past that might have been, and to this present *happy* reunion.'

They drank, and Amina came into the room. She was tall, big-boned like many Berber women, with a complexion of gold-dust, solemn black eyes, and braided hair. She greeted Maurice demurely but, unlike Ahmed, her manner had an inner quality. She was very sure of herself. At dinner, immaculately served by Ahmed, her replies were monosyllabic, though Edward had obviously taught her good English. The food was excellent – Anglo-Moroccan: avocado pear, a kous-kous, and orange soufflé. The wine was rough Moroccan, very potent. Maurice drank profusely, feeling himself mellow – a handsome Berber woman, a beautiful Moroccan boy – in other circumstances, what a delicate choice. Over the second brandy, after Amina had left them, he became muzzily sentimental. 'Straordinary thing, our meeting like this, after all these years. Lucky for me, too.'

'I was glad to be of assistance to you.'

'Lot of bridge over – I mean water over – the bridge.'

'You can't quite forget the past, can you? You should. You've become rich, I've become – not, with Amina, quite respectable – but safe, and not unhappy.'

Out of this semi-drunken stupor Maurice heard himself saying: 'And, as you've so kindly told me, *you* can go home to England whenever you want.'

'Do you want to so terribly?'

'Yes, no, I don't know. I'm successful, make a lot of money, only slightly shady. But you know the English Tangerines, they're all like me, for one reason or another they can't or won't go back to England. They play bridge and have boys. I don't play bridge.'

There was a silence, then Edward said, 'Another brandy, or what about bed? You must be tired after the excitement of the day.'

'Bed,' Maurice's voice was thick.

'Ahmed's gone to his quarters. Can you find your own way?'

'Of course.'

Clad in Edward's borrowed pyjamas, Maurice sat on the edge of the comfortable bed, reviewing hazily the day's events. What a coincidence, after all these years Edward coming to *his* rescue. And he seemed to bear no grudge – a really decent fellow. And the temptations – Amina and that Arab boy – in other circumstances either would have been equally desirable. But he had to admit he had drunk too much. He tumbled into bed and soon was snoring asleep.

He awoke to the hazy realization that someone seemed to be trying to climb into his bed. To his muzzied exclamation 'What are you doing?', he received only an urgent 'hush'. The body then inserted itself, and for the next hour his sophisticated and still somewhat drunken palate was satiated. Everything he had ever desired seemed to him to be fulfilled. It might be Amina, it might be Ahmed, he was too bemused to care. At last it was over. As it climbed out of bed he muttered, 'Who are you?' 'Hush,' it replied, and vanished through the window.

When Maurice awoke, the sun was streaming through the window. Ahmed was padding round the room. For a moment Maurice felt nothing, apart from the slight bewilderment that attends the last steps of a hangover. Then he remembered and turned sharply on Ahmed. 'What are you doing here?' he asked. Ahmed came to a sort of attention. 'My master,' he said, 'asked me to see if you were still sleeping.'

No, it couldn't be Ahmed, he *must* have known if it was a boy. 'What time is it?'

'Nearly eleven o'clock, sir. My master asks if you would like your breakfast here, in this room.'

Maurice raised himself, looked at the open window, leading on to an enticing terrace. 'Yes, I would,' he said, and later, as he sipped the fresh orange juice, sampled the crisp toast, and drank what certainly was *not* Nescafé, his mind cleared. It had been a dream, the sort of lascivious dream which increasingly as one grew older became very nearly a substitute for the real thing. There was nothing to worry about. From his terrace, he could see the small bungalow he had glimpsed as Edward had driven him past it last night. Who lived there? An outside hand? But Edward had said he ran the small farm without any help. Ahmed? He asked him when Ahmed came to announce that his bath was ready. 'Me? No, sir, me live in *this* bungalow.'

'Then who does live there?'

Ahmed shrugged, but there was a hint of unease in his manner. 'My master keeps it private.' He left the room.

Maurice took his bath, dressed, and made his way to the sitting-room. Edward was awaiting him. 'Sleep well?'

'Beautifully, thank you.'

'No hangover?'

'Not a trace, thanks to your excellent wine.'

'Come, Maurice, a rough red Moroccan? How many brandies out of that flask before I rescued you? You had two after dinner.'

Maurice grinned uncomfortably. 'You always lectured me in the old days.'

'Did I? Perhaps I ought to have. Anyway, the mechanic from the garage has been to have a look at your car. Temporarily it's a complete write-off. The garage is sending you a replacement to get you back to Tangier.'

'It's very good of you.'

There was a silence. Suddenly Maurice wanted to get away. He had the illogical feeling that he was on treacherous ground, but he could not explain why. Edward, opposite him, seemed the same bland, totally forgiving friend. Mainly to find something to say, he asked: 'By the way, who lives in that little bungalow by the gate? I was looking at it from my terrace just now.'

Edward rose suddenly from his chair, stood over Maurice. 'I'm glad you asked that question. Perhaps as a very old colleague, you are entitled to know my secret.' He paused. 'Amina and I have a daughter. She's a strange – I'll be frank – a very oversexed child. It is she who with her companion lives in the little bungalow.'

Maurice felt bemused by this unexpected confidence, rather touched in fact that old Edward should have told him. 'It must have been quite a problem' – it seemed best, as it were to shrug the whole thing off.

'We had a bit of a scare last night,' Edward said. 'The companion rang through that Daisy had escaped. We were afraid she had made, as she has before, a bee-line for Ahmed's bedroom – it's next to yours. Luckily, her companion rang back again almost at once to say Daisy had returned. So we didn't have to disturb you.'

Maurice sat still, his mind racing. So the dream might have after all been reality. And – there was an undercurrent, he realized, in Edward's dispassionate account of a personal tragedy. He could not guess its impact, but it spelt danger. 'It must have been hell for you,' was all he could manage.

Edward smiled. 'You don't know the worst yet, Maurice. My daughter is a leper.'

THE WINDOW WATCHER

Dulcie Gray

It was nearly a year since the idea had come into her head; shortly after they had moved into their present flat, in fact. And tonight when her parents were out she'd be watching those two in the house opposite again, through the window, to see the next act in their drama.

They all thought she was a fool. Everybody did. Simple, they called her. But she wasn't simple at all; she was very complicated. Now she had created an absorbing peep-show, which she herself could control, and where the puppets were humans, and rich humans at that. It was enormously exciting. She was the puppet master – the ring master at a circus – or the director of a daily television serial (except that she directed these people's lives). Almost, she was God.

Her parents were getting ready to go out. Her brother had already gone out, and in half an hour she could turn off the lights, and pull back the curtains and, if her puppets were at home, the show would begin.

She had a feeling that they would be at home. It wouldn't be her fault if they weren't, and they had fallen for the rest of the bait she'd set them, almost too easily. So why not this time?

When her parents had been moving to this present apartment, Jennifer hadn't been particularly interested at first. In fact she had been dead bored, because she hadn't seen the possibilities of the place. They'd been in so many flats in her seventeen years of existence, and each one had been as uninteresting and ugly as the one before; exactly like this one, except for its location, which was why it was quite a few weeks before she realized how different it really was after all.

Jennifer's parents ran a shop. At least her father had been the manager at a succession of tobacconist and sweet shops –

and her mother always helped him. (Except of course that her help was always called assistance.) There was a chain of these little shops in North London and her father was moved from one to another, because he was quite good at his job, and, with Mother to assist him, he was considered one of the chain's best men. Not that he was paid much, but it was enough to keep the family in reasonable comfort in the jerry-built little homes with which he was provided, 'gratis and for nothing', as he always said when he wished to be smart and funny. And now he ran the tobacconist-cum-sweet shop-cum-paper shop in Gosforth Gardens, in Bayswater.

Jennifer was very large. She had a blank face, protruding eyes, dark, greasy hair, and a shapeless figure. Her legs were enormous. Her mouth was slack and her hands were permanently red. She was also subnormal mentally, they all said, and emotionally retarded, whatever that might mean. But this time, with her present idea working so well, she hadn't been mentally subnormal had she? She'd been as bright as those two rich people opposite. Brighter. And they were so rich that they could afford that huge house, and not only one new car, but two: a Jaguar and a Jensen. So who was the fool now?

It had all begun the first evening she'd been left alone in the flat. She was always being left alone these days, because she was an embarrassment to her family when they went out. When she'd been smaller, her parents had been careful never to leave her on her own unless they couldn't help it in case she got up to 'something unfortunate', as her mother put it. 'Getting up to something unfortunate' was like the time she set the curtains in the bedroom on fire, for fun, and they had to have the fire brigade, or when she put the sick kitten in the fridge for the night to see what would happen to it (it died), or when she gave all her brother's clothes to a man who called for charity, because she hated her brother. Now she'd got something better to do, and her parents, though they had no idea what was keeping her so happy, sensed it, and had thankfully taken advantage of it.

The flat was right over the tobacconist's shop, but its living-room window looked away from the main road, and straight across at the big houses which surrounded the Gardens, which gave the district its name. The big houses were five storeys high, and had pillars, and were faced in white stucco. The block of flats in which Jennifer's parents lived was built in yellow brick, and had concrete steps and picture windows, and the walls were always cracking because they were made of breeze blocks and concrete, which hadn't been dried out for long enough before the flats were occupied. So naturally, although Jennifer hated the people in the houses opposite because they were rich, it was interesting to see how the rich lived. And from where she now lived, she could now see how, with great clarity. And you could say that again!

None of the people opposite seemed to think it necessary to draw the curtains at the back of the houses. Perhaps they thought it was unimportant that people like Jennifer could see what they were doing, almost as if Jennifer and people like her were too unimportant to have an independent existence; certainly too unimportant to call for any protective measures on hot summer nights. Anyway, this was how it all began.

Jennifer's parents went out, leaving her to her own devices, and brother Tommy went out as usual with that crashing little bore Marlene with whom he was going steady. They were to be married in the autumn, by the way, and Jennifer wasn't allowed to be a bridesmaid. Too simple again, apparently. Well, one day Jennifer would get her own back. There'd be a time and a place, and a method. Jennifer would see to that. But first she'd let them marry. That way she could get them out of her home. Anyway, on that first night alone in the new flat she'd watched the telly for a bit, and suddenly a row had broken out in the street below the windows. Jennifer had looked out, but hadn't been able to see what was going on very well, so she'd switched off the lights, and looked out again. The row was between two lots of servants belonging to the big houses. Two women were fighting, and two men were shouting out something in Portuguese or Spanish or something, and trying to get them apart. All the servants of the houses round here were foreign. And that made them interesting too. It was almost like being in another country on this side of the flats.

It was then that Jennifer had seen her two 'rich specials', as she called them from now on. They were both glamorous to look at. Both of them were fair, both of them were tall. She was wearing a long green silk dress. He was in a dinner jacket, and Jennifer was fascinated. They were standing by a door, clearly lit in the frame of their own window, and they were obviously saying good-bye to some equally well-dressed guests. It was hard to see much of the furnishing of the room, as it was plainly in the narrow part of an L-shaped room, but downstairs the curtains were also drawn back, and the cook, the butler, another male manservant, and a girl of her own age were also clearly visible; the cook washing up, the girl bringing piles of plates and cutlery to her at the sink from a table nearby, and the butler and second manservant leaving the kitchen immediately they heard the guests leave the upper room.

The guests all went and presently the two menservants returned. The girl helped to dry the dishes, and she also stacked cutlery and glass in a dish-washer.

And upstairs the two glamorous ones settled themselves down in two arm-chairs, one on each side of the window, to have a smoke. Presently he beckoned the woman in the green dress to his chair, and she went over to him, and knelt at his feet, gazing adoringly up at him. He took her face in his hands, and gently kissed her on the mouth, then he began caressing her, and put a hand on one of her breasts. She pulled his head down passionately, and they began kissing in earnest.

Jennifer watched them with a strong sense of disturbance. She was both excited and revolted. The man was very handsome. Too handsome, and the woman too servile; too adoring. They were behaving disgustingly. People shouldn't be allowed to behave like that in public. Jennifer felt alternately very hot and very cold, and her mouth was going dry. Finally the man pulled down one of the shoulder straps of the woman's evening dress, and the woman laughed, and said something, and they both got up and left the room. And about time too! In a few seconds a light in the room higher up was switched on, and the man came towards the window, and drew the curtains. End of the first tableau.

From then on, watching them became Jennifer's favourite occupation – and, presently, an obsession. She found out all she could about them. They were called Dyer. He was a merchant banker, and they had been married a year. She was the daughter of Sir Fraser Cotswold – and had been a débutante three years before that, which made her only three years older than Jennifer. Somehow this added to Jennifer's growing hatred of her. To be so young, so pretty, so cared for, and so rich. It was much too much. She must be taken down a peg. He must, too, because he had chosen her in preference to Jennifer, and because he loved her. And with not just a decent, ordinary love, but this filthy revolting kind.

Jennifer sent the first letter six weeks after she had first seen them. It took her much time and thought to write and she discarded several attempts before she was satisfied. In small capital letters, and as neatly as possible, she wrote; 'Mr Dyer, do you know about your wife, when you are out all day? She's getting talked about.' She addressed it to M. Dyer, Esq – which was the first time she'd put 'Esq' on any letter (which gave her quite a thrill), and she'd dropped it through the letter box, on a day when her parents would be out of the way all evening.

The results were entirely satisfactory. The 'specials' had had people in for a party again, over the way, and after this lot of guests had gone, they went over to the two arm-chairs as usual, and he'd pulled Jennifer's letter out of his pocket and handed it to his wife. He'd been smiling, but not very gaily, when he had produced the letter and he was obviously watching closely for her reactions to what she read. She'd frowned, shaken her head, and then laughed. He hadn't laughed back. Then they had talked a good deal, at first calmly, and then more excitedly. Finally she had said something which had made him angry and he'd hit her across the face. She'd sprung backwards with the flat of her hand across her mouth – a curiously theatrical gesture – and then she'd left the room. He'd stayed behind for a long time. So long in fact that Jennifer had had to stop watching, so as to be in bed by the time her parents returned. They always liked her to be in bed by their return although Jennifer was seventeen. And she didn't mind. She liked bed.

A month later she had telephoned Mr Dyer and it gave her great delight to see him rise from the window chair and cross out of sight to the other side of the room to answer her. When he came back, his wife had argued again, and this time she had run out of the room in tears, slamming the door behind her.

Two months went by before Jennifer attempted to make any further move. The situation in the house opposite was developing satisfactorily unhappily. The 'specials' seldom both sat at the window together now, and when they did, he was usually reading the paper and drinking something brown out of a large cut-glass tumbler (whisky?) and she was reading a book. They seemed to be on terms of formal politeness.

Suddenly there was an exciting innovation. One night another man sat opposite Mrs Dyer in the window seat, and Mr Dyer was nowhere to be seen. Although the new man and Mrs Dyer sat at some distance from each other, it was clear that the man admired her and that though the woman didn't seem to be encouraging this, she appeared to be pleased with what he had to say. From now for the next few weeks, the man appeared every Tuesday evening and soon they were gazing into each other's eyes, in what were obviously long silences. What's more there was never a light on in the kitchen when he came to visit, so Tuesday must be the servants' night off. So what about that for excitement? Then another night as he got up to go, and she rose to say good-bye, the man took her in his arms and kissed her. The woman freed herself with some sort of remonstrance, but she showed no sign of displeasure. Things were hotting up, it seemed. Time for Jennifer to get going again.

The next morning she wrote a second letter. 'Dear Mr Dyer. On Tuesday evenings your wife makes love to another man. Do you mind? Don't tell her you know, but why not come back early and catch them at it?'

So as to be able to watch the sequel the following Tuesday, Jennifer had to engineer an invitation out for her parents, by telephoning Auntie Elsie, and managing to indicate that her mother and father expected to be asked for that evening. The ruse worked, the invitation came, and her parents left the flat at eight o'clock. By now, the new man and Mrs Dyer had established themselves in their usual places. By nine-fifteen they were holding hands, and by nine-thirty, they were in each other's arms. Suddenly the drawing-room door was flung open and the husband, wife and lover were all framed in the window together.

A tremendous quarrel took place. Once it looked as if the men would fight, but the woman prevented it. The husband stormed at her, the lover looked threatening again, and finally the woman led her lover out of the room, and the husband poured himself a drink. He drank it standing, and was helping himself to another when the woman returned. Now they raved and gesticulated, and as he'd done once before, Mr Dyer slapped his wife's face. This time she didn't flinch, but said something which sent him berserk. He took her throat in his hands and she struggled furiously, kicking out at him, and trying to wrench herself away. She managed to get free at last and ran for the door, but he went for her again and she picked up the table-lamp and held it above her head. He tripped over the chair, which made Jennifer laugh a bit, but in doing so, he kicked his wife in the stomach and she doubled up, as the heavy gilt lamp crashed down on her husband's head.

Jennifer was laughing out loud, now, in her excitement and pleasure.

The woman knelt by her husband's body, then sobbing, she ran out of the room, and a light showed on the very top floor. Presently, she came back accompanied by the cook, and while the cook, too, burst into tears, Mrs Dyer ran towards the telephone.

Well, what a to-do! Now what? Jennifer looked at her watch. Heavens – time for bed, and she'd better hurry! No point in upsetting her parents, and tomorrow she'd find out what had happened.

She did. The news was everywhere. In all the shops, in the areas by the kitchens of the big houses, and in all the highways and byways near Gosforth Gardens. Mr Dyer had had an accident. Mr Dyer had died in hospital.

He had died! He had died! He was dead! Dead! Dead! Dead!

Jennifer was marvellously excited. Fabulous how her plan had worked! But fab! And now she could add one last twist. She could pay out Mrs Dyer for ever, for being so pretty and so rich.

Jennifer dialled the police station, and when a voice answered her, she said, 'I want to report a murder, please. My name is Jennifer Wates, of 17 Gosforth Court, Gosforth Street. I'm ringing from there now.' Her blood was racing, and she had never felt happier or more alive. Real zingy she felt. Swinging.

'A murder?'

'Yes, please.'

'I'll put you through.'

'Thank you.'

Another voice came on the line. 'Detective Inspector Jones here,' it said.

'This is Jennifer Wates, of 17 Gosforth Court, Gosforth Gardens,' said Jennifer, lisping, as she always did when she got excited. 'Last night I saw Mr and Mrs Dyer, of 3 Gosforth Place, having a quarrel. She hit him with a heavy lamp. I saw her do it. It was deliberate. The windows of our living-room look straight on to the drawing-room at the back, and I saw it all. They hadn't drawn the curtains. He was taken to hospital, I heard, and I thought he might recover, so I didn't report it, but now I hear he's dead, so I felt I ought to.'

'I see.' The Inspector sounded wary. 'Would you like to come down here and make a report, Miss Wates?'

'No thank you,' replied Jennifer, primly. 'I think my mother and father would prefer you to come here. They wouldn't like people to see me at a police station.' She stuttered on the last word.

'Good, then I'll be right along. Thank you, Miss Wates.'

'Thank you, Mr Detective.'

Jennifer replaced the receiver. She went to the kitchen and took a Mars bar out of a tin in the cupboard. She knew she shouldn't eat so many sweets because they'd make her even fatter than she was now, but what the hell? You didn't get thrills like this every day and what better way of celebrating than with a Mars bar?

She took the Mars bar back to the living-room and lay flat on her back on the sofa, licking at it blissfully, gloating with happiness. This was her first revenge. Her first pay-back to the world at large for the fact that she was simple, and ugly, and unloved. And from now on, who cared? She could have a super time. She could pay out Marlene and Tommy for being normal and happy, and Mrs Spriggs down the road because she avoided Jennifer's eyes even when she talked to her, and the young man in the butcher's who laughed at her. And everyone. And one day she'd even pay out her mother. Who knows? This was the life. There were so many things to be done, it made your head reel.

There was a ring on the front door bell. Jennifer put down the Mars bar, and smoothed down her dress.

She opened the door. The Detective Inspector was real dishy. 'Miss Wates?' he enquired politely.

'Miss Wates,' replied Jennifer gravely.

She had arrived.

SPINALONGA

John Ware

'The Greek generals have commandeered the boat,' said
Angela, my wife. The hotel manager made suitably soothing
noises. 'It's just for this morning the military require it,' he
said. 'You can go to the island this afternoon.'

In the eastern-most part of Crete, when the summer tem-
perature reaches 85 or thereabouts around noon, a cooling
north-west breeze springs up. This makes conditions inside the
landlocked bay of Minos Beach ideal for swimming and sun-
bathing. But out in the open sea, around the headland opposite
St Nicholas, there was quite a swell. The Greek boatman, with
no Board of Trade regulations to worry him, had loaded the
smooth cover of the hold with chairs from the resort to
accommodate his many extra passengers and when his mate,
an inexperienced helmsman, let the boat wallow sideways, the
chairs slid all over the place.

'It's highly dangerous,' shouted the middle-aged English
industrialist from the Midlands. 'Turn back ... Turn back!
We'll go tomorrow,' he added, as the handsome Greek sailor
eyed him in a way which clearly said, what about my fares?

So turn back we did, running for the shelter of Minos Beach
and a lazy afternoon.

'Nine o'clock in the morning,' the boatman reminded us.

Just as I expected, half-a-dozen passengers failed to make it
at nine next morning, so we had a less crowded boat, around
which we could stretch our legs and the nice German could
move around to operate his superb camera equipment.

A few miles up the coast, at some time a barrier reef had
emerged to separate one bay from another and during the
Venetian occupation of Crete they constructed a canal to link
the blue waters together. Derelict windmills stand sentinel at
the entrance and along the banks. There is no sign of human

occupation, but a cantilever bridge suggests the recent past.

'Desolate,' I said to Bill, a fellow-guest from the hotel.

'Eerie,' said his wife Phillipa.

'It's nothing to Spinalonga,' he said. 'Spinalonga was a leper island. The poor devils were sent there to die. Nothing has lived there since – not even a lizard.'

He stood up. 'There it is, ahead.' And suddenly everyone seemed to see it together. The German's wife, a rather ugly, dyed redhead, sat forward in her chair. Their pretty little daughter got up and went forward a few paces, gazing intently ahead. My wife and I stood, and I noticed that everyone had fallen silent.

Ahead was the usual humped brown island. But the crown of this was dominated by a huge fortified citadel and on the quayside below were grouped several ruined buildings. Stone ramparts stretched on either side and disappeared round the bend of the island. Up the rocky slopes ran a narrow road with loose stone walls holding back the earth. Nothing grew on the walls and the only vegetation seemed to be the dried brown grass and a few very old trees.

Suddenly everyone began talking again.

'What are you thinking?' I asked my wife.

'I can only think of a Huxley title,' she replied. '*Eyeless in Gaza.*'

The huge mediaeval Venetian fortress indeed stared from great eyeless sockets across the waters.

'It withstood a siege of forty years by the Turks after they had overrun Greece and taken Crete,' said Phillipa.

'No geraniums. I should have thought the walls would have been covered with geraniums,' said Angela, continuing to stare fascinated as the island loomed large upon us.

'Half an hour here,' said the boatman.

'Can't we snorkel?' chorused the wives.

'It takes half an hour to walk round the island,' said the boatman by way of answer.

'Nevertheless,' said my wife, 'I'll take the snorkel and my bathing costume.'

'Me too,' said Phillipa. 'Look down there at those lovely rocks.'

Like the buildings behind it, the small quayside was crumbling away. 'The only boats that ever come here are tourist boats,' explained Bill, who had been to the island before.

The boatman's mate took us across the rubble to the concrete road. It climbed steeply up in front of us. Behind us was a tunnel. 'That's where you'll come out after making a complete circle,' he said.

My wife slipped back and dumped her swimming kit in the shade of one of the buildings. We noticed that there were broken electric cables hanging from the walls.

'Yes, the Germans fortified it during the war,' said Bill. 'But neither the Greeks nor the Allies occupied it once the Germans had gone. Left it to the skeletons of the lepers,' he added, and I noticed Angela shivered. 'Let's get back into the sun,' she said.

The usual blazing hot morning was developing as we toiled up the roadway towards the top of the first ramparts, which went straight down into the sea. Through a gap in the wall on the right we saw a wooden cross and, entering, we found ourselves in a walled cemetery. A small building on the left seemed to have been some form of chapel and to the right, between the graves and the rampart, was a double row of concrete paving stones.

Two of them were askew and I noticed they had iron handles by which they could be raised or lowered into position. Fascinated by thoughts of what might lie beneath, I went over to the one which most exposed the hollow below and peered in. Grinning up at me in a hideous rictus was a skull, detached from the doubled-up bones of a skeleton. The graves were no longer than three feet, so that the joints of the corpses had to be broken and the skeletons bent double to get them in.

'My goodness, look at this,' I said, awed. But Angela had seen enough. 'I don't want to look,' she said. 'There's a skull in this one,' and she pointed to the other open grave near where she was standing, 'so I suppose yours is the same, only

probably worse. Come on,' she added, hurrying out through
the entrance back on to the road, where I followed her at a
more dignified pace, but nonetheless glad to turn my back on
the desolate scene.

A few yards further up we came to a small whitewashed
church, with rusted bell hanging at a crazy angle, as though
some bellringer had suddenly stopped ringing as the bell
swung out and it remained petrified in that position. A broken
wooden door hung loosely ajar and we went in.

There were some broken chairs strewn about and on a shelf
between what was probably the vestry by which we had entered and the dark interior of the church stood several ikons in
various stages of decay. I picked one up. It was like a small
cheap Victorian photoframe with the gilt peeling off it. The
picture was woven on tapestry and showed the figure of Christ
crucified. It was beneath glass. 'Always wanted an ikon,' I
said. 'I'll take this. No one can want it round here.'

'You can't,' said my wife. 'It's sacrilege.'

'Then I'll buy a Russian one in London,' I said. I glanced
into the dark interior and made out a huge figure of Christ
painted on the wall, but I was too nervous to investigate closer.
My wife was already disappearing through the doorway. Impulsively I slipped the ikon into the back pocket of my shorts,
intending to hide it in the holdall in which we carried the fins
and snorkels. My wife shivered again as she came out into the
sunshine. 'Creepy,' she said.

Bill was wrong about nothing living there, for as we
approached a mass of crumbling houses on each side of the
road which had now become a narrow concrete path, two
kestrels went screeching into the sky from a mouldering back-
yard. One of them kept sweeping down towards us, its glorious
red-and-brown feathers glistening in the sunshine as it tried to
lure us away from the spot where we had obviously disturbed
the nest.

'Perhaps they have some babies,' said Angela. She tried to
get a photograph of one of the parents, hovering almost
motionless overhead.

'Don't waste the film,' I warned her. 'We've only got two left.'

I turned to look back the way we had come and there, standing outside the little white chapel, his eyes fixed on us, stood a young Greek priest, bearded and in flowing cassock.

'I thought the island was deserted,' I said. 'There's a priest on it, anyway.'

Angela, a few yards ahead, swung round. 'Where?' she asked.

I turned back, but he was gone.

'Well,' I said, a little uneasily, 'he must have followed us out of the church. He was standing in the path looking up here. I must say he's pretty agile to disappear like that.'

'What did he look like?' asked Angela.

'Like you say they all look, dear. Like Makarios – only young. No grey hairs but a full beard.'

'Shoes or sandals?' she asked, and I saw she was not taking me seriously. I felt annoyed.

'You'll see him because he can't spend all day in that ruin.'

The tumbledown houses climbed away, on one side, towards the huge round citadel. On the other, they backed down towards the edge of the cliff. There was a road on the right, and down a steep cobbled incline and through a beautifully shaped archway I could see a small jetty jutting out into the sea. I made Angela go down and pose under the archway. It made a perfect photograph with the deep blue sea behind. 'Only one left now,' she said.

As I lowered the camera, I saw for the first time a white village across on the mainland opposite the jetty. As I looked closer I saw it was completely derelict and crumbling like everything on Spinalonga itself. I wound the camera on to its last exposure and as I did so I was conscious of someone at the top of the incline. I looked up and there stood the priest staring at us. I spun round triumphantly to Angela, who was gazing across the water at the ruined town on the opposite bank.

'Shoes or sandals, indeed!' I said. 'Look for yourself.'

She turned round and gazed at me in wonder.

'Not me, you idiot! Up there on the path.' I pointed at the priest. But there was no one there.

'Well I'll be damned, he's playing hide and seek.' Angela began to snigger.

'I tell you he was standing right there looking down at you. He watched us take the photograph.'

'Looking at you then,' she said, 'not me. What have you been doing? Desecrating the shrine?'

I turned instinctively to hide my back pocket.

'Oh, come off it,' I said. 'If we hurry up to the path we're bound to see him!'

'If there's anyone to see,' she replied, not hurrying. Sure enough, there was no one about when we got back to the path.

We continued round the island. On the leeward side ferns and trees had grown out of the walls and pavement, but after the kestrels had subsided, the still air seemed more charged with brooding silence than before.

Suddenly we came to the tunnel, long and curving and carved out of the rock which overhung the path. But nowhere was it in complete darkness. As we came out at the other end we saw the boat by the jetty.

'Well, it's not taken half an hour and I'm for a swim,' said Angela. I looked up the steep incline which we had climbed when we first set off. At the top of the first section was the little walled cemetery. There was no one in sight.

'I think I'll go and photograph the cemetery,' I said, and set off up the slope while Angela disappeared into the building to change. I heard Phillipa's voice and, somewhere round the corner, Bill's. 'They're swimming-mad,' I grumbled as I toiled up the slope in the now-fierce sunlight.

Halfway up the path a huge tree sprang from the wall and threw out a heavily leafed branch almost blocking the way. I pushed through it and it was as though I had pushed through a deep velvet curtain into another world. Only the same fierce sunlight beat down upon the same concrete beneath my feet.

As I turned into the cemetery I gave a start, for there was the bearded priest waiting for me! He stood over the open grave which I had previously examined. I was near enough now to see his features and the thoughtful brown eyes gazing at me, almost I thought, with a touch of sorrow.

He spoke in a slow precise English. 'I saw you pick it up and you are quite right, no one will need it here. But are you sure you need it?' He smiled, showing perfect white teeth through his black beard and moustache. But was I right in sensing a hint of menace in the benevolence of the smile?

I felt embarrassed yet reassured that he had seen me take the ikon. It confirmed that he had been in the dark interior of the church all the time.

'I thought of buying a real one in London,' I said feebly. 'But this seemed to be in need of an owner.' I tried a smile which I thought disarming enough to let him know I was no petty thief. He drew himself up to his full height, which must have been at least six-foot-two, and the brown eyes stared hard at me. 'This *is* a real one,' he said with dignity. 'It belonged to the unfortunate buried here,' and he pointed into the open grave.

Suddenly, seeming to recover himself, he said, 'Help me to replace the stone. It is not right that the dead should be exposed.'

'I was going to take a photograph,' I said.

'Let us restore the stone first,' he said. 'You did not want to take the grave open?'

Of course, that was just what I had intended, but I felt his admonishing gaze so intently that I could only lie.

'Of course not,' I replied, 'it was your picture I wanted. Who opened the grave?' I added hastily, walking over and preparing to grasp the other handle.

'Tourists,' he said contemptuously. 'Can't let the dead lie in peace.' He looked down at the grave. 'These are the graves of lepers, unknown and unmarked. See,' he said, pointing, 'this poor unfortunate had osteomyelitis as well as leprosy. You can see it in the deformed bones.'

I looked down and saw again the hideous skeleton. 'Where ...'

He anticipated my question. 'They made rough coffins of thin wood, like your orange boxes, very flimsy, which soon perished. But they also just wound the body in a cloth. Over there in the corner,' and he pointed to the small building I had taken for a chapel or resting place, 'they often burnt the body in the coffin because they knew leprosy was contagious.'

He smiled again – brilliantly – and we both bent and lifted the stone back into position. It was not very heavy for two, but I noticed the other stone, which had not been moved so far off the grave, was already back in position.

'I could manage that myself,' he said, following my glance. 'Now, take your picture.'

I went back a few paces and got him in the viewfinder looking straight into the lens. 'Smile again,' I said, pressing the lever. He gave a swift flash of his teeth, and then walked past me towards the entrance even before I had wound the film on. I followed him, anxious to see which way he would go. Again he anticipated my question. 'My flock,' he said, sweeping his arm round to encompass the whole island.

'But I thought no one lived here?'

'Well, we have visitors ... like yourself for instance ... and those who expose the graves,' he said and quickly added before I could ask the questions buzzing through my mind. 'You have been through the village.'

He pointed beyond the chapel from where I had taken the ikon.

'But it's all in ruins.'

'Nevertheless, that is my way, and I must go. *Pax vobiscum*.' As I stood groping for words, he added, 'Take care of the ikon,' and strode away upwards.

'Yes,' I said, 'er ... good-bye.' He was already several yards away and I noticed the end of his long cassock stirred the dust. Beneath it the worn heels of dull black shoes appeared and disappeared. 'That's something for Angela to know,' I thought flippantly, and I turned down the path.

As I reached the bough which blocked the way with its heavy foliage, I looked back. He was standing perfectly still on the path outside the chapel, looking at me. Although I waved he made no response.

I passed the tree and immediately could hear the sounds of Angela and the others, and the chugging of the engine which the boatman had just started. Bill came out of the water first. 'Tell him to take us right round the island, not straight back,' he said. I welcomed the chance. That way I'm bound to see the priest and convince Angela, I thought.

'What have you got in your pocket?' asked Bill.

'It's an ikon I found in the ruined church. But Angela said not to take it as it would be sacrilege. So not a word to her. But when I went up to photograph the graveyard there was a priest who had seen me take it and he said it was all right. It belonged to the skeleton in the open grave and he asked me to help him put the stone back. The skeleton was all deformed, by the way. Did you see it?'

Bill, who had been eyeing me suspiciously, burst out laughing. 'What priest? Wait till Angela hears this. You'll be in trouble going back for that thing and now inventing a phoney priest to cover up your tracks. Wouldn't do it if I were you,' and he slapped me heartily.

I quickly pushed the ikon deeper into my pocket as I saw Angela coming up the jetty with her snorkel in her hand.

'There *was* a blasted priest up there,' I cried. 'He puts back the gravestones which the stupid tourists remove. You'll see them covered up if you like to go back there, and I couldn't have done it alone.'

Bill grinned wider than ever and Angela, arriving, wanted to know what was going on. Bill didn't give me away. 'Says he met a priest and helped him to put gravestones back,' he laughed. 'Oh, that,' said Angela, joining in the fun. 'He's been seeing this priest all over the island.'

As she said this, the boatman was stepping aboard. He heard and crossed himself. I began to get annoyed with everyone, including myself. 'I've just explained to Bill that the priest we saw —'

'*You* saw,' interrupted Angela.

'And you would have seen him too, if you had walked quickly enough,' I said. 'And what is more, he wears shoes,' I added in triumph.

'And I suppose you took his photograph?'

'And so I did. And you'll see he wears shoes.' In fact, I couldn't remember whether these were visible in the photograph I'd taken or not.

She decided to be sympathetic, which I hate more than any of her moods. 'Then that'll be the last one, dear,' she said.

'God!' I cried. 'There *was* a priest up there, looking exactly like a young Makarios. We'll probably see him as we go round the island.'

The two boatmen together were about to cast off as the Germans came aboard. Surely they must have seen the priest? The German looked incredulous like the rest. 'I never saw anyone,' he said.

'How could a priest today know whose ikon it was, anyway?' Bill whispered to me when Angela was out of earshot. 'The skeleton he claims owned it has been dead two hundred years or more.'

I suddenly felt the same sick fright I had felt when I saw the priest in the cemetery, but I controlled my panic, for I recalled his deep brown eyes and friendly expression and the tone of his voice.

'He would know who owned all the things in the chapel,' I said feebly. 'Wait till you see his picture . . .'

Peer as we might as we rounded the island, there was no priest to be seen. I became more disgruntled and while Angela was looking elsewhere I slipped the ikon down to the bottom of the holdall.

When we got back to London, I took the rolls of film to Kodak in Regent Street, and within the week they came back. We put the reel through the viewer. There was number 35, the photograph of Angela under the archway, and then the photo of the cemetery basking in the white sunlight, the wooden cross on the left, the priest in the centre, and the graves with their covers in place.

'There, you see!' I cried triumphantly to Angela.

Something about the figure of the priest was wrong, though. I stared. The cassock, the shoes, yes ... but the face? Dear God, it was a skull, eyeless, teeth drawn back in a hideous rictus! And the so-piously clasped hands – claws rather, held something. An ikon!

A dreadful suspicion shot through my mind.

'What? Where?' said Angela, staring blankly.

Without answering, I rushed upstairs to get the holdall which I had not yet unpacked. Fumbling inside, I found only my swim trunks and flippers and snorkel. There was no ikon.

Feeling vaguely sick, I sat back and began to rub my hands. The itched. I looked at them. On the backs of both hands were strange little yellowish-brown lumps and reddish spots, one or two of them already festering.

AGGROPHOBIA

L. Micallef

She was a large girl with glowing spectacles. She radiated vitality even at three AM in the listless atmosphere of the seedy cafe off Shaftesbury Avenue. Smoke and frying-fat fumes lingered indecisively on the stairs and wreathed indolently upwards to the street. Three boys rattled coffee cups in time to the juke box, casting occasional glances of contempt at the thin drab in the corner, slouched over a cigarette and persisting in attempts at jocular familiarity with the proprietor, who ignored her as he served.

A mixed, middle-aged party, sobering up noisily on braised steak, scattered peas over their table. Now and then a shabby boy or girl would wander in, make furtive enquiries about the proprietor's Irish girlfriend behind the soft drinks bar, and drift out again. A young Rasputin-faced man with straggling hair took a seat opposite a feeding couple and sat staring at the woman, willing her to notice the contrast between her well-filled plate and his empty mouth. She looked uncomfortable but warded off his silent begging by speeding up her chewing rate.

The girl with spectacles looked around eagerly at it all and addressed the boy beside her. 'It's fascinating, really fascinating!' she enthused. 'And awfully – *conducive*. There's more material here than anywhere I've been.'

The boy screwed his sharp Cockney features into an appearance of interest. 'Material?' he queried.

'Yes, I'm taking anthropology next semester. Last year it was psychology. I'm interested in People.' Her Californian voice, thick and soft as the ice cream in the glass dish before her, vibrated earnestly. 'I just can't be mathematical about people, though. I mean, I can't make statistics of them.

They're all so – individual. Especially in London. I just love London. It's so *safe*.'

The boy's drooping eyelids jerked up. 'Safe?'

She finished her ice cream and clattered the spoon into the dish. 'Sure, safe. You don't think I could wander around at night, alone, collecting people, in New York or Los Angeles or any city Stateside, do you? You English are just so civilized, it's unbelievable.' She looked at him with benign interest. 'You use places like this a lot?'

He shrugged, stirring his coffee. 'There's always people here.'

'Say, you like people, too? That's great! You a student or a writer or anything?'

He shook his head, dully.

'A poet? No, well, do you mind telling me what you do do? I mean, I don't mean to be nosy but you understand that you're one of these people here and I've got the opportunity of talking with you, which I appreciate very much, believe me. You don't mind answering questions, do you?'

He shrugged.

'Well, that's really great of you.' She whipped a neat notebook and pencil from her jeans pocket and crouched over them. 'I don't want you to think I'm making a *specimen* of you – I'm just too human myself to be a people-user, but I'm meeting so many interesting individuals this vacation that I can't keep track of them all.' She placed a warm hand on his arm. 'Oh, they're deeply in my consciousness, believe me, as real faces, as *friends*, but I'll have to pick up the details when I get home and need the material for my research study. You understand that, don't you?'

He nodded.

'Oh, you're really nice – er – what's your name? Tom? Say, that's nice. My name's Alfrida. I really appreciate your co-operation, Tom. You've always lived in London, have you?'

Half an hour later she had an encapsulated version of the dossier on the desk of Tom's probation officer, a set of documents that drove that official to despair but filled Alfrida with delight.

'It's really wonderful, Tom, you being raised in such over-crowded conditions, and still living like that, and being in those reform schools and everything, and still being a people lover. I mean, you've never gotten away from people, have you?'

He shrugged.

'Haven't you ever wanted to, Tom? Like, having day-dreams of the lonely horizon where there's room to throw a shadow, make a single silhouette? The Cowboy Image is very potent in an intensified urban environment, Tom, I've got books on it. Mmmh?'

He drank coffee, disinterestedly. She persevered. 'Open spaces, Tom. Don't you ever dream of, want, *desire* Open Spaces?'

He set his cup down sharply and looked at her. She blinked at the sudden alarm in his eyes. 'No!' he told her. 'No.'

Her nose twitched excitedly. 'Tom' – laying a hand on his shoulder – 'Tom, does that expression mean something to you? Open Spaces?' She shook him gently but eagerly. 'Open Spaces, Tom. *Open Spaces* . . .'

'Gerroff!' He shook her away and stood up. 'Get lost, will you?' He picked his way through the tables and made for the stairs. She followed him out to the street and ran after him as he hurried along it.

'Tom, where are you going?'

He shouted back at her as he strode away. 'To find more people – and that don't include you, nosy-knicks! Shove off!'

She was a large girl with long strong legs and she quickly caught up with him. She took his arm pleadingly. 'Tom – Tommy – I can help you. Please let me help!'

'Don't need no help.' He went on his way doggedly. She clung to him. 'Tommy, it's a common complaint amongst overcrowded people – rats get it —'

'Rats to you too, girl.' He dragged her up the Avenue, his small wiry body surprisingly resistant to her attempts at restraint. With sour amusement he allowed her to stay with him as long as he determined the direction, heralded on all sides by their echoing footsteps. He suddenly became aware of this and stopped, looking huntedly around at the wide street. 'Christ, it's empty, init? Never seen it so empty.'

'You're afraid, Tom. You've got to admit that. You're afraid of empty, open spaces.'

He turned on her and pulled himself free, glaring furiously. 'Get away! I won't warn you again, you —!' He began to run. When he reached the Circus and stood looking with relief at the groups of young people, sauntering or sitting around Eros, she was still with him, panting a little, her spectacles shining earnestly, her voice urgent.

'Agoraphobia, Tom. That's what you're suffering from.'

He was trembling slightly, but had regained some of his humour. 'Yeah, girl, you know all about the old aggro, don't you?'

'Huh?'

He strolled off, grinning. She tried other tactics. 'Tom,' she suggested softly, 'why don't we go to my place? There's coffee and we can talk – huh?'

'Sorry, you're not my type.' His grin widened sarcastically.

'No, honestly, Tom, I mean just that. Coffee and talk. I've got a lovely little place – up in Hampstead. You know Hampstead, Tom?'

'Ow yes. Aye was born there. Home from 'ome, 'ampstead. May awnty resides there in 'er summer villa.'

'That's great, Tom – how about it, huh? It's a real lovely little room, and you're not going any place else, are you?'

He stopped and looked at her, a mischievous glint in his eyes. Then he shrugged. 'Okay.'

She beamed triumphantly and looked around for a taxi. When she found one she urged him into the back and muttered something to the driver before getting in beside him.

He stared sardonically out of the window as they passed swiftly through the silent streets, pretending to ignore her ceaseless chatter. 'I have this theory, Tom. People with your problem – I don't think it's just overcrowding, it's the *contrast* of being overcrowded with the way people used to live, in the beginning. Race memory. You know Jung, Tom?

'Well, when there weren't so many people they needed each other. The plains were full of danger. If one person was caught alone in the open with the primitive weapons they had then, he didn't stand a chance against the wild animals. Only together could they reverse the situation and be predators instead of prey. They were afraid of open spaces, Tom, because they had good reason to be.'

His lips curved in a cynical smile but he gave no other sign of listening to her. Undeterred, she continued to sermonize earnestly.

'But nobody really likes too many people around him all the time. He never really gets used to being closed in by buildings. Even if he doesn't think about it, he subconsciously resents it, and really *fears* it. People are a danger. But then when he feels like that, even without knowing it, his mind reverts to the opposite – no people at all, *alone*, and his race memory goes back to what it meant to be alone, on the plains, in danger. So he chooses this fear instead of the other, because —'

He closed his eyes and leaned back against the seat but she babbled on until the taxi stopped. She looked out of the window and nodded. 'We're here.' She got out quickly and paid the driver who grimaced at the tip and, reversing abruptly, roared off into the darkness like a curse.

The boy was puzzled. ''Ere – we're at the 'eath. Where do you live, then?'

She took his arm comfortably. 'The other side of the hill. It's a short-cut. We'll soon be there.' The walked over the grass, the boy uneasy as he looked around at the bare landscape, relieved only by the dim outlines of trees. The sky was clear but moonless and the stars were already fading. A grey pre-dawn pallor was growing from the east. The girl talked quickly as if to distract him from his surroundings.

'So you see, Tom, a sensitive person like you would be aware of all this, without knowing why, or what to do about it.

You know, intelligence has nothing to do with education. I think you're a very intelligent person, Tom.' She squeezed his arm with affection. 'I want to help you.'

'Yeah?' His eyes turned from side to side, nervously.

'I think this problem of yours is the basis of all your troubles – the reform schools and everything. Insecurity takes many forms, Tom. You never did tell me just why you were – er – sent away. Would you like to tell me about that?'

They had reached the top of the hill, which levelled out before them, becoming a smooth, raised plain. The boy stopped with quickened breathing. ''Ere – where are you taking me? I don't see no houses around 'ere!'

His voice was sharp and high, but she led him onwards, ignoring his growing panic. 'Any minute now, Tom. You just can't see very far in this light.'

She nudged him to return his attention to the conversation. 'Why did they put you in reform school, Tom?'

'Uh? Oh, I beat up some kids.'

'Both times?'

'Yeah.'

'What did they do to you, Tom, these kids?'

His shoulders were hunched and he still cast quick, uneasy glances around him as they walked. 'Don't remember. First time was at a school picnic at Brighton, on the Downs. This kid and me, we got left behind. Then there was the time Fred an' me went 'itch-'iking —'

He stopped, disengaged himself firmly from her clutch, and took two steps forward, peering into the gloom. 'You've bin 'aving me on, haven't you?' His tone was definite, his face hard.

She sat down on the grass. 'Yes, Tom. We're nowhere near anywhere. We're alone on the Heath and we're going to stay here until you're cured of your condition.' She patted the ground beside her. 'Come here, Tom. You won't find your way out, not until daylight. Do the thing you fear and the death of fear is certain. You'll be grateful to me for the rest of your life.' She was quietly confident.

He stood very still, contemplating her. When he spoke his voice was flat and controlled.

'Maybe I will.'

She crossed her ankles and folded her arms as he wandered idly for a few minutes until, looking at the ground, he stooped to pick up something. 'I'm glad you're taking it so well, Tom,' she said, warmly. 'I'm glad you can see it my way.'

He straightened and came back to her, tall against the dim skyline. 'Now here's my way, girl.' His voice was gentle. 'I try not to bother about this *condition* of mine too much, but I read things now and then that makes me think, though I don't want to.' He stood over her, hands clasped behind his back. She beamed encouragingly up at him.

'Like those parks in New York,' he continued steadily. 'They 'ave to keep them full of people 'cos they've found out that some other people get hurt when they find themselves alone there. An' that's because some *other* people get ideas when they see nothin' around but trees and land and just one other 'uman, right in the middle, like a rabbit.

'They get these thoughts, see, and they can't do nothin' about them. Even if they'd read all your books about the races an' memories and that. They get these different sorts of ideas and they can't help themselves.'

He hunkered in front of her, smiling softly. 'Like me an' Fred when the lorry dumped us off on Salisbury Plain. Suppose the bloke thought it was funny. There he was, alone all night, in the dark. An' I got this feeling.' His face was suddenly radiant as his smile widened into joy and his hand came swiftly from behind his back, clutching a large, sharp stone.

'Like an 'unting feelin', girl,' he explained, smashing her spectacles with his first blow. She screamed, clawing at her eyes, writhing, blood trickling between her fingers. She looked clumsy and ridiculous, lying there, plump thighs straining at jeans, sandals twisting off under the frantic kicking of heels, so he broke her hands with two more knocks of the stone – expert knocks, born of the skilled ease of the natural hunter.

She huddled her arms to her chest, moaning. Shreds of eye membrane and splinters of glass mingled in the pulped bridge of her nose. Her legs, instinctively protective, crept towards her body, so he broke the kneecaps and shin bones and they retreated, twitching. Then he smashed her arms, starting at the wrists and progressing methodically to the shoulders.

'The trouble with Fred,' he confided, ripping off her clothes, 'was that he was bigger 'n me. He knocked me out before I really got going. An' when I came to 'e 'ad me in for assault and battry and I'd forgotten why.'

He licked his lips when all of her quivering flesh lay exposed and helpless before him.

'Cor, you're big, too, ain't you, girl? Lovely. Lots more of you to go yet, before we put you out of your misery. Pity I 'adn't a knife . . .'

Dawn's first light crept over the Heath, revealing a dense cluster of bushes some distance away. He thrust the stone into his pocket and began to pull the girl's moaning mass towards them, gathering up the tatters of her clothing and bundling them under his arm. 'Gotta make the most of you, girl. Gotta make you last all day. Mightn't get a chance like this again, 'cos I forget easy, see? I forget 'ow much I enjoy it.'

He trailed her across the grass, being careful about blood, and stored her in the thicket. Then he sat down beside her and taking out the stone again, poised it over her mouth.

'Nice an' nooky in 'ere, girl. Cosy. I don't like open spaces, much, do you?'

AWAKE, SLEEPING TIGRESS

Norman Kaufman

I hardly know where to begin, I'm so distressed. I suppose I should feel some sense of shame too, though God knows I'm no pillar of moral righteousness. Such an idea would be laughable – if I felt like laughing. But it's already a week since it happened and I'm still upset about it . . .

I'd known her for about three months, see – she was my landlady, you understand. I had answered an ad I saw in a newsagent's window, you know the sort of thing, rooms to let, hot and cold water, blah blah blah. Apply Miss Hannam at such and such an address. Which I did – and got my first shock.

For Miss Hannam was a hundred years old; and if you doubted her, she would point with simple pride to the telegram framed over the mantelpiece of her grubby little hovel (for that's all it was, so help me), a telegram that offered sincere congratulations to Eliza Mary Hannam upon reaching her century. It was signed with the Queen's signature, and that was that: one couldn't very well argue with Her Majesty's say-so. Not that there were many doubters really, because Eliza Mary *WAS* old, and she looked old and she acted old; and no one ever said to her, Oh Miss Hannam I would have thought you were about seventy if I didn't know different, fancy you being as old as *THAT*, well well well . . . Mind you, there weren't that many folk who spoke to her at all, what with her being so ancient and living in such a dank and dismal dump as she did: there was even talk of her not being quite – well, quite natural (maybe she – ha ha – maybe she's a witch, my dear – ha ha ha, silly really, but you don't know *WHAT* goes on these days, do you, dear, and she certainly looks the part, don't you think, mmm?)

Well, certainly she was no witch – but just as certainly she was far from normal. You can take my word for that; and if I tell you a bit about her, you'll understand that I'm piecing it together both from what I've heard by keeping my ears open, and by what Authority told me when it was all cleared up, so don't think I've got any particular insight, because the following is the truth as I saw it.

There wasn't much fun in Eliza Mary's life right from the word go – for she was born on the last day of 1869 in a damp, rat-ridden tenement house in North London. But she survived, despite the limitations of her time and her environment, and she grew up and went to school and thence into service with a Society family of some note. There was in fact very little to single her out from the tens of thousands of young women in similar circumstances; until one day the younger son of the household, one Simon de Vere Ffoulkes, felt a little flighty, a little full of *joie de vivre* and the joys of youth, not to mention a flagon of rather strong wine. Whereupon he took it upon himself to waylay twenty-four-year-old Eliza Mary Hannam at the top of the stairs by the broom cupboard – first of all ascertaining that Lord and Lady de Vere Ffoulkes were absent from the house, and that the rest of the family and servants were otherwise occupied.

In years to come, Simon would sometimes talk about the incident as if in a dream. For the rest of his days he would never forget the look on her face as he whispered his insidious come-on into her ear, as he guided her gently but ever so firmly into the broom cupboard, shut the door, and switched out the light. For Eliza Mary was – how can I put it? – she was blank, she was not even struggling, not even pretending just for the sake of it. In a word, the idea of resistance was completely beyond her ken, it never even occurred to her.

I must add here that it is my intention as far as possible to be as vague as I can be about the more tasteless side of this account, without, I hope, blurring the reader's own mental images. Suffice to say then that he lay her back on that dusty floor and (forgive me, I must be discreet) robbed her of her maidenhood. Yes I know it's a quaint phrase, but those were

Victorian times, remember... But I digress – what I must immediately point out is that Simon failed to enjoy any of it, and no more did his friends enjoy it, those of whom saw fit to follow Simon's example 'just to see what happens'. But regardless of the man involved, Eliza Mary never changed in her attitude, either mental or physical: without doubt she herself felt no bodily or emotional stimulation whatsoever. And such a one-sided arrangement was always enough to quench the fire in any man's loins.

The years went by and Eliza Mary was thirty and forty and then fifty, and the novelty of using her body had long since worn off; but it didn't matter to Eliza Mary because it never had mattered, had it? As far as she had been concerned, if the master's son and his friends and acquaintances wanted to do that thing to her, then all right, fair enough, it was fine with her, she was in service, she was beholden to the family, she was there to please, although come to think of it they didn't usually seem overjoyed afterwards, but that wasn't her fault, was it?

The fact is that Eliza Mary had been born with what latter-day psychiatrists would have termed a stunted libido. Quite simply, she grew to maturity with absolutely no knowledge of the basics of sex, attributable to this strange mental blockage that somehow refused to allow knowledge of this kind to infiltrate her mind and brain and ken. In addition, she had lost both her parents when very young, and her formative years had been governed by a termagant of an aunt who looked on her as an unpleasant duty rather than her late brother's child: certainly she would have brooked no mention of *THAT WORD* in her household.

So there it was. And the years continued to speed by, she watched her friends dying off, and suddenly the calendar said 1940, then 1950, and 1960 ... Simon de Vere Ffoulkes was now just a long-dead memory, the aunt was nought but dust in the family crypt... But something was happening to Miss Hannam, something that was little short of beyond comprehension, and certainly beyond belief; but I hope you do believe me, for it did happen: dear God yes, it happened all right.

She woke up one morning, ninety-one and a half years of age, and she lay there in bed, and it was as if the dawning sun had come up out of the heavens and finally liberated the mental obstruction that had held such a restraining hand on her instincts throughout her life. Suddenly, she realized, in a frightening flash of awareness, suddenly she knew. She *KNEW*. And with this first conscious wakening thought came an odd feeling of – what was it, the birth of a lust in her that she had never known as a young woman, all those wasted years ago?

Thus, incredibly, it began: the slow burning of a desire for a male that transcended all else, that sat with her and slept with her and ate with her, that lived by her side for almost a decade. For at last she knew. She felt. She believed. And ... it was too late. She was old, oh so old: she was lined and bent and unalluring and unwanted. What mental torture she underwent can only be guessed at.

Then came the last day of 1969 and the telegram. Three days later, a young man looking for cheap digs knocked on her door.

A brief word about myself, if I may be permitted. I'm twenty-three and admit to looking thirty: but I've always stoutly maintained that I don't mind this in the least, because I enjoyed every minute of getting into such a state in the first place. My whole *raison d'être* was women: I lived by them and for them, and if there were no women in the world I think I would have died long ago of a broken heart. All my spare cash, all my time and energy and consuming, boiling lustfulness, went into the Chase. By trade I was a van driver, and my wage was far from lavish – but women cost plenty, I don't need to tell you that, and I needed a base from which to carry out my errands of prey, or even to lure my (willing?) victims back.

Of course, when I got to the house and saw the state it was in, well, I did feel the first pangs of disappointment. I suppose I should have known it was too good to be true, at twenty-five bob a week, but ... I reasoned to myself that a small heater would soon disperse the damp patches and that a lick of paint might do the dismal walls a whole heap of good, and who could find such a cheap lodging-house in London anyway? So: arrangements were made for me to move in right away, and in I came; and whilst I was slightly put off by the musty-smelling landlady of apparently vast age, I was content enough.

I'm just about coming to the difficult part now, so I hope you'll bear with me if I appear to ramble a bit, if my words and phrases appear to stumble and slide about, because though it's a week back now, the sweat still stands out on my face when I think of it, and it's hard to write when your hands are slippery with perspiration and with the tears that roll quite naturally down my face and on to my fingers...

It was pure bad luck that she should have found those canvas bags. There were three of them and they all had various reference numbers and 'Trustee and Continental Bank' stencilled across them. Or maybe it wasn't bad luck, maybe it was my own stupidity that I didn't ditch them somewhere immediately after the raid. But she found them, and she could still read papers, could Miss Hannam. And she was not a fool. Bank clerk wounded in £3,000 hold-up, she read. Police looking for a man in late twenties or early thirties, broad-shouldered, around six feet tall... No, Eliza Mary, despite her years, was no fool; and perhaps when she found them she might have considered going to the Law – if only she had been normal. But as it was, she took them and she hid them away in a safe place. And at breakfast-time the next day, she told me what she'd done, this wheezing, hump-backed, stinking old —

At first I was all bluster, I suppose; and then, realizing the uselessness of it, I wondered if I ought to strangle the old loon. But maybe she saw that spark in my eyes, for she advised me gently to forget any homicidal instincts I might have, since she had already left a little letter with her bank, informing them of my name and description and the whereabouts of the canvas bags. On the envelope she had written: 'To be opened only in the event of my unnatural death'.

So what did she want in return for her silence, I wanted to know, all sullen-like, because I knew when I was beaten. Well, she hesitated before she answered, and her rheumy eyes lighted up as if a switch had been pressed deep inside her, releasing some dormant vitality, some hidden need. And I looked at her, thunderstruck, aghast: for I knew, I knew before she spoke. And my insides turned to water.

To love me, she croaked. That was all: but I turned and stumbled to the sink and brought up an undigested breakfast. I heard her murmur something about tonight at eight, and then she drifted out; but I could not have replied through the dry retches that threatened to choke me.

There was no out for me, that much I could see. I certainly wasn't clever enough to have murdered her in a manner that would have looked like a natural death; and I think I would have stopped short of murder anyway, it just wasn't in me. At least, that's what I thought at the time: but if I'd have known then how I would feel afterwards, then yes, perhaps I might have done away with her. The sickness is still here in my throat as I write, just as it was as I approached her room at eight that night.

She sat there in the old rocking-chair by the bed as I entered, her gnarled fingers busy with knitting-needles and wool. Knitting! The sheer incongruous horror of it, in the light of what she proposed we do together, was almost more than I could bear. But as I waited on the threshold, she nodded and smiled, laid down the needles and the wool, took off her spectacles and told me to undress her.

I stood transfixed, the first beads of sweat already popping out on my forehead, the first clutch of nausea tugging at my stomach. But ... this thing had to be done. It was my future I had to safeguard.

I reached out trembling fingers, and she got to her feet, and stood there, waiting, waiting, that slight smile still on her face, and – so help me – a thin trickle of saliva at the corner of her mouth. My hands dropped to my side for a moment, I swallowed hard as my stomach contracted, my mind in agony.

And then, with an effort of will such as I have never experienced, I reached out to her again.

As I look back now, I can see us both there like actors in a
charade, and I marvel, with all modesty aside, I marvel at my
own self-control. She stood there in silence as my anguished
fingers fumbled at the dirty black gown that swathed her
crooked form. Her deep-set eyes peered at me hungrily as I
peeled the garment from her and cast it on the dusty floor.
Only the rise and fall of her chest showed that she lived...I
tore blindly at her underclothes, her filthy underclothes that
reeked like her of decay; I heard her give a little sob, and I felt
the tears start from my own eyes, and I wondered what was
going on inside that mind of of hers...

*So at last it is here: this is what I have waited for, this is
what I have read about and dreamed about for all these years
past...This man is young and strong, and this will be wonderful, I know it. He is beginning to shake and tremble, and
he is crying, and I can smell the sweat on him. My own heart is
throbbing, my chest is heaving now, there is this new emotion
clawing at me, I can hardly catch my breath...*

Through the haze of abject dread that palsied my limbs, I
watched as she wavered in front of me, trying – dear God! –
trying to smile a seductive smile. She was naked – I had made
her so – and she was waiting now as I too undressed, waiting
for me to come to her and to join with her in the act of love. I
looked at her as the sick loathing constricted my throat: I
looked at the thin white hair and the sunken cheeks and the
toothless mouth; at the flat chest and the obscene swollen belly
and the fleshless flanks. And as if in the grip of some awful
nightmare, I moved towards her, found myself touching the
mottled body, felt the stink of the dirt in my nostrils, felt the
bile in my mouth as the veined arms encircled me and drew
me so gently towards the bed. I felt the scream rising up in my
chest, the sweat of pure terror stinging my eyes...I can't, I
heard myself rasp out, it's no use, there's no feeling, there's
nothing, there's nothing, there's —

And then suddenly my screaming stopped. For it was a lie,

a *LIE*, you understand? Yes, there *WAS* something, there *WAS*, and I thought I was going to die : my body was stirring with a sudden aching desire for this hundred-year-old woman. I was consumed with self-hatred, and loathing for this evil body that lay beneath me; but I could not move away, and I could not speak any more, and soon my whole being was fused with hers, and we moved as if we were one, and she writhed and scratched and tore at me, transported into the shadowy regions of passion that transcends all limitations of time; and as if from a great distance I heard us calling out for each other, our bodies soaked in perspiration, our eyes blinded with tears, the vomit from us both thick between our chests.

Finally, I got to my feet, stood there shuddering, looking down at her as my breath came in great heaving gasps; and through the yellow mists that dulled my sight, I saw that Eliza Mary was dead, her gummy mouth stretched in a half-smile, the glitter of lascivious pleasure and a new understanding still there in her set, lifeless eyes.

THE DEAD END

David Case

1

The waiter splashed a little wine in my glass and waited for me to taste it. Across the table, Susan was studiously avoiding my gaze. She was looking out of the leaded window at the blur of motorcars moving past in Marsham Street. The waiter stood, blank faced and discreet. This was a place where we had often been very happy, but we weren't happy now. I nodded and the waiter filled our glasses and moved away.

'Susan . . .'

She finally looked at me.

'I'm sorry.'

Susan shrugged. She was very hurt and I was very sad. It is a sad thing to tell the woman you love that you aren't going to marry her, and I suppose I could have chosen a better place than this restaurant, but somehow I felt I needed a familiar place, where we could be alone but have other people surrounding us. A cowardly attitude, of course, and yet it had taken great courage to break the engagement. I wanted nothing more in the world than to marry Susan, and now it was impossible.

'I've been expecting it, Arthur. It wasn't really such a shock.'

'Susan.'

'I could tell, you know. It's been different. You've been different. Ever since you returned from South America, I've been expecting this. I expect you met someone else there . . .'

'No. Please believe that.'

She gave a bitter little smile across the table.

'I love you, Susan. As much as ever. More. Now that I realize how much I'm losing, I want you more than ever.'

'Arthur, you haven't even made love to me since you came back. How can I believe you?'

'I can't, Susan.'

'Then tell me why.'

I shook my head.

'You owe me that much, Arthur. At least that much. Some explanation. Whatever it is, I'll understand. If there's someone else, if you're tired of me, if you simply want your freedom, I'll understand. There'll be no bitterness. But you can't simply break it off like this, without even telling me why. It's inhuman.'

And perhaps she would have understood. Susan, of all people, might have understood. But it was too horrible and I couldn't bring myself to tell her. I couldn't tell anyone. I didn't even tell the doctor who examined me what he was supposed to be looking for. It was a terrible secret, and I had to bear it alone.

'Susan, I can't tell you.'

She looked towards the window again. The leaded panes distorted the outside world. I thought she was going to cry, then, but she didn't. Her lip trembled. Waiters moved efficiently past our table, and the other customers wined and dined and pursued their individual lives, while I sat there alone. Susan was there, but I was alone.

'If only you hadn't gone,' she whispered.

Yes. If only I hadn't gone. If only a man could relive the past and undo what had been done. But I had gone, and I looked down at the wine shimmering in my glass and recalled how it had happened; recalled those monstrous things which had been, and could never be undone . . .

It is hard to believe that it was only two months since the director of the museum called me to his office on a grim London afternoon. I was excited and expectant about his summons, as I followed the echo of hollow footsteps through those hoary corridors to his office. I was well aware that Jeffries, the head of the anthropology department, planned to retire at the end of the year, and had hopes of being promoted to his position. I can recall the conflicting thoughts that bounded in my head, wondering if I wasn't too young to expect such promotion, counterbalancing this by mentally listing the well-received work I'd done since I'd been there, remembering that many of my views were opposed to the director's, but knowing him as a man who respected genuine disagreement and sought out subalterns who did not hesitate to put forth their own theories, and also, perhaps mainly, thinking how delighted Susan would be if I could tell her I'd been promoted and that we could change and hasten our plans in accordance with my new position. Susan wanted children, but was prepared to wait a few years until we could afford them; she wanted a house in the country but had agreed to move into my flat in town. Perhaps, now, we would not have to wait for these things. Visions of happiness and success danced in my head that afternoon, as they do when a man is young and hopeful.

I was only thirty-one years old that day, although I'm old now.

It was two months ago.

Doctor Smyth looked the part of a museum director, the template from which all men in that position should have been cut. He wore an ancient and immaculate double-breasted suit crossed with a gold watch chain, and reposed like a boulder behind a massive desk in his leather-bound den.

'Ah, Brookes. Sit down.'

I sat and waited. It was difficult to feel so confident now that I faced him. He filled a blackened pipe carefully, pressing the tobacco down with his wide thumb.

'Those reports I sent on to you the other day,' he said. He paused to touch a match to the tobacco, and I watched it uncurl in the flame. I was disappointed. I'd hoped this meeting would be far more momentous than that. A haze of smoke began to drift between us.

'You've studied them?'

'Yes, sir.'

'What's your opinion?'

I was mildly surprised. I'd been surprised when he sent them to me. They were the sort of thing one usually takes with a grain of salt, various unsubstantiated reports from Tierra del Fuego concerning a strange creature that had been seen in the mountains; a creature that appeared vaguely manlike, but behaved like an animal. It was reported to be responsible for destroying a few sheep and frightening a few people. The museum receives a good many reports of this nature, usually either a hoax or desire for publicity or over-stimulated imagination. True, there had been several different accounts of this creature with no apparent connexion between the men who claimed to have seen it, but I thought myself too much a man of science to place much faith in rumours of this sort.

And yet Smyth seemed interested.

'Well, I don't really know. Some sort of primate, perhaps. If there is anything.'

'Too large for a monkey.'

'If it weren't South America, I'd think possibly an ape . . .'

'But it is South America, isn't it?'

I said nothing.

'You mentioned a primate. It isn't a monkey, and it can't very well be an ape. What does that leave?'

'Man, of course.'

'Yes,' he said.

He regarded me through the smoke.

I said: 'Of course, the Indians in that area are very primitive. Possibly the most primitive men alive today. Darwin was certainly fascinated by them, running naked in that climate and eating raw mussels. This creature might well be a man, some hermit perhaps, or an aboriginal who has managed to avoid contact with civilization.'

'And more power to him,' Smyth said.

'I should think that's the answer.'

'I doubt it, somehow.'

'I don't see . . .'

'Several aboriginals have been known to have seen this

creature. Surely they would have recognized him as a man like themselves.'

'Perhaps. But there's certainly no proof to suggest it is something less than a man. I'd rate the plausibility of anything else well behind the Abominable Snowman, and you know my views on that.'

Smyth smiled rather tolerantly. I had done some research on the Yeti which had been well received, but my conclusions had been strictly negative. Smyth was inclined to admit the possibility of such creatures, however.

'I thought much the same way, at first,' he said.

'At first?'

'I've given it considerable thought. I was particularly impressed by the story that half-breed fellow told in Ushuaia. What was his name?'

'Gregorio?'

'Yes, that's the one. Hardly the sort of thing a man would imagine without some basis in truth, I should think. In fact, I sent a wire to a fellow I know there. Man named Gardiner. Used to be a manager with Explotadora, when the company was really big. Retired now, but he figured he was too old to start a new life in England and he stayed there. Splendid fellow, knows everyone. Helped us considerably the last time we had a field team out there. Anyway, he replied, and according to him this Gregorio is a fairly reliable sort. That got me wondering if there mightn't be more to this than I'd supposed. And then, there's another angle ...'

His pipe had faltered. He spent several moments and several matches lighting it again.

'What do you know of Hubert Hodson?' he asked.

'Hodson? Is he still alive?'

'Hodson is several years younger than I,' Smyth said, amused. 'Yes, he's still very much alive.'

'He was before my time. Not highly regarded these days, a bit outdated. I've read him, of course. A renegade with curious theories and an adamant attitude, but a first-class scientist. Some of his ideas caused quite a stir some twenty years ago.'

Smyth nodded. He seemed pleased that I knew about Hodson.

'I'm rather vague on his work, actually. He specialized in the genetics of evolution, I believe. Not really my line.'

'He specialized in many things. Spread himself too thin, perhaps. But he was a brilliant man.' Smyth's eyes narrowed, he was recalling the past. 'Hodson put forth many theories. Some nonsense, some perhaps not. He believed that the vocal cords were the predominant element in man's evolution, for instance – maintained that any animal, given man's power of communication, would in time have developed man's straight spine, man's thumb, even man's brain. That man's mind was no more than a by-product of assembled experience and thought unnecessary to development. A theory of enormous possibilities, of course, but Hodson, being the man he is, threw it down like a gauntlet, as a challenge to man's superior powers of reasoning. He presented it as though he preferred to cause consternation and opposition, rather than seeking acceptance.

'It was much the same with his mutation theory, when he claimed that evolution was not a gradual process, but moved in sudden forward spurts at various points in time, and that the time was different and dependent upon the place. Nothing wrong with these ideas, certainly, but his manner of presentation was such that the most harmless concepts would raise a hue and cry. I can remember him standing at the rostrum, pointing at the assembly with an accusing finger, his hair all wild, his eyes excited, shouting, "Look at you! You think that you are the end product of evolution? I tell you, but for a freak Oligocene mutation, you would be no more than our distant cousins, the shrews. Do you think that you and I share a common ancestor? We share a common mutation, no more. And I, personally, find it regrettable." You can imagine the reaction among the learned audience. Hodson merely smiled and said, "Perhaps I chose my words rashly. Perhaps your relation to the shrews is not so distant after all." Yes, I can remember that day clearly, and I must admit I was more amused than outraged.'

Smyth smiled slightly around his pipe.

'The final insult to man came when he claimed all evolution had been through the female line. If I remember correctly, he stated that the male was no more than a catalyst, that man, being weaker, succumbed to these irregular mutations and in turn was merely the agent that caused the female to progress or change, was only necessary to inspire the female to evolve, so to speak. Men, even men of science, were hardly prepared to countenance that, naturally. Hodson was venomously attacked, both scientifically and emotionally, and, strangely enough, the attacks seemed to trouble him this time. He'd always delighted in the furore before, but this time he went into seclusion and finally disappeared entirely.'

'You seem to know a great deal about him, sir,' I said, 'Considering he's rather obscure.'

'I respected him.'

'But how does this tie in with the reports from South America?'

'Hodson is there. That is where he went when he left the country twenty odd years ago, and he's been there ever since. That's why you've heard nothing from him for the last generation. But God knows what he's doing there. He's published nothing, made no statements at all, and that's very unlike Hodson. He was always a man to make a statement simply for shock value, whether he really believed it or not.'

'Perhaps he's retired.'

'Not Hubert.'

'And you believe that his presence is connected with those reports?'

'I have no idea. I just wonder. You see, no one knows exactly where he is – I don't expect anyone has tried to find out, actually – but he's located somewhere in the Chilean part of Tierra del Fuego, in the south-western section.'

'And that's where the reports have come from,' I said.

'Exactly. It just makes me wonder a bit.'

We both pondered for a few minutes while he lighted his pipe again. Then I thought I saw a flaw.

'But if he's been there for twenty years ... these reports have all been within the last six months. I don't see how that would tie in.'

'Don't you?'

I didn't. He puffed away for a while.

'This creature which may, or may not, have been seen. It was as large as a man. Therefore, we may assume it to be full grown. Say, twenty years old, perhaps?'

'I see. You believe – I mean to say, you recognize the possibility – that Hodson may have heard something about this creature twenty years ago, and went to investigate. That he has been looking for it all this time.'

'Or found it.'

'Surely he wouldn't keep something of that enormity secret?'

'Hodson is a strange man. He resented the attacks that were mounted against his ideas. He might well be waiting until he has a complete documentation, beyond refutation – a life's-work, all neatly tied up and proven. Perhaps he found this creature. Or creatures. We may safely assume that, if it exists, it had parents. Possibly siblings, as well. I think it more likely that Hodson would have discovered the parents and studied the offspring, or the whole tribe. Lived with them, even. That's the sort of thing he'd do.'

'It seems – well, far-fetched, sir.'

'Yes, it does, doesn't it? A science fiction idea. What did they used to call it? The missing link?' He chuckled. 'The common ancestor is more accurate, I suppose.'

'But you can't really believe that a creature like that could be alive now?'

'I admit it is most unlikely. But then, so was the coelacanth, before it was discovered alive.'

'But that was in the sea. God knows what may exist there. We may never know. But on land, if a creature like that existed, it would have been discovered before now.'

'It's a wild, barren place, Tierra del Fuego. Rough terrain and a sparse population. I say only that it is possible.'

'You realize that the Indians of Tierra del Fuego are prehistoric, so to speak?' I said.

'Certainly.'

'And yet you feel there is a chance this creature might be something other than one of them?'

'A possibility.'

'And still a man?'

Smyth gestured with his pipe.

'Let us say, of the genus homo but not of the species sapiens.'

I was astounded. I couldn't believe that Smyth was serious. I said, with what I thought admirable understatement, 'It seems most unlikely.'

Smyth looked almost embarrassed. When he spoke, it was as though he was offering an explanation. He said, 'I mentioned that I have great respect for Hodson. And a great curiosity. He's not a man to forsake his science, and he's spent the last twenty odd years doing something on that island. That in itself is interesting. Hodson was primarily a laboratory man. He had little time for field work and believed that to be the proper task for men with less imagination and intelligence – believed that lesser men should gather the data for men of his own calibre to interpret. And then, quite suddenly, he disappears into the wilds. There has to be a reason, something to which he was willing to dedicate the rest of his life. And Hodson placed the highest possible value on his life, in the sense of what he could accomplish while he lived. It may have nothing whatsoever to do with these reports. Quite likely it doesn't. But whatever he is doing is definitely of interest. Whatever he has accomplished in twenty years is bound to be fascinating, whether it is right or wrong. I've often considered sending someone to locate him, but always put it off. Now seems the perfect time to kill two birds with one stone. Or, perhaps, the same bird.'

I nodded, but I was in no way convinced.

'I expect you think I'm grasping at a straw,' Smyth said, noticing my hesitation. 'I knew Hodson. Not well, not as a friend, but I knew him. You'd have to know him to understand how I feel. I was one of the last people he spoke with before he vanished, and I've always remembered that conversation. He was exuberant and excited and confident. He told me that he was working on something new, something very big. He even admitted that the results might disprove some of his earlier theories, which was very impressive, coming from a man who had never in his life admitted he might be mistaken. And he said that this time no one would be able to scoff or doubt or disagree, because when he was finished he would have more than a theory – he would have concrete proof.'

Smyth tapped the ash from his pipe. He seemed tired now.

'You've never been to South America, have you?' he asked.

'No.'

'Would you like to?'

'Very much.'

'I think I'd like to send you there.'

Smyth opened a drawer and began thumbing through some papers. There were handwritten notes in the margins. He said, 'The place to start will be Ushuaia. I'll wire Gardiner to expect you, he should be helpful. You can spend a few days there checking on the reports in person. Then try to locate Hodson. Gardiner might know where he is. He'll certainly know where he buys his supplies, so you should be able to work back from there.'

'Are you sure he gets his supplies from Ushuaia?'

'He must. There's nowhere else anywhere near there.'

Everything seemed to be moving very fast suddenly.

'Now, I'd better arrange a hotel for you,' Smyth said, turning a sheet to read the margin. 'The Albatross or the Gran Parque? Neither has hot water nor central heating, but a dedicated scientist shouldn't mind that.'

I tossed a mental coin.

'The Albatross.'

'How soon will you be able to leave?'

'Whenever you like.'

'Tomorrow?'

I believe I blinked.

'If that's convenient,' Smyth said.

'Yes, all right,' I said, wondering what Susan would think about it with no time to get used to the idea.

'Fine,' Smyth said, and the interview was over. I was amazed and sceptical, but if Smyth had respect for Hodson, I had respect for Smyth. And the prospect of field work is always exciting.

I rose to leave.

'Oh, Brookes?'

'Sir?'

I was at the door and turned. He was filling another pipe.

'You know that Jeffries is retiring at the end of the year?'

'I'd heard as much, sir.'

'Yes. That's all,' he said.

Then I was very excited.

Tierra del Fuego.

Delighted as I was at Smyth's open hint of promotion, I think I was even more excited about the opportunity to visit that fascinating archipelago. I suppose that every anthropologist since Darwin has been fascinated by the opportunities existing there to study primitive man. Separated from the South American mainland by the Straits of Magellan and divided between Argentina and Chile, Tierra del Fuego consists of the large island, five smaller islands, numerous islets, peninsulas, channels, bays and sounds crouched beneath the low clouds and fierce winds where the Andes stagger down, stumbling across the straits and limping out to fall, at Cape Horn, into the mists at the end of the world. There was little there to attract civilization, 27,500 square miles of rugged wilds with sheep, lumbering and fishing, a recent discovery of poor oil in the plains to the north-east – and the fascination of Stone Age man.

They were there when Magellan discovered the land in 1520, and named it the land of fire because of the signal fires that smouldered along the windy coast, a group of human beings that time and evolution had overlooked, leading their natural and prehistoric lives. And they are still there, diminished by contact with civilization and unable to cope with the fingertips of the modern world that have managed to grope even to this forsaken place, reduced to living in wretched hovels on the outskirts of the towns. There are few left. These creatures who could face the wind and snow without clothing could not face the advance of time.

But surely not all had succumbed. And this, I felt, would prove the answer to the rumours of a wild creature, that it would be an aborigine who had refused to give up his dignity and forsake his wild freedom, and still ran savage and naked through those mountains and canyons. It was a far more feasible solution than Smyth had put forward, and no little opportunity for study in its own right. I believed that was what Hodson had been doing all these years, but that Smyth, never a sceptic, was so overpowered by the force of this man that his imagination had run wild; that he could have believed anything in relation to Hodson.

Or was Smyth, perhaps, testing me in some fashion? Could he be inviting me to draw my own conclusions as the future head of my department?

It was an intriguing thought, and I was quite willing to stand the examination. I needed no unfounded rumours or vague speculation, the opportunities of Tierra del Fuego were enough in themselves.

I had only one reservation. What was Susan going to think of this immediate and prolonged parting? I knew that she would put forth no objections, she was not the sort of woman who would interfere with a man's work, but I knew she would be disappointed and disturbed at our separation. I wasn't happy at the thought of being away from her either, of course, but this feeling was tempered by my excitement. It is always harder for the one who stays behind.

We had never been apart before. We'd met some six months before and become engaged within a fortnight – one of those rare and remarkable meetings of mind and body that seem destined to be, a perfect agreement in all things and a blissful contentment when we were together. We were old enough to know that this was what we wanted, and all we wanted, with no doubts whatsoever about our future. I knew Susan would understand the necessity for the separation, and had no qualms about telling her; I worried only that she would be saddened.

Susan was preparing dinner at her place that evening. She had a small flat in South Kensington where she practised her culinary arts several times a week, not as the way to her man's heart, which she already had, but through a splendidly old-fashioned idea of being an ideal wife. I was still in an excited mood as I walked to her place through the late afternoon, scarcely noticing the steady drizzle as a discomfort, although possessed of a feeling that all my senses were alert, that I was aware of everything in the slightest detail. The sky was darkening and the street lamps had come on, pale and haloed. The traffic was heavy but strangely silent. Pedestrians hurried home from their work, collars up and heads lowered. They all seemed very dismal and drab to me, creatures of humdrum habit who could not but envy my life and future, my woman and my work, had they known. I would have liked to stop some passing stranger and tell him of my success, show him a photograph of Susan, not through vanity as much as a feeling of gratitude. It was the first time I could remember wanting to tell someone about myself. I had few friends and most of my acquaintances were professional, and had never felt the need before. But then, I had never felt this happy anticipation. I quickened my pace, anxious to be with Susan.

I had a key to her flat and let myself in at the front door, walked up the two flights to her floor and entered. The flat was warm and comfortable, the gramophone was playing a record of baroque harp and recorder and I could hear Susan manipulating utensils in the tiny kitchen. I stood in the doorway for a moment, appreciating the way Susan had decorated the room, with great care and taste and little expense, and feeling the contentment that always filled me when I was there. I realized then just how much I was going to long for Susan while I was away.

Susan heard the door close and came into the room. She was wearing a simple black dress of which I was exceptionally fond and her hair fell to her shoulders with all the tones and shades of a forest fire. She smiled as she crossed the room and we kissed. Then she must have seen something in my expression, because her forehead arched in query.

'You look thoughtful, darling.'

'I was thinking.'

'Oh?'

I moved to the couch. She didn't press her question.

'Dinner in fifteen minutes,' she said. 'Sherry?'

'Fine.'

She poured the sherry from a cut-glass decanter and handed me a glass, then sat beside me on the couch, curling her long legs under her. I sipped the drink and the record ended and rejected. The Hebrides Overture began to play.

'What about?' she asked then.

'Two things, really. I was talking with Smyth today. He made a point of mentioning that Jeffries is retiring.'

'But that's wonderful, Arthur.'

'Oh, it's nothing definite. I mean, he didn't tell me I was in line for the position or anything.'

'But he must have implied it.'

'Yes, I suppose so.'

'Oh, darling, I'm so pleased.' She kissed me lightly. 'I know you'd hoped for it. We should celebrate.'

I smiled, not too cheerfully.

'Is anything wrong?'

'No, not really.'

'You hardly seem elated.'

'Well, there's another thing.'

'Good?'

'In a way. It's just that – well, I don't know what you'll think about it.'

She looked at me over the rim of her glass. Her eyes were green and lovely. She was very beautiful.

'Tell me,' she said.

'I have to go to South America.'

She blinked.

'Oh, not to live or anything. Just a field trip for the museum. A wonderful opportunity, really, except it will mean being away from you for a while.'

'Did you expect me to object?'

'I knew better than that.'

'How long will you be gone?'

I wasn't at all sure. I said, 'Two or three months, I suppose.'

'I'll miss you very much, darling. When will you have to leave?'

'Tomorrow.'

'So sudden? But why?'

'Well, it's an idea Smyth has. I don't agree with him, but either way it's a marvellous opportunity. And my promotion might well rest on what I do there.'

Susan pondered for a moment, then smiled. It was all right. She understood, as I'd known she would, and conflicting emotions struggled for only that moment before yielding to logic rare in a woman.

'I'm happy for you, darling. Really I am.'

'It won't be long.'

'You're very excited about it, aren't you?'

'Yes. It's a splendid opportunity. Except for being away from you.'

She dismissed that with a gesture.

'Tell me about it.'

I talked for a while, telling her about Tierra del Fuego, Hubert Hodson, the recent reports and my own ideas about them. Susan listened, interested because it interested me, and getting used to the idea of our separation, balancing it with the advantages that would follow my potential promotion. Presently we had dinner with candlelight and wine, and Susan

was as lively and cheerful as ever. I loved her very much. I
could already feel the pain of parting, the emotional tone of
our last evening together and a touch of the thrill that would
come when we were together again on my return.

We took our brandy out to the little terrace that ran around
the side of the building and stood hand in hand at the railing,
looking out across the dark canyons of the city. The lights of
the West London Air Terminal loomed garish and gaudy
above the rooftops. They reminded me of my flight, making
the prospect more concrete and immediate, and perhaps they
did the same for Susan. She became solemn, holding my hand
tightly.

'God, I'll miss you so much,' she said.

'Me too.'

'No longer than you have to, darling?'

'No longer.'

'I'll be awfully lonely.'

'So will I.'

She looked at me then, feigning a frown of deep concern.

'Not lonely enough to seek solace in the arms of another
woman, I trust,' she said. But she said it as a joke, to dispel
the tension. Susan knew I wanted no one but her, and never
would. I'd never imagined a time when I would place a
woman ahead of my work, but if she had asked me not to go, I
would have remained with her.

Ah, why didn't she?

2

I refilled my glass.

Susan hadn't touched her wine. I recalled how happy we'd
been the night before I'd left, and the contrast made our
sorrow worse. If it could possibly be worse. The waiter looked
towards our table to see if we wanted anything and looked
quickly away. A man dining alone across the room glanced ap-

preciatively at Susan, admiring her long legs and amber hair,
then lowered his gaze as I looked at him. Susan would have no
trouble finding a new man whenever she wanted, and this
bitter knowledge sent a chill down my backbone, all the colder
because I knew she wanted no one but me, and because I
could never marry her. My hand trembled with the weight
of the bottle and my heart trembled with the weight of
despair.

Susan looked up through her lashes, a glance that would
have been flirtatious had her eyes not been dull with grief.

'What happened in Tierra del Fuego, Arthur?' she asked,
pleading for an answer, a reason which might make her sorrow
less through understanding.

I shook my head.

I couldn't tell her.

But I remembered . . .

I flew from Buenos Aires to Ushuaia.

In the footsteps of Darwin, the modern speed seemed wrong
and disappointing. Darwin had been there on HMS *Beagle*
from 1826 to 1836, exploring the channel on which Ushuaia
was situated. It was called, appropriately enough, the Beagle
Channel. But I flew in from Buenos Aires in five hours, seated
next to a middle-aged American tourist and disturbed by the
thought that there could be nothing left for discovery in a town
with an airport and the beginnings of a tourist trade.

The tourist wanted to talk, and nothing short of direct
impoliteness would have silenced him.

'Going to Ushuaia?' he asked.

I nodded.

'Me too.'

That seemed obvious enough, since that was where the
aeroplane was headed.

'Name's Jones. Clyde Jones.'

He had a big, healthy face clamped around a huge cigar.

'Brookes.'

Jones extended a wide hand. He wore a ruby ring on his

little finger and an expensive camera on a sling around his neck. His grip was very firm. I suppose he was a pleasant enough fellow.

'You a Limey? I'm a Yank.'

He hesitated, as though wondering if this required another handshake.

'You a tourist? I am. Travel a lot, you know. Since my wife died I travelled all over. Been in your country. Been all over Europe. Spent two months there last summer, saw it all. Except the communist parts, of course. I wouldn't want to go there and give them any foreign exchange.'

'Quite right,' I said.

'Did you know this Ushuaia is one of the southernmost communities in the world? I want to see this Ushuaia. Don't know why. 'Cause it's there, I guess. Like mountain climbers, huh? Ha ha.'

I looked out the window. The flat tableland and glacial lakes of the north were behind, and the terrain was beginning to rise in rugged humps and twisting rivers, glimpsed through clouds as heavy and low as the smoke from Jones's cigar. It was exciting land, but I was depressed. Jones did not seem interested. I suppose he saw nothing that was not framed in his camera's lens. He chatted away amicably, and I was seized with a feeling that I had been born too late, that nothing new remained to be discovered, and that all one could do now was study the past.

And no man has ever been more wrong.

Everything seemed much brighter after we landed.

The airport was on the edge of the town, and Jones shared a taxi with me. He was staying at the Albatross, too. The taxi was a huge American model, as modern as a missile, but somehow this didn't trouble me, now that I was in contact with the land. It was as if the motorcar were out of time and place, not that the land had changed. Jones may have felt something of this anachronism, as well, for he became quiet and almost apprehensive, perhaps sensing that he didn't belong here, that the soul of this place had not yet been sucked into the tourists' cameras. I looked from the window and became excited once more as we jolted through the streets.

Ushuaia looked like a Swiss mountain village set on a Norwegian fiord. Sharp-spined wooden chalets leaned on the steep hills and a glacier mounted the hill behind, impressive and impassive. Farther to the west the high peaks of Darwin and Larmeinto rose into the low clouds. The taxi slowed suddenly, throwing me forwards on the seat. We had braked behind a man on horseback, sitting slumped in his poncho. The horse moved sedately up the middle of the road. The driver sounded the horn and the rider, if anything, slumped more and carried on at his own pace. The driver cursed, revving the monstrous engine in helpless frustration and moving his hands in wide gesticulation. I was pleased.

The taxi stopped at the Albatross and we got out. The wind was dipping and swirling through the streets. It was late afternoon. Jones insisted on paying the fare and waved away my protest, saying I could stand him a drink later. He was shivering in his Brooks Brothers suit. We had to carry our own bags in to the desk while we registered, and I walked up to my room while Jones looked about for a page boy or a lift. I was gratified for the chance to be alone, and pleased with my room. It was primitive and satisfying, although I don't suppose Jones was too happy about such accommodation.

I washed and shaved with cold water and went to the window to look out. It would soon be dark, and I thought it too late to call on Gardiner that afternoon. This didn't displease me. I was far more anxious to pursue my own wanderings than Smyth's theory, and although I was certainly anxious to meet Hodson it was more because he was an eminent and interesting theorist in my own field than because he might provide a link in the implausible chain of Smyth's reasoning. I decided to spend what remained of the daylight in roaming about the town, getting the mood of Ushuaia as a fulcrum towards understanding the land.

I hoisted my suitcase to the bed and opened it, found a

warmer coat and put it on, put a notepad and pencil in the pocket and left the room. I had to pass the entrance to the bar on the way out, and glanced in. Jones was already there, chatting in familiar tones with the barman. He didn't notice me. It was cold and damp in the street and the vortex of wind had straightened and came more steadily from the south. I turned my collar up and lighted a cigarette in the shelter of the building, then walked out to the street. The wind fanned the cigarette until it burned like a fuse, bouncing sparks as I turned my head.

I had a street map of the town, but didn't use it. I had no particular destination but walked in the general direction of the port, down steep streets lined with the trading companies that supplied the whole area, facing that powerful wind. Motorcars and horsecarts shared the streets with an assorted population of many nationalities and many backgrounds; English, Spanish, Yugoslavian, Italian, German – the racial mixture that invariably gathers at a frontier, colonialists and conquistadors, sailors and settlers, farmers and shepherds, the leftover dregs of the gold rush and the seepage from the oil fields in the north, men who had come to seek and men who had come where they would not be sought – and, of course, the few tourists looking disgruntled and uncomfortable and wondering what had possessed them to come here. This was a rich lode indeed for a social anthropologist, but that was not my field, and I had only a mild interest in observing the men who had come here. I wanted the men who had been here long before anyone came, and there were only a few natives in the town. They had been drawn towards this outpost of civilization but had not been integrated into its core; they had stopped and clustered at the outskirts.

Standing on the quay, I looked into the hard water of the Beagle Channel and the deserted islands in the mist beyond. The water ran in jagged lines of black and white, and a solitary hawk circled effortlessly in the air currents above. A man, almost invisible inside an ancient leather coat, led a loaded llama straight towards me, forcing me back from the water. He didn't notice me, although the beast turned a curious eye as he lumbered past.

I turned back up the incline. My heavy coat was proof against the cold, but the wind slid through the fabric and cascaded my hair over my brow. The sensation was not unpleasant, and I felt no urge to return to the hotel yet. I turned in the opposite direction and climbed away from the centre of the town.

Night was deepening the sky beneath the darkened clouds when I found myself at the end of the modern world – the outskirts of Ushuaia. I had a very concrete sense of standing at a barrier. Behind me electric and neon blanketed the town, the light confined within the limits. This was the point to which civilization had penetrated, although it lay in a thin veneer within the boundaries, its roots shallow and precarious, a transplant that had not yet taken a firm hold. Before me the land broke upwards and away, jagged and barren and dotted with clusters of sheet-metal shacks painted in the brightest tones, oranges and yellows and reds. The thin chimneys rattled bravely in the wind, and the smoke lay in thin, flat ribbons. Kerosene lamps cast futile pastel light in the doorways, and a few shadowed figures moved.

This, then, was where the natives lived. This was where they had been drawn, and then halted, those who had surrendered. And beyond this fringe, perhaps, were those who had refused to yield to the magnet of time.

I walked slowly back to the hotel, and slept well.

3

I awoke early in the sharp cold. The window framed a rectangle of bright and brittle light blocked on the opposite wall. I dressed quickly and went to the window, expecting to see the sun, but the light was filtered through a tissue of cloud, diffused throughout the sky. It left the streets strangely without shadow or contrast, and made the day seem even colder than it was. I put an extra sweater on before going down to the breakfast room. No one else was there yet. A fire had been lighted but hadn't yet taken the chill from the room, and I didn't dawdle over my coffee. I wanted to send a wire to Susan to let her know I had arrived safely, and then I had to contact Gardiner. I was just leaving when Jones came in, looking haggard and bleary. He smiled perfunctorily.

'You tried that pisco yet?' he asked.

I didn't know what pisco was.

'The local booze. Grape alcohol. Gives a man a wicked hangover, I'll tell you.'

He shook his head and sank into a chair. He was calling for black coffee as I left. I wondered if he'd ever managed to get out of the hotel bar the night before. And yet, in his fashion, he would learn things about this town that I would never know.

I walked to the telegraph office and sent the wire to Susan, lighted my first cigarette of the day and started back toward the hotel. Three hawks were perched, evenly spaced, on the telegraph wires, and I wondered, whimsically, if they would be aware of my message darting beneath their talons. A taxi had pulled up at the hotel to let a passenger out, and I asked the driver if he knew where Gardiner lived. He did, and I got in the back seat, smoking and looking out of the windows. We drove out past the ancient Indian cemetery on the crisp morning road, with crackling tyres and white exhaust, on a day that made me feel very much alive.

Gardiner's big house was stuck against the glacier in two-dimensional silhouette. I walked up from the road and Gardiner opened the door before I had knocked. He wore a red wool dressing gown and held a gin and tonic.

'You must be Brookes.'

I nodded.

'Smyth wired me to expect you. Thought you'd be here last night.'

'I got in rather late.'

He stepped back and let me in. He hadn't shaved yet, and had vaguely waved the gin in lieu of a handshake. We went into a large room curiously devoid of furnishings. A beautifully engraved shotgun hung on the wall and there was a sheepskin rug by the fire.

'I hope I'm no trouble,' I said.

'Not at all. Glad to help if I can. Glad to have some company. Gin or brandy?'

'It's rather early.'

'Nonsense.'

He gave me gin and we sat by the fire.

'Smyth said you've been very helpful to us in the past,' I said.

'I'm no scientist, but I expect I know as much about this place as anyone. Been here thirty-odd years. Not much to do here now. A little shooting and a lot of drinking. Used to be different in the old days, before the land reforms whittled the company away.' He shook his head, not necessarily in disapproval. 'But that won't interest you.'

'Well, I'm more interested in the natives.'

'Of course.' He looked thoughtful, shaking his head again. 'There were three tribes when the white man came here. The Alacalufs, the Yahgans, and the Onas.' I knew all this, but was content to listen. 'They were absolutely prehistoric, stark naked savages. Probably very happy, too. They didn't understand the white man and they didn't trust him. Good judges. They were even rash enough to steal a few of the white man's sheep, and the white man shot a few of them, of course. Did them a little harm. But then the enlightened white men came. The missionaries. They came burning with the fever of reform and saw these unfortunate lambs of God running about naked and indecent and, in the fashion of their kind, gave them blankets for warmth and modesty. The blankets hadn't been disinfected, so they also gave them plague. Killed off all the Onas and most of the others. But, oh well, we couldn't have them trotting about naked, could we?'

Gardiner sighed and poured another gin.

'Will you stay here?' he asked.

'I'm already at the hotel.'

'Ah.' I think he would have welcomed a guest. 'Well, how can I help you, then?'

I told him about the rumours and reports, and what Smyth thought possible. Gardiner nodded. He'd heard them himself, of course.

'Would you think there was anything in it?' I asked.

'There must be something. All rumours have some basis in fact. But I doubt if it's anything very interesting. Nothing like Smyth suggests. I've never seen or heard of anything like that before, and if something did exist it surely would have been discovered before. Left some evidence of its existence, at least.'

'That's what I thought.'

'I should think perhaps a wild dog, or possibly a man — maybe even an escapee from the penal colony, living wild.'

'That would account for the dead sheep. But what about this man who claims to have seen it? The one Smyth queried you about?'

'Gregorio. Yes. Of course, when I answered Smyth's wire, I didn't know what he was interested in Gregorio for. I thought he might be contemplating using him for a guide perhaps, and he's reliable enough for that sort of thing. But as far as his account of this strange creature —' he paused, as if giving it every consideration. 'Well, I suppose he did see something that frightened the hell out of him, but I'm sure it wasn't what he thought it was. He's a superstitious, imaginative sort of fellow, and he certainly hasn't tried to capitalize on the story so I expect we can discount the possibility that he made it up. He hasn't said anything about it for some time.'

'I'd like to talk to him.'

'No harm in that.'

'Do you know where I might find him?'

'Yes. He lives in a shack just west of town. Scrapes out a

living as a freelance farmer and tourist guide, now that they have started to come.' Gardiner shuddered at the idea of tourists. 'Speaks English well enough. I shouldn't offer him much money, though, or he's liable to feel he owes you a good story and embellish it.'

'Anyone else I should see?'

'You might have a chat with MacPherson. He has a small farm near here. Had a few sheep destroyed. He'll be more accurate than Gregorio.'

MacPherson was one of the names I remembered from the reports Smyth had received.

'Where will I find him?'

'He's in town right now, matter of fact.'

'That will be convenient. Where?'

Gardiner was pouring another drink.

'Where else?' he said, smiling. 'At the bar of the Gran Parque. I'll drive you in and introduce you, if you like.'

Gardiner drove an ancient Packard with considerable panache. I asked him about Hodson as we rumbled ponderously into town.

'Hodson? Haven't seen him in years.'

'Smyth seemed certain he was still here.'

'Oh, he's here. But he never comes into Ushuaia.'

'Any idea where he lives?'

'Not really. He's an unsociable type.' Gardiner seemed scornful of such behaviour. 'He's out in the mountains some-where. Graham might know more about it. He runs a trading company and I think Hodson gets his supplies there. But he never comes in himself.'

'If you'll introduce me to Graham —'

'Certainly,' Gardiner said, concentrating on the road with both hands on the wheel. He wore string-backed driving gloves and a flat tweed cap. We came over a sharp rise and there was a horse and rider blocking the road, slowly moving towards us. We seemed to be moving frightfully fast. I started to shout a warning but Gardiner was already moving, shifting down with a fluid sweep of the lever and letting the engine howl. He didn't bother with brakes or horn, and scarcely turned the steering wheel. The rider hauled the horse around in a rearing sidestep and the animal's flank flashed by my window. Remembering the taxi driver's difficulty, I decided that Gardiner must have a considerable reputation.

'Certainly I shall,' he said.

The trading company was on our way and we pulled up in front. The old Packard ran considerably better than it stopped. It rocked to a halt like a weary steeplechaser refusing a jump. Gardiner led the way into a large building cluttered haphazardly with a catholic selection of goods and supplies. Graham was a dusty little man behind a dusty wooden counter, and when Gardiner introduced us, he said, 'Baa.'

I expect I looked startled.

'Local greeting,' Gardiner said. 'Has something to do with sheep, I assume.'

'That's right,' Graham said. 'Baa.'

'Baa,' I said.

'Brookes is trying to get in touch with Hodson. Does he still trade with you?'

'That's right.'

'Do you know where he lives?' I asked.

'Nope. Never see him. Haven't seen Hodson in three or four years.'

'How does he have his supplies delivered?'

'He doesn't. Sends a man to fetch them.'

'Well, do you know anyone who could take me to him?'

Graham scratched his head.

'Can't think of anyone off hand. Funny. I guess the best thing would be to wait for the man who fetches his supplies.'

'That would do. If I could speak to him the next time he comes here.'

'Can't speak to him.'

'Oh?'

'Can't speak. He's a mute.'

I felt rather frustrated. Gardiner was grinning. He asked, 'Does he come frequently?'

'Yeah. Has to, pretty much. See, Hodson's camp or whatever it is, is up in the mountains. Probably over on the Chilean side. There aren't any roads up there, so he has to take the things on pack horses. Can't take very much stuff on horseback, so he has to come in every few weeks. Should be coming in any day now, matter of fact.'

'Could you let me know when he does?'

'Guess so.'

'I'm at the Albatross.'

'Yep.'

'I'll be glad to —'

'Not necessary,' he said, foreseeing the offer of money. 'If you need any supplies yourself, buy 'em here.'

That was something I hadn't thought of.

'What will I need to reach Hodson's?'

'Hard to say, since I don't know where it is. You'll need a horse and pack. I can get something ready for you, if you want Have it waiting when Hodson's man arrives.'

'That will be fine.'

I wasn't sure how fine it would be. I hadn't been on a horse for years, but some obscure pride rose up in a dubious battle against the urge to ask him to find me a docile animal. The pride won. I suppose I was already being affected by contact with these self-sufficient frontiersmen.

We went back to the car.

'It's a rather rough trek up those hills,' Gardiner said, as he started the engine. He let it idle for a moment. Perhaps he'd seen my doubts mirrored in my expression. 'I suppose you can handle a horse all right?'

'I've ridden,' I said. 'Not for some time.'

'Best to let the horse pick his own way. Good, sure-footed animals here.'

'Well, the worst I can do is fall off.'

Gardiner looked horrified.

'A gentleman never falls off,' he said. 'He is thrown.'

He was chuckling happily as we drove off.

MacPherson wasn't in the Gran Parque.

This distressed Gardiner, who hated to have people behave out of character, and hated to have his predictions proven wrong. We found him in the next bar down the street, however, so it wasn't too unjustifiable. MacPherson was classically sandy haired, proving that truth has less regard for triteness than literary convention. He was standing at the bar, talking with a villainous-looking man with a drooping moustache and splendidly hand-tooled boots.

Gardiner drew me to the bar at the far end.

'He's talking business. We'll wait here until he's finished.'

'What a remarkable looking fellow.'

'Mac?'

'The other one. Looks like a Mexican bandit.'

Gardiner grinned. 'He is rather traditional, isn't he? A Yugoslav. Free zone trader.'

'What would that be?'

'A smuggler. Works from here up to Rio Grande through the Gortbaldi Pass. Quite a bit of that goes on. This fellow is very respected in his line, I understand. Not that I would have any dealings with him, of course.' Gardiner looked amused. The Spanish barman came over, running a rag along the bar, and Gardiner ordered gin and tonics, after checking his wristwatch to make sure it wasn't yet time to switch to the afternoon whiskies. I expect he lived by a rigid code in such matters. The barman set the drinks down and wiped his hands on the same rag he'd wiped the bar with.

Gardiner said 'Cheers,' and took a large swallow.

I was unaccustomed to drinking this much, and certainly not this early in the day, and sipped cautiously. Gardiner drank fast. I could see that Clyde Jones, in many ways, would fit into this society much more readily than I; that my first impression had been hasty and ungracious and single-minded. But I resisted the temptation to drink more quickly.

Presently the Yugoslav departed, walking very tall and

proud with his spurs clanking, and we moved down the bar.
Gardiner introduced us and I bought MacPherson a drink. He
drank Scotch, but I expect his code was more accountable to
nationality than chronometry.

'Lived here long?' I asked.

'Too long,' MacPherson said. Then he shrugged. 'Still, it's
not a bad life. It's all right.'

'Brookes is interested in this thing that's been killing your
sheep,' Gardiner said.

'Oh?'

'Came all the way from London to investigate it.'

'I don't suppose there are many natural predators here, are
there?' I asked.

'Ah, there's the odd fox and the hawks and such. Never
been anything like this before, though.'

'It's a curious business, from what I've heard.'

'It is that.'

'What do you make of it?'

He considered for a few moments and a few swallows of
Scotch, the skin on his brow like furrowed leather. 'Well, it's
not serious, really. Not enough damage been done to do me
any financial harm. I guess I lost half a dozen sheep all told.
But it's the way they were killed that bothers me.'

'How was that?'

'Well, they were torn apart. Mutilated. Throats torn out
and skulls crushed. Never saw anything quite like it. Whatever
did it is not only powerful but vicious. And the strangest part
is that my dogs seem helpless.'

Gardiner signalled for another round of drinks, and
MacPherson seemed to be thinking deeply while the barman
brought them.

'Have you tried to find it?'

'Of course. I almost had it once. That was the strangest part
of all. It was a month or so ago and I was sort of keeping an
eye out for it. Had my gun with me, and four good dogs. Well,
we found a sheep that had just been killed. Couldn't have been
dead more than a few minutes. Torn to pieces. I put the dogs

on to it and they started howling and growling and sniffing
about, then they got the scent and took off after the thing. The
land's rocky and I couldn't see a trail myself, but the dogs had
it sure enough. I followed them and they tracked it a few
hundred yards in to a ravine. I thought I had it then for sure.
But when I was coming up behind, the dogs suddenly stopped
dead and for no reason I could see, the whole pack started
yelping and came running back with their tails between their
legs. Made the hair stiffen on my neck, I'll tell you that. They
came back so fast they almost knocked me down, and they all
crowded around my legs, whimpering. Gave me a funny sensation, that. I kicked 'em and beat 'em but damned if I could
make them go into that ravine. Even when I went up to the
edge myself, they wouldn't follow. I looked around a little,
walked along the edge for a little way, but it was rocky waste-
land with heavy undergrowth all along the bottom and I had
no chance of finding it without the dogs. But I was sure that it
was in there, waiting.'

He paused. He looked a little shaken.

'Matter of fact, I was scared to go in after it.'

MacPherson didn't look the type to be afraid of much.

'Any trouble recently?' I asked.

'Oh, it's still there all right. Whatever the hell it is. I've
tried setting traps for it and poisoned one of the carcasses, but
it did no good. Cunning brute. I got the idea, you know the
feeling, that it was watching me all the while I was putting the
traps out.'

'Could it be a wild dog or something of the sort?'

'I doubt that. No dog could have put the fear into my pack
that way. And no dog could've crushed those sheep's skulls
that way, either. No dog I ever saw.'

'A man?'

'Maybe. I thought of that. Used to have a few sheep carried
off by the Indians. But they always stole them to eat. This
thing just mangles them and leaves them where they died.
Maybe eats a mouthful or two, the carcasses are so shredded I
can't really tell. But no more than that.'

'Few animals kill purely for pleasure,' I said. 'Wolverine, leopard maybe . . . and man, of course.'

'It it's a man, it's a madman.'

MacPherson bought a round. I had a glass in my hand and two waiting on the bar now, and felt that I'd soon be in no condition to pursue any investigations.

'Would it be possible for me to stay at your place if I find it necessary to look for this thing?' I asked.

'Surely. I don't know if you can find it, but I'll give you every help I can. I'll have to take you out, though. You'd never find my place on your own. It's in the mountains west of here and there are no roads and only crude maps. I'm not even sure if I'm in Chile or Argentina.'

'I have some other things to do first,' I said. 'I may not have to take advantage of your hospitality.'

'I hope you get the bastard. What gun are you using?'

It took me a moment to comprehend that.

'I didn't come to shoot it,' I said.

MacPherson blinked.

'Then what the hell are you going to do?'

'That depends on what it turns out to be.'

MacPherson snorted. Then he looked serious. He said: 'Well, it's none of my business, but if you're going to look for this thing, you'd better take a gun with you.'

'Surely it wouldn't attack a man?'

MacPherson shrugged.

'You haven't seen those sheep, son. I have. Believe me, you better take a gun.'

The way he said it was quite impressive.

It was past noon now, and Gardiner had switched to Scotch. MacPherson approved. We had not had lunch, and Gardiner and MacPherson both seemed content to spend the afternoon at the bar. I'd had more than enough to drink, and the barman brought me a coffee with the next round. A few more customers wandered in and stood at the bar, talking and drinking. I noticed them vaguely, my thoughts on what MacPherson had told me. It was virtually the same story that I'd read in the reports, but hearing it in person, and seeing the man who told it, was far more effective than reading it in the grey safety of London. I was far less sceptical, and ready to believe a great deal more. Perhaps the alcohol had stimulated my imagination; it had certainly fired my impatience to get to the bottom of the mystery. I was convinced now that something very strange indeed was roaming those all but inaccessible mountains, and much too excited to waste any more time in that bar.

'Would this be a good time to see Gregorio?' I asked.

'Good as any,' Gardiner said.

'If you could direct me —'

'I'll drive you there. It's not far.'

He looked a shade disappointed at the prospect of leaving the bar.

'That's not necessary. Actually, I could use some air to clear my head. I'll walk.'

'Are you sure?'

'Absolutely. It'll give me an opportunity to look around a bit more, too. I couldn't see much at the speed you drive.'

Gardiner laughed. He was possibly a certain degree in his cups by this time. MacPherson seemed absolutely impervious to intoxication. I took my note pad out to write down the address, but Gardiner laughed more at this, and when he'd given me the directions, I saw why. They were accurate but somewhat unusual. Gregorio lived in the third orange shack on the western approach to town. There was a grey horse in a tin shed beside the shack. The shed was green and the horse was gelded. It was surely a more exact method of location than street names and postal districts, as any stranger who has asked directions in London will know.

I finished my coffee.

'One last drink before you leave?' Gardiner asked.

'Not now, thanks. Will you be here?'

'Undoubtedly.'

I turned to leave and Jones came walking down the bar. He

was wearing a purple sports shirt and smiling. His hangover
seemed to have been effectively reduced by drowning.

'Hello there, Brookes. Have a drink?'

'I can't just now. I have some business to attend to.'

He looked disappointed. He had a very American friendli-
ness, and was probably lonely. I introduced him to Gardiner
and MacPherson and he shook hands eagerly.

'You fellas live here? Quite a place, this.'

Jones bought drinks and merged easily into the group. I felt
obliged to wait for a few minutes and not leave him with
strangers, but it proved unnecessary. He was perfectly suited
to the situation. When I left, Gardiner was telling him how the
Explotadora company used to virtually rule the territory and
give the governor his orders, and Jones was agreeing that
government by private enterprise was vastly superior to
Democrats and communism.

I walked out beyond the town.

The wind was stronger here, without the shelter of the
sturdy buildings of the town. A *pasajero* rode past me, leading
a pack horse burdened with all his possessions and trailed by a
pack of mangy mongrels. There were shacks on both sides of
the road, hideously bright and clattering metallically. Indians
sat huddled in the doorways and on the crooked steps. Men of
ancient leather and twisted cord, their eyes turned listlessly
after me, not really interested but simply following a motion,
the same way that they watched a ragged newspaper tumble
before the wind; sullen and listless and uncomprehending,
perhaps sensing their lives were changed and unnatural, but
not recognizing their defeat. A few sheep grazed behind the
shacks, facing away from the wind with splendid unconcern,
placid and eternal, and forming perhaps the only bridge between the present and the past.

Gregorio was sitting on a gnarled log beside his door, smoking a hand-made pipe. God knows what he was smoking in it.
He wore a poncho with a hood roughly sewn on and shadowing
his eyes. His hands were strangely delicate, despite the horny

calluses, the fingers long and mobile. He peered at me suspiciously. He'd had enough experience of civilization to be wary, unlike the Indians who had watched me walk past.

'Are you Gregorio?' I asked.

The head nodded under the hood.

'You speak English?'

He nodded again.

I squatted down beside him.

'My name is Brookes. I'd like to speak with you for a few moments if you can spare the time.'

There was no reaction.

'I'll gladly pay you for your time.'

He nodded again. I began to wonder if he actually did speak English.

'It's about the creature you claim ... the creature that you saw in the mountains.'

Gregorio rustled within the poncho and the hood fell back from his head. He had hair like black wire and a face like a Cornish farmhouse, sombre, grey and grim. But his eyes were bright with intelligence and perhaps something else – perhaps it was fear.

'*Bestia hombre*,' he said. His voice rasped. I felt certain then, looking into his face, that this man was not faking or pretending. He had seen something and that something was very terrible indeed.

I took a small bank note from my pocket and offered it to him. He took it without looking at it, with a vestige of pride long vanquished by necessity. He held it crumpled in his palm.

'Tell me what you saw.'

He hesitated.

'Is that enough?'

He motioned with the hand holding the note, a scornful gesture. 'It is enough,' he said. His English was surprisingly clear, with a faint North American intonation. 'It is not a good memory, Señor.' He puffed on his pipe, his lean cheeks sinking inwards. I felt he was gathering more than his thoughts, and waited anxiously.

'When I tell them, they do not believe me,' he said, turning his eyes toward the town. 'They laugh. They think I see things that are not there.'

'I believe you.'

His eyes shifted back to me.

'I've come all the way from London to speak with you, and to find what you saw.'

'You will look for this thing?' he said, incredulously. He couldn't believe that anyone would voluntarily seek the creature he had seen – or thought he'd seen. A curious mixture of disbelief and respect moved his expression.

'Yes. And I will find it, if you help me.'

'Help you?'

'Tell me all you can remember.'

'I will tell you, yes.'

'When was it that you saw this thing?'

'It was some weeks ago.' He shrugged. 'I have no calendar.'

'You were in the mountains?'

He nodded and looked westward. The land rose steadily away from us and the clouds seemed to tilt down to meet the far mountains. Gregorio stared into the distance. And, without looking at me, he began to speak. His voice moved musically over the foreign English words, but it was music without gaiety, a tragic overture introducing his sombre theme.

'I was looking for work on the sheep ranches. I had the horse and two dogs.' He stabbed the stem of his pipe toward the green tin shack. 'That is the horse. The dogs —' he hesitated, his face still turned away from me, and I saw the cords knot in his neck. 'The dogs were running after me. They were happy to be away from this town, in the mountains. They were good dogs. One especially, a dog of great courage and strength. El Rojo he was called. His breeding one does not know, but his loyalty was firm. He was mine many years, although I had been offered much money for him.' He paused again. His hands were restless. Then he seemed to shrug, although his shoulders did not actually move.

'We rode on a narrow trail through trees. The trees there

lean and turn because of the great wind. The wind was very loud then, and the horse made great noise on the rock. It was becoming night. I do not know what hour, I have no clock. But it was time that I make camp, and I looked for a place. I went from the trail and was among dark trees. And then there was no noise. It was like a storm about to break, that silence. But there was no storm, the sky was clear. It was something else. I knew it was not good. The dogs also knew. The little dog cried and El Rojo had stiff hair over his neck. I felt the horse tremble between my knees. All up my legs I feel this, and the eyes are white, the nostrils wide. I kicked at the horse with my heels, but it did not walk.'

Gregorio turned to face me then. His face was terrible. He was reliving those moments vividly, and perhaps this was how his face had appeared then. He seemed scarcely aware of me, his eyes turned on the past.

'Then I heard the sound of this thing. It was a snarl. Not like a dog. A warning, perhaps a challenge. I am not sure what it was. I turned to the sound and then I saw it. It was in a thicket, but I saw it plainly. I looked at it, and it looked at me. We regarded one another. I was unable to move and my throat would not work. My backbone was of ice.

'It was not tall. It bent forwards with long arms. Its chest was huge and shoulders heavy. There was much thick hair, and where there was not hair the skin was dark. For some time we do nothing, and it made the sound again. The hindquarters raise, as if it is stiffening its tail. But it has no tail. Something was beneath it. A sheep, I think. It was woolly and red with blood, and this thing was red at the mouth. Blood dropped heavily from the teeth. But they were teeth. They were not fangs of a beast, they were teeth. And the eyes are on me all this time. It has the eyes of a man . . .'

He was staring into my eyes as he said this. His pipe had burned out, but his teeth were clamped on the stem. I didn't move, afraid to break the memory that held him, and the belief that gripped me.

'I wished to run from this thing, but the horse was filled

with fear. It would not run. And I, too, am frozen. Only El Rojo has sufficient courage. He feared nothing, that dog. He moved toward the thing. The other dog was not so brave. It ran. The movement makes the horse able to run, also, and he followed after the dog. The horse ran faster than he could run. Faster than I think any horse can run. I am a horseman. All my life I have ridden horses, and I knew this horse well. But Señor, I could no more stop this horse than stop the wind. And I did not want to.'

He was aware of me again, and I thought the story was finished. But he lowered his face and spoke again, more softly.

'But I looked back,' he said. 'I could not look away from this thing. I saw the dog make a circle on stiff legs. The dog is snarling with bare fangs, and then the thing moved to the dog. The dog was not fast enough. Or the thing is too fast. They are together on the ground then, and I could see no more. But I can hear what happens. I can hear the cry of the dog, the sound of pain and death. It is loud, then it is not so loud, and when I can hear the dog no longer I hear the sound of this thing. It is not like before. It is more terrible. It is the worst sound a man has ever heard. There was nothing I could do. I could not stop the horse for a long ways, and when finally I did I was trembling more than the horse. I thought of the dog. I loved that dog. But I did not go back.'

Gregorio lapsed into silence. He seemed sad and exhausted. The note was still clasped in his hand. I waited for several moments before he raised his head.

'That is what happened,' he said.

'Do you have any idea what it was?'

He shrugged.

'Could it have been some animal. Some animal you have never seen before?'

'It was a man.'

'It was dark you said . . .'

'The light was sufficient.'

'A man then. An Indian?'

He shook his head patiently.

'A man and a beast,' he said. 'A beast-man. A man like no man ever was.'

A man like no man ever was? Or is?

I left him then. I said that I might wish to talk with him again and he shrugged. He was filling his pipe again, and when I looked back from the road he was slumped on the log exactly as he'd been when I came. I was profoundly affected by his tale. I believed him. He might have been mistaken, but he had not deceived me. He had seen something much too terrible to be imagined, and the emotions of his memory were far too genuine to be feigned. Somewhere in those trackless and forsaken wastes, a creature existed. I did not know what it was, but I knew that I had to find it.

I thought of MacPherson's advice.

I did not like the idea of carrying a gun, but I decided that I should. There was another idea that I liked considerably less . . .

4

I spent the next three days in Ushuaia.

It gave me the opportunity to observe these primitive people, as I'd wanted, but my interest in this pursuit had greatly waned. I regarded it now as something that had been done by others before me, interesting enough but hardly a challenge, compared to the possibilities of a new discovery. The tales I had heard from Gregorio and, to a lesser extent, MacPherson, had inflamed my imagination. I had never been a man to draw easy conclusions from incomplete data, and yet the same idea that had seemed absurd when Smyth presented it to me in his quiet, dark office, and the same statements I had passed over lightly in the objective reports that reached the museum, took on a new reality now, just as the clouded sky cast a new light over this land.

I was consumed by an impetuous urge to proceed with my investigations, and frustrated by the need to wait. But the first essential was still to locate Hodson. That was why Smyth had sent me, and it would have been foolish to follow another line of research until I'd seen him, and settled my mind one way or the other on that account. And it seemed there was no way to find Hodson until his man arrived for supplies.

I went to Graham's every morning to inquire, and be disappointed. Graham had prepared a knapsack and saddlebags for me, and arranged with the stables down the street to have a horse ready to be hired at any time. The knapsack contained a portable stove and foodstuffs in lightweight plastic containers, along with other articles which surprised me, but which Graham thought might possibly prove handy if not essential in traversing that rugged land: a small hatchet, a folding knife, several lengths of rope and cord – things of potential value in survival, rather than in comfort. There was also a sleeping bag and groundsheet. It hadn't occurred to me that I might be spending a night in the open, and I was grateful for Graham's foresight, although not so pleased by several tales he told me of men who had been lost in the mountains. With his guidance, I purchased a suitable outfit of clothing for the trek, heavy whipcord trousers, wool plaid shirt, quilted windbreaker with hood attached, and sturdy, treble-soled boots equally suited to riding and walking over broken land. I felt a certain satisfaction in being so well prepared which somewhat mollified my impatience.

In the meanwhile, I spent the days walking miles into the country on all sides. I wore my new clothing, getting accustomed to the freedom of this new manner of dress at the same time as I felt myself becoming acquainted with the land. I made no particular effort at observation, and made no entries in my notebook. Whatever I learned was simply absorbed without conscious effort, coming through the senses while my mind turned over manifold plans and possibilities. I didn't attempt to restrict my thoughts to what I knew, or could be proved. It was out of character for me, but I was out of the

world I knew, and anxious to enter the world of which
Gregorio had spoken.

There were aspects of his story that fascinated me, that had
the solid ring of truth, fantastic as that truth might be. These
were not the things that seemed to have affected Gregorio
most, however. He had seemed most impressed by the creature's eyes, but I passed this over. Many animals have eyes
that seem almost human in their intelligence, often the most
loathsome creatures, rats and moray eels for instance. Gregorio
could easily have been misled in this. But he claimed it had
teeth, not fangs, and referred to its foreward or upper limbs as
arms, not the legs he would have attributed to most animals –
small points he had not pressed unduly, but which convinced
me. And, more than anything else, there was the action he'd
described – the raising of a non-existent tail. I have often
wondered why mankind emotionally resents the tail that his
forebears carried; why that is so frequently the point chosen
when a man without knowledge scorns the process of evolution. For the same reason that he portrays the devil with a tail,
perhaps? A feeling of superiority for the misguided reason
that man has lost a useful and functional part of his anatomy.
Surely a man like Gregorio would have given a tail to a fig-
ment of his imagination, or added one to a trick of light upon a
superstitious nature. The tail is an integral part of bestial evil,
and it seemed reasonable to assume that he would have. But he
hadn't. The thing had no tail, and moved as if it had.

My mind danced back through the aeons, obscuring fact
with fancy and the present with the past, jamming two dimen-
sions into one space, in my readiness to believe almost anything. I built fantasies of unbelievable intricacy and detail, and
was content not to hinder the construction of this fragile
architecture of the imagination. And, in this structure, there
was the cornerstone of truth. For somewhere, sometime there
had existed a creature which was less than man, and in many
ways less than an ape, at some point where the distant line
forked and began to pursue constantly diverging trails. It had
happened once, at some point in time, and evolution has a

pattern we have not yet mapped, a stamp that surely may be repeated in different places, when the time of those places is right. I had always believed in the likeliness of simultaneous evolution, finding it far more plausible than since-sunken land bridges and fantastic ocean emigrations on crude rafts, to account for the presence of mankind in the New World and the islands. The only new concept was the timing, and this problem did not seem insurmountable now that I was at a place like this, a land untouched by change as the world aged around it. Could the old pattern have begun again, working here along the same old lines that had populated the rest of the world in forgotten ages? The same evolution, a million years behind?

My wild musings surprised me, as I realized what I had been considering. And yet I didn't scoff at the thought.

On the evening of the third day I walked out beyond the new Italian colony and turned from the path to ascend a rocky incline. The stones were soft beneath the heavy soles of my boots, and I carried a stout walking stick, using it as a third leg against gravity. Some small creature scurried unseen through the brush as I scrambled on to the flattened top of the hillock. A solitary beech tree twisted up from the undergrowth, and an owl hooted from the line of trees fringing a ridge to the north. It was raining lightly, and the wind was drifting higher than usual. I stood beneath the tortured limbs of the tree and lit a cigarette, looking out towards the west. I could not see far in the darkening mist, but I knew that somewhere out there were the mountains and canyons, the unmarked Chilean frontier and, somewhere beyond that, the place where I would find Hodson. I wondered what chance I would have of finding him if I were to set off myself, and the thought tempted my impatience. But it would have been more than hopeless. I had to wait.

Presently, aided by my stick, I clambered back down the incline and walked back to town through the soft, dark rain.

I encountered Jones on the stairs the next morning, and we

descended together. I had intended to go to the breakfast-room, but I saw that it was occupied by three widowed tourists who had arrived the day before amidst cackling disorder. They were calling for separate bills and debating over who had devoured the extra doughnut. I believe they were from Milwaukee. I turned into the bar with Jones.

We sat at the bar. Jones had Pernod with his black coffee.

'Women like that make me ashamed to be a tourist,' he said. The nasal tones still reached us, although we felt quite sure the ladies wouldn't come into the bar. 'That's the trouble with tourists. They get some place and then, instead of relaxing and enjoying themselves they rush about trying to see everything. Laden with guidebooks and preconceived ideas of what they must look at. Now me, first thing I do is find a nice sociable bar and have a drink. Get to meet some of the people. That's the way to be a tourist.' He poured some water into his Pernod and admired the silicone effect as it clouded. ''Course, you're lucky. You can travel without being a tourist. Gardiner was telling me how you were a famous scientist.'

'Hardly famous.'

'What's your line?'

'Anthropology. I'm on a field trip for the museum.'

'You don't work on atom bombs and things, huh?'

He looked vaguely disappointed.

'Decidedly not. My work lies towards discovering where mankind came from, before it is gone.'

Jones nodded thoughtfully.

'Yeah. Still, I guess we got to have those atom bombs and things since the commies got 'em. Better if no one had 'em. You work for a museum, huh? I like museums, myself. Been in all the big museums all over the States and Europe. Not 'cause I think I got to, though. Just 'cause I like 'em. We got some fine museums in the States, you know. Ever thought of joining that brain drain? A scientist gets lots better money back home than you get over in England.'

'I hadn't considered it, no.'

'Ought to. I mean, science and all is fine, and that England's a great little island, but a guy's got to earn a decent living for himself, too. That's right, isn't it? You got to look after yourself first, before you can look after the rest of the world. That holds for science and politics and charity and everything.'

'You have a point.'

'Want something with that coffee?'

'No, thank you.'

'I don't usually drink much at home, myself. But when I'm travelling, a little drink relaxes me. I like drinking in your country. Those pubs are fine things, 'cept they're never open when a guy's thirsty.'

The barman refilled our cups, and poured Jones another Pernod.

'What you doing here, anyway?' Jones asked me.

I almost launched into a detailed explanation, but caught myself in time.

'Studying the natives, more or less,' I said.

'That so? Ain't much to study, is there? I mean, they're sort of primitive.'

'That's why I'm studying them.'

'Oh,' said Jones.

A boy was standing in the doorway, blinking. It was the boy from Graham's trading company. I raised a hand and he saw me and came down the bar.

'Mister Graham sent me over. Said to tell you that Hodson's man is here.'

'I'll come with you,' I told him.

'Want a drink before you go?' Jones asked.

'Sorry. I don't have time.'

'Sure. Business before pleasure, huh?'

I left Jones at the bar and followed the boy out to the street. It was a bright morning, unusually warm. Half a dozen hawks were circling against the sun. I felt stimulated as we walked toward Graham's. This was what I'd been waiting for.

There were three horses tied in front of the trading post, and Graham was busily gathering the various supplies, referring to a handwritten list. He glanced up as I entered, and nodded toward the back of the room.

'There's your man,' he said.

It was dark in the shadow of crates and shelves, and for a moment I didn't see him. Then, gradually, the outline took shape, and I believe my mouth may have gaped open. I don't know what I'd expected, but certainly not a man of such ferocious and terrifying aspect. He was gigantic. He must have stood closer to seven feet than six, a massive column of splendidly proportioned muscle and sinew, wearing a *caterino* over chest and back, leaving shoulders, arms and sides bare. He was standing completely motionless, huge arms crossed over his massive chest, and even in this relaxed position the definition of his muscles cleaved darkly against the brown skin. The man's countenance was in accord with his body, his features carved from mahogany with a blunt chisel. A dark rag was knotted across his wide forehead, just above the eyes, the ends of the knot hanging loose and frayed and his hair a ragged coil over the edge.

Graham was grinning.

'Quite a lad, eh?'

'Rather impressive. Any idea what tribe he could belong to? He doesn't look like any of the Indians I've seen around the town.'

'No. I heard somewhere that Hodson brought him down from up north. The Amazon, I think. As his personal servant. Can't see why he'd want something like that around the house, though.'

'And he can't speak, you say?'

'I never heard him make a sound. Dumb, I reckon. Brings a list of supplies and waits while I get it packed and loaded, then he's off again. Brings a cheque on Hodson's bank every few months to settle the account, but I don't think he knows what it is.'

'Can you communicate with him?'

Graham shrugged.

'Sure. Sign language, same's I talk to any of them that can't understand English. Simple enough. Universal.'

'Could you ask if I may accompany him?'

Graham frowned.

'Well, I can tell him you're going. Don't really know how I'd ask. No sense in it, anyway. He's got nothing to say about it. Can't tell you where you can go, and it wouldn't do to give him the idea he could. I'll just let him know you're going with him, and you'll have to do the rest. Keep up with him, I mean. Not that he might try to lose you, but I wouldn't be willing to bet he'd wait for you if you dropped behind. Probably wouldn't even notice.'

'I see.'

'You shouldn't have to worry about keeping up, since he's got two animals to lead. Can't go too fast. But he'll probably just keep right on going until he gets there, so it may be a long haul in the saddle.'

'I'll manage.'

'Sure. No worries.'

Graham finished gathering the supplies into a pile by the door. The Indian paid no attention to either of us. He hadn't moved since I'd entered. I noticed that he carried a machete in his waistband and wore nothing on his feet. He fascinated me, and I could hardly take my eyes away from him.

'You can start loading these on the horse,' Graham said to the boy. Then he held his hand up. 'Wait. You better get Mister Brookes' horse over from the stables first. Get it saddled and ready to go before you load the pack horses.' The boy went out. Graham went behind the counter and brought out my saddlebags and knapsack.

'Now we'll see what we can get across to him, eh?' he said. I followed him to the back of the room. The nearer I got, the bigger the Indian looked. I didn't actually get too near. Graham began making hand signs, simple symbols that I could have done as well myself. He pointed at me, at the Indian, and then out toward the horses. Then he made a few subtler movements. The Indian watched it all with absolutely no change of expression, no comprehension but also no disagreement, and it was impossible to know how much he understood.

'That's about all I can do,' Graham said.

'Does he get the idea?'

'God knows.'

'Should I offer him money?'

Graham frowned.

'I don't suppose he uses it. Probably doesn't know what it is. You might offer him something else, a present of some sort. Damned if I know what, though.'

I rejected that idea as being too much like baubles and beads for the savages. Graham and I went back to the door. The Indian still hadn't moved. I looked out and saw the boy leading my horse around the side of the building. The animal wasn't too large and didn't appear frisky, walking with its head down. It had high withers and a long, arched neck.

'Not much to look at,' Graham said. 'You don't want a spirited animal on a trip like this. This one is placid and sure-footed, it should be just the thing.'

'I'm sure it will be fine,' I said, wondering if Gardiner might have influenced the decision. The horse stood with wide spread legs and drooping back while the boy saddled it, but it looked sturdy enough – more bored than aged or tired.

I put my knapsack on. It felt comfortable. The boy began carrying Hodson's supplies out to the pack animals and loading them with quick efficiency, while Graham and I watched from the doorway. I lighted a cigarette, feeling a nervous energy tightening in my belly, a core of anxiety wrapped in the spirit of adventure.

Graham motioned to the Indian. The horses were ready. The Indian moved past us and over us, and went down the steps. He tested the straps and balance of the packs, his biceps ballooning as he tugged. Then he gathered the leads into one and moved to his mount. There was a blanket over the horse's back, but no saddle, and the Indian was so tall that he virtually stepped on to the animal. He arched his back and the horse moved off at a walk, the pack animals following.

I mounted and settled. Graham came down the steps.

'Good luck,' he said.

The anxiety was gone now. I felt fine. I felt like thundering out of town in a swirl of dust. But I heeled gently and we moved off at a walk, behind the pack animals, which was much more sensible.

5

The Indian paid no attention to me as I rode behind him. He seemed totally unaware of my presence, an eerie feeling once Ushuaia was behind us, and we were the only two people in sight. We went at a moderate pace and I kept about ten yards behind the pack horses, realizing again how much energy it takes to ride a horse over broken ground, even at such a slow gait. The Indian, however, seemed to use no energy. He rode with an easy grace, his long body relaxed and shifting to the horse's motion, a technique well suited to a long journey, functional rather than stylistic. Although his horse was of a good size, it looked more like a burro beneath this vast man, and his feet almost brushed the ground.

The sun was abnormally bright and I began to sweat in my heavy clothing, and down my temples. After a while I shrugged out of the knapsack and balanced it on the pommel while I took the quilted windbreaker off and stuffed it in the saddle-bags: slid into the knapsack again. During these gyrations I dropped farther behind, and had to urge the horse into a trot to catch up. The ground was firm and the gait jarred me. I knew I was going to be stiff and sore in a short time, but discomfort earned in such a genuine way didn't bother me; the slight ache of bones and joints lends a certain awareness of one's body and of being alive. It would be a dull existence without pain.

The landscape changed gradually.

We had passed the farthest point of my walks, and I observed this new terrain with interest. The contours were

lunar. Large, smooth boulders loomed on all sides and our
path wound around and between them. There were few marks
of civilization here. Indeed, few signs of life. A few stunted
trees grew between and above the rocks, dull moss covered the
stony surface, the odd wild sheep peered at us from impossible
perches, an ostrich raised its curious head and turned its long
neck until it resembled one of the twisted trees. I had had
some idea of making a rough map of our journey, but gave the
idea up without attempting it. The landmarks were all of a
sameness that made recognition difficult – impossible, with my
limited knowledge of cartography and compass reading. I
knew only that we were heading westward, but not directly.
The trail, where there was a trail, curved and zigzagged,
following the broken face of the land. We were climbing
steadily, the land rising and falling in changing pattern, but
always drawing higher in the end. The sun pursued us until it
drew level to the north of us, following its eternal path over
the equator, and our truncated shadows shifted away from it.
The light caught blinding points in the rocks. Time lost objective meaning for me, I was dulled by the heat and the motion
and the unchanging contours, and did not even refer to my
wristwatch. I'd had no breakfast, and my stomach was empty,
but the effort of opening my pack and eating in the saddle was
too great. My throat was parched, but I did not raise the
waterbag. I slumped in the high Spanish saddle and rode on.

And then, some time in the afternoon, I became aware that the
land had changed. It had been an unnoticeable transition, but
suddenly we had come into the genuine foothills, the rising
plain was behind us and we were ascending into the mountains.

There was no longer even the semblance of a trail, and the
going was more difficult, the trees thicker and the rocks higher.
The Indian seemed to know the way without having to pay
attention, turning and detouring for no apparent reason, but
never pausing or backtracking. My horse was placidly confident of his footing. Loose rocks clattered from beneath his

hooves, soft mud sucked at his legs between spaces of bare rock, but he never faltered; he lurched but recovered instantly and smoothly. Graham had made a wise selection.

The sun had outdistanced us. It slanted into my face now, hotter than before. I turned to look behind, and found that the plains were already hidden by the folding hills. I knew that I was lost; that I could never have retraced our path back to Ushuaia. I wondered whether we had yet crossed the frontier into Chile. There was no possible way to tell, and it didn't matter in the slightest. Time and distance had both become completely subjective, and my mood was almost stoic; eventually we would be at our destination, and what more did I need to know or concern myself with?

It was in this mood that I nearly rode past the Indian before I noticed he'd dismounted; I didn't, in fact, notice until my horse had the sense to stop. I slid stiffly from the saddle and stretched. It must have been mid-afternoon. Our steady pace had taken us quite a distance, but the path had been so devious that it was impossible to estimate how much actual progress had been made.

We were in the shadow of a large, flat-sided overhang of rock, and trees grew all around, draped with thick yellow moss and stretching down to the dense shrubbery of the undergrowth. The moss stirred restlessly, and cast tangled, shifting shadows. I started to ask my silent companion whether we were halting very long, and then realized the futility of that. He was squatting beside the horses, thigh muscles bunched as great in circumference as a normal man's torso. There was a leather pouch at his waistband and he drew some coarse bark from it and commenced to chew it. The aromatic fumes hung on the air: Winter's-bark, stimulant and tonic, and apparently all the nourishment that vast body needed for this tedious journey. I watched his jaws work methodically and opened my own pack. I had no idea if there would be time to prepare a meal, and had a hasty bite of dried meat and a bar of chocolate. I would have had time for nothing more. I had not even fastened my pack again before the Indian stood up and

approached his horse, stooping under the overhanging limbs.
My muscles throbbed as I hauled myself back into the saddle,
but my seat was all right. The Spanish saddle was very comfortable with its high, square cantel. I pushed my horse up
level with the Indian as he started off, and volunteered with
obvious gestures to take my turn leading the pack horses. He
didn't actually refuse. He simply failed to acknowledge the
offer, and a moment later I was once more trailing along behind.

Some time later, we came to a shallow stream bordered by
steep, soft banks, and moved along beside it for a while. The
water ran in the opposite direction, strangely rapid for such
slight depth and bursting over the rocks that lined the bed.
Trees burrowed their roots down to the water and mossy limbs
stretched over in an arch. We weaved through the foliage and
the moss clung to my shoulders, the soft earth gripped the
horses' hooves. The Indian had some difficulty leading the
pack horses here, and had to move slower. I was closer behind
him, wanting to make sure we followed in his exact footsteps,
close enough to notice the long scar that ran diagonally over
his naked ribs, down to his hip. It was an old scar and not very
visible against his dark, dust-covered skin, but it must have
been a hideous wound when it occurred, a deep gouge with
lesser marks on either side, not clean enough to have been
caused by a knife or bullet and yet following a straight course
that seemed to imply a purpose to the infliction. Perhaps the
talons of some powerful beast, I thought, and wondered what
animal might have dared attack this giant.

We came to a break in the bank, where the land had cracked
and folded back in a gully, and here the Indian urged his
mount down, leaning back from the waist as the horse slid
down on stiff legs. The pack horses followed him down reluctantly and my horse stopped, tossing his head nervously and
looking for an alternative route. I tugged the reins and heeled
to little effect. The Indian was already moving away, riding up
the centre of the stream, and I felt a moment of panic thinking
I might not be able to get the horse down and would be aban-

doned here; I heaved heavily on the reins, bringing the horse
around and off balance. He sidestepped and missed the edge of
the bank and we went down sideways, the horse snorting and
kicking, and somehow managed to stay upright. I took a deep,
relieved breath, and the horse shook his head, then started off
again behind the others. The bed was strewn with rocks and
the pack animals kicked spray up at me. It felt refreshing. We
rode through the water for some time, perhaps an hour, and
then ascended the far bank, lurching and heaving up through
the slippery mud.

The land had changed once more on the far bank of the
stream. We were traversing dense forest. The rocks and boulders were still there on all sides, but they were hidden and
engulfed by the trees and shrubbery. The undergrowth was
heavy, and I could not see the horse's legs beneath the knees,
yet he carried on steadily enough on this invisible ground.
Moss braided my shoulders and clung around my neck like
Hawaiian leis. It was cooler here, the sun blocked out and the
earth damp. I put my windbreaker on again. We passed
through an open space and back into the shade, through
patterns of light and shadow, moving chiaroscuro imprinted on
the senses. I was still sweating, but the moisture was cold, and
I was aware of my discomfort now, the blunted sensations of
the hot afternoon sharpened unpleasantly. I became conscious
of time again, hoping we had not far to go, and looked at my
watch. It surprised me to find it was seven o'clock. We had
been riding, virtually without pause, for ten hours. The Indian
seemed as fresh as he had when we started, and who knew how
long he'd ridden to reach Ushuaia that morning. It seemed
impossible that anyone, even that extraordinary man, could
have travelled through this terrain through the night, and yet
we pushed on with no sign of a halt.

We emerged once more into an open space, a hill scarred
with stumps. A waterfall sparkled from the ridge to the south
and a fallen tree leaned like a buttress against the cliffs below.
Halfway up the hill we passed a grave, an indented rectangle
of earth and a weathered wooden cross lashed, leaning, against

a stump. It amazed me. What solitary shepherd or recluse woodchopper had died in this forsaken place, and who had been here to bury him? Yet, in a way, this forlorn grave gave me a sense of security. I was not at the end of the world, man had been here before, if not civilized at least Christian, and they would be here again. In Ushuaia I had burned with the urge to get away from civilization and to explore undiscovered secrets in forgotten lands, but somewhere along this tedious journey those thoughts had modified and science had yielded to instinct. I would have been very happy indeed to have a drink with Clyde Jones at that moment . . .

We approached the top of the hill and yet another line of trees, silhouetted in tormented tangles against the darkening sky. Small birds watched from the safety of the limbs and butterflies waifed through the vines, catching the last sunlight in their brilliant wings. We drew near and I started at the sudden battering of wings, jerking around to look as a dark form rose up beside me, hovering for a moment and then rising slowly and heavily – a giant condor, a dozen feet between its wingtips, elevating from some disturbed feast. The Indian seemed as unaware of it as he was of me. I shivered and bent over the pommel. We brushed a tree, the rough surface scraping my cheek, but I was too exhausted to feel the pain, scarcely aware of the mountains ahead, capped with snow and fingers of white running down the slopes. They did not seem high, and then, dimly, I realized that we were high; that we had come to the peak of this range of hills, and a long valley was spread out before us.

I gripped the pommel and relaxed my aching knees, knowing I would be unable to go much farther, hoping we would be there soon, or that night would come and force a stop. It couldn't be long now, the mist was low and the light feeble. The horses were tiring, too, heads down and legs weary and uncertain. We were moving on level ground, crossing the flattened top of the hill towards the descent. A jagged arroyo yawned before us, we passed along the ridge and came out through a field of blasted and broken trees where the wind

snarled. There was no shelter here, and the wind had con-
quered. It was moaning over us, and then, suddenly, it was
raging and howling across the surface of the land. It struck
without warning, nearly dragging me from the saddle. The
horse whinnied and I clutched at mane and pommel and
leaned far over. Even the Indian seemed to sway in the unexpected blast. Streamers of yellow moss ran over the ground
and a dead tree cracked and splintered. This was not the swirling wind of Ushuaia, but a straight shot from beyond the
shoulder of the world, hauling the clouds behind it.

Clinging tightly to the horse, I faced into the wind. I caught
my breath. I was looking out beyond those last rocks that
stumbled from the edge of the land and sank beneath the
towering walls of clouds, looking over the edge of the earth.
For an instant the view was clear, and then the rain whipped
in and the mists blanketed the sea. It was, in the lapse of
seconds, black night.

Even the Indian yielded to this storm. He turned the horses
back to the treeline and dismounted in the scant shelter of a
rock castle, towers and pillars and spires of ancient stone,
stroked smooth on the southern side and harbouring tenacious
moss on the north. The horses stood quietly, facing the rocks,
their tails rippling as the wind curved around behind, while he
unburdened them of their packs. This, obviously, was to be
our home for the night, or the duration of the storm. I didn't
know which; I didn't know if the Indian had intended to stop
or if the storm had brought about the decision, and didn't care
about the reason, so long as we had halted. I could scarcely
slide from the saddle, every joint was stiffened and I ached
through the length of my bones, as though the very marrow
had petrified.

I unsaddled the horse and unpacked my sleeping bag and
groundsheet, going through the motions mechanically. I
hobbled the horse and put the feeding bag on as Graham had
demonstrated, feeling hollow with hunger myself but much too
weary to make the effort of eating. The horse shuffled off to
join the others, dark outlines against the trees, grouped to-

gether. The Indian was wrapped in a blanket, lying close to the base of the rocks. I could barely see him. The end of his blanket was lifting as the wind tried to find us, curling around the edges and lashing through the columns, and then hurtling on to vent its fury in the trees.

I slid into the warmth of the sleeping bag, too numb to feel the hard ground under me, and looked up at the raging sky. Darts of rain stabbed my eyes and I turned toward the rocks. I thought for a moment of Susan, of the comfort of being with her in her flat, and decided I was mad to be here, as I drifted into sleep.

Some sound awakened me.

It was early and bright. The world was fresh and clean, and the wind had risen up above the clouds again. I sat up, all my muscles objecting, and saw that the Indian was already arranging the packs. I wondered if he would have ridden off and left me sleeping, and felt certain he would have, through indifference rather than maliciousness.

It was agony to slide from the sleeping bag, and I recalled my thoughts of the morning before – that I didn't object to genuinely earned discomfort – and decided that this principle could be taken too far. But necessity forced me on.

My horse stood patiently while I saddled him and removed the hobble. The Indian was already moving off through the broken trees as I painfully hauled myself into the saddle. My stomach muscles ached and my thighs throbbed as they gripped. I doubted that I could last through another day like the last, and yet there was no choice now. I couldn't turn back and I couldn't go on at my own pace, I had to follow the Indian at whatever speed he travelled, and pray we found Hodson before I collapsed.

Strangely enough, however, this second day was not so bad once it had started. We were descending now, and this threw new muscles and balance into use, fulcruming against the grain of the old stress, but my body was deadened and the pain was a dull constant which could be ignored. The muscles, being used, did not stiffen. I found it easier to keep my balance without conscious effort, and was able to eat dried meat and chocolate from my pack without slowing or faltering. Perhaps we travelled at a lesser pace, as well, for the horses must have been feeling the efforts of the long day before. Only the Indian seemed incapable of fatigue, and he was wise enough not to push the animals beyond their endurance.

At first I kept my mind from my discomfort by observing the landscape, and after a while my thoughts turned inward and dwelt on any number of unrelated subjects. When I came back to reality from these wanderings, I was surprised to discover how well my body was standing up to the rigours of the journey – far better than I would have thought myself capable of when I lurched painfully into the saddle that morning. There was a touch of pride and self-respect in this, and there might have been vanity as well, but for the example of the Indian riding on before me, relentless and enduring, and looking at him I felt that it was only luck that kept me going.

I had no idea how far we'd travelled when, in the late afternoon, we came to Hodson's.

6

We came around a fold in the hills and Hodson's house was below us, in the basin of a narrow, converging valley. The sun was in the west. It lighted the surrounding hilltops but hadn't slanted down the valley, and the house was shrouded in gloom. It was a bleak structure, rough grey wooden walls and a corrugated iron roof, protected from the wind by the shoulders of land that rose on three sides and a sheer rock face towering behind.

I was surprised. I'd expected something more, or something less – either a rough field camp or a civilized home, perhaps even a laboratory. But this was a crude, makeshift building, sturdy enough but poorly finished. Still, it fitted in with what I knew of Hodson. He wasn't a man who needed or wanted the fringes and frills of modern convenience; perhaps, with no income I knew of and only his limited personal funds, he could afford nothing else.

We followed a hard dirt track down the incline, where two rises rolled together. As the angle of vision changed, I noticed that the house seemed connected with the rock face behind – not leaning against it for support, but actually protruding from the rock, making use of some natural crevice or cave.

We had reached the bottom of the descent and turned toward the house when a figure emerged and stood by the door, watching our progress. A stocky man, solid on widespread legs. I recognized Hubert Hodson, from photographs taken a generation before, a little heavier, a little greyer, but the same man, sturdy and imposing in woollen shirt and heavy boots. His face was windburnt and tanned, and his brow was as corrugated as the roof above him. He was watching me, and he didn't seem pleased.

We halted in front of the house and the Indian slid from his horse. I nodded to Hodson. He nodded back and turned to the Indian, his hands moving rapidly. The Indian replied in the same fashion, and glanced towards me. I believe it was the first time he'd actually looked at me. Hodson made a final, terminating gesture, and walked over to stand beside my horse. His shirt was open halfway down, his chest hard and matted with hair. He looked more like a lumberjack than a scientist, and his obvious strength would have impressed me, had such feelings not been overwhelmed by observing the giant Indian.

'You wanted to see me?' he asked.

The Indian had apparently understood that much.

'Yes, very much.'

Hodson grunted. 'Well, you had better come in. Leave your horse, the Indian will take care of it.' I thought it curious that he referred to his servant that way, instead of by name. I dismounted and handed the reins to the man, and he led the horses around the side of the house. Hodson had gone to the door and I followed. He'd started to enter the house, then

stepped back to let me go through first, a perfunctory politeness that seemed to show a determination to keep our meeting
on a formal basis. Courtesy had never been associated with
Hubert Hodson.

'I saw you coming,' he said. 'Thought you'd most likely
been lost in the mountains. A mistaken idea, obviously.
Always been a fault of mine, leaping to the hasty conclusion.
Well, I'm usually right, anyway.'

The interior was as bleak as the outside. We stood in a
barren room with home-made furnishings and bare walls, one
small window throwing insufficient light. Two doorways led
out at the other side, hung with curtains of strung beads.
There was one battered leather chair, the sole acquiescence to
comfort.

'Who are you?'

'Brookes. Arthur Brookes.'

'You know who I am,' he said. He held his hand out,
another surface politeness. His grip was unconsciously powerful. 'Afraid I can't offer you much hospitality here. Have a
seat.'

I sat on a straight backed chair that wobbled on uneven
legs.

'This is luxury after a night in those mountains.'

'Perhaps.'

'Your servant sets an inexorable pace. A remarkable man. I
don't know his name —'

'I call him the Indian. I expect you did, too. Mentally, I
mean. Anyway, he can't speak so there's little sense in giving
him a name. Always better to classify than denominate. Avoid
familiarity. Once you label a thing you begin to think you
know what it is. Clouds the issue. Trouble with society, they
designate instead of indicating. Give everything a name
whether it's necessary or not. Etiquette. Confusion. Nonsense.
But I expect I'd better give you a drink, for all that.'

This brisk monologue pleased me. I saw he was still the
same Hodson I'd been given to expect, the same iconoclast and
rebel, and that seemed to indicate that he would still be carry-

ing on with his work – and furthermore, that he might be willing to talk about it. That was a paradox in Hodson. He denied society and civilization, and yet burned with the need to express his ideas to his fellow men, needing the objects that he scorned.

'I've some brandy. Not much. Plenty of the local stuff, if you can take it.'

'That will be fine.'

Hodson clapped his hands loudly. He was watching me with an expectant expression. A movement caught my eye at the back of the room and I glanced that way. I saw a young woman come through one of the beaded curtains, started to look away and then found myself staring at her. She was coming towards us, and she was absolutely splendid.

I don't believe I've ever seen such a magnificent physical specimen, and there was little cause to doubt my perception because she was wearing no clothing whatsoever. Hodson looked at me and I looked at the girl. She was tall and lithe, her flesh burnished copper and her hair so black that it reflected no highlights at all, an absence of all colour. She smiled at me inquisitively, flashing teeth in a wide mouth and eyes as dark as her hair. It is extremely difficult to manage a polite smile of greeting in such circumstances, and Hodson was amused at my effort.

'This is Anna,' he said.

I didn't know what to do.

'Anna speaks English. Anna, this is Mister Brookes. He has come to visit us.'

'How do you do, Mister Brookes,' she said. She held her hand out. Her English was flawless, her handshake correct if somewhat disturbing. 'It is very nice to have a guest. I don't think we have had a guest before?' She looked at Hodson.

'Bring Mister Brookes a drink, my dear.'

'Oh yes. Of course.'

She smiled again as she turned away, her firm breasts in profile for an instant, and her buttocks inverted valentines rolling tautly together as she walked away. She left the same way she'd entered, moving through the beads with supple grace, not the acquired poise of a woman but the natural rhythm of some feline animal.

Hodson waited for me to comment.

'A charming young lady,' I said.

'A trifle disconcerting, I suppose?'

'I must confess I was a bit taken aback. By her symmetry, of course, not her nakedness.'

Hodson laughed.

'I wondered how you would – but no matter.'

I felt I'd passed some examination, although I wasn't sure how he'd graded my reactions.

'She is an Indian?'

'Yes. Not a local, of course. From the Amazon. I found her there when she was just a baby – must be fifteen years ago or more. Bought her on a whim of the moment.'

'Bought her?'

'Of course. What else? Surely you didn't think I stole her? Or does the idea of purchasing a human being offend your morality?'

I didn't like that.

'My morality is unequivocally subjective. But I notice you've given her a name. Unlike the Indian. Would that be significant, in any way?'

Hodson frowned and then grinned.

'It was necessary to the experiment. I had to give her an identity, in order to see how it developed. But, I must admit, it would be rather difficult to refer to Anna as, say, the subject under observation. Some matters defy even my principles.'

Anna returned with two glasses, gave us each one and left the room again. Hodson pulled a chair over and sat facing me, balanced on the edge as though the interview would not be lasting very long.

'Now then. Why have you come here, Brookes?'

'I'm from the museum. You know Smyth, I believe. He sent me to find you.'

'Smyth?' His face was blank for a moment. 'Yes, I know

Smyth. One of the more sensible men. Knows better than to scoff without comprehension. But why did he send you here?'

I took my cigarette case out and offered Hodson one. He declined. I wondered if a direct approach would be best. Hodson would certainly resent anything else; would slice through any oblique references with his sharp perception. It had to be direct. I lighted a cigarette and proceeded to tell him about the reports and Smyth's deductions. He listened with interest, hands resting over his knees, eyes shifting as though they reflected the thoughts behind them.

'And so I'm here,' I said.

Hodson leaned back then, crossing his legs. 'Well, I hardly started these rumours,' he said. 'I don't see any connexion with my work.'

'Just an idea of Smyth's.'

'An erroneous idea.'

'Surely you've heard these rumours yourself?'

'No reason to make that assumption. I am, as you can see, completely isolated here. My only contact with the world is through the Indian.'

'Well, you've heard them now.'

'What you've told me, yes.'

'Don't they interest you?'

'Unfounded and fantastic.'

'I thought so. Smyth didn't. And now that I've spoken with these people . . .'

He waved a hand.

'Genetics is my line. This wouldn't concern me, even if it were possible.'

'Yes, I know your work. Tell me, what has kept you here for twenty years?'

'That same work. Research. Paper work, mostly. Some experimentation. I have a laboratory here, crude but sufficient. I stay here for the isolation and lack of distraction, no more. You were mistaken to assume that my research had any connexion with the area in which I chose to pursue it.' He drained his glass.

'You see, Brookes, I have the unfortunate trait of optimism.
I overestimate my fellow man constantly. When I am surrounded by other men, I invariably try to give them the benefit
of my work. It's disrupting, takes time, and proves less than
useless. That's why I'm here, alone, where my progress can
continue peacefully and steadily. It's going well. You are, in
point of fact, the first distraction I've suffered in years.'

'I'm sorry if —'

He waved the apology away.

'I understand your interest,' he said. 'I've observed these
people. Anna, for instance, is a fascinating study. One of the
few people in the world who is completely natural and un-
spoiled. Been kept from the degrading influence of society.
Not necessarily modern society, either. All society corrupts. If
I hadn't bought her she'd be ruined already, filled with super-
stitions and legends and taboos and inhibitions. Sometimes I
actually believe that the so-called primitive man is more
degraded than civilized man; more governed by superstruc-
ture. She came from a savage tribe and has become a superb
woman, both physically and emotionally. Her nakedness, for
instance. She is as immune to the elements as she is to shame,
as innocent of the wiles of a modern world as she is the
sacrifices and bloody religion of her parents. If I had met a
woman like Anna when I was a young man, Brookes, I might
have – oh well, I suppose I was born a misogynist.'

Hodson was becoming excited. He was a talker, denied the
opportunity for twenty years, and although he might not have
wanted to, he was talking.

'Or the Indian,' he said. 'The intellect and the instincts of
an animal, and yet I have his total devotion and loyalty – not
an acquired trait, like patriotism, hammered into the young by
conditioning, but a natural loyalty such as a dog gives to his
master. It doesn't matter if the master is kind or cruel, good or
bad. That is irrelevant. A most interesting aspect of natural
man.'

'Then you are studying these people,' I said.

'What?' Hodson blinked. His face was flushed beneath the

weathered skin. 'Not, not studying. A sideline. One can't help observing. It has nothing to do with my work.'

'Will you tell me about that work?'

'No,' he said. 'I'm not ready yet. Soon, perhaps. It's a new field, Brookes. Unrelated to the study of primitive peoples. I leave that to the social anthropologists, to the do-gooders and the missionaries. To you, if you like. You're welcome to them.'

'And these rumours?'

'I may have heard something. Perhaps an aborigine or two just trying to live their own lives. They'd be enough to shock anyone who saw them, and of course no one has ever told them it's wicked to kill sheep.'

'That, too, would be of immense interest.'

'Not to me.'

'You surprise me.'

'Do I? That's why I'm here, alone. Because I surprise people. But I have nothing for you, Brookes.'

He waved towards the window. The sun was coming in now, as it settled into the western junction of the hills, blocking a shallow parallelogram on the floor.

'You may seek your wild man out there. But you'll find no clues here.'

And that positive statement ended the initial phase of our conversation. We sat in uncomfortable silence for a time. I felt a sense of futility and annoyance that, after waiting so impatiently in Ushuaia and then undertaking that arduous trek through the mountains, it had all come to nothing. I blamed myself for expecting more than I reasonably should have, and felt irritated at Hodson, even while I admitted his right to resent my visit. Vexation does not depend on justice.

Hodson seemed to be pondering something that didn't concern me or, more likely, something he didn't wish me to be concerned with. My presence both pleased and disturbed him, and he seemed undecided whether to treat me as the conversational companion he'd been without for so long, or the disturbance he wished to avoid. I felt it best to refrain from intruding on his thoughts, and sat quietly watching the dust dance in the oblong of light beneath the window.

Presently he clapped his hands again. Anna must have expected this, for she appeared instantly with fresh drinks, flashing that searching smile at me, undoubtedly puzzled at my visit and, I think, enjoying the change in daily routine. She moved off reluctantly, looking back over her shoulder with interest that was innocent, because she'd never learned that it wasn't.

Hodson began to talk again. His mood had changed during those minutes of silence, and he wasn't expounding now. It became a mutual conversation. We talked in general terms, and Hodson was interested to hear of some of the latest theories which hadn't yet reached him here, although he expressed no opinions and no desire to go into them in depth. I referred to some of his own earlier work in this context, and he seemed pleased that I knew it, but passed that same work off as misguided and outdated. This turn of the conversation came naturally, and brought us back to his present work, from a new angle, and he had lost his reticence now.

'For the past twenty years or more,' he said, 'I have been mainly concerned with the replication processes of the nucleic acids. I believe – I know, in fact – that my work has progressed far beyond anything else done in this line. This is not conjecture. I have actually completed experiments which prove my theories. They are immutable laws.'

He shot a quick glance at me, judging reactions with his old desire to shock.

'All I require now is time,' he continued. 'Time to apply my findings. There is no way to accelerate the application without affecting the results, of course. Another year or two and my initial application will be completed. After that – who knows?'

'Will you tell me something about these discoveries?'

He gave me a strange, suspicious look.

'In general terms, of course.'

'Do you have any knowledge in this field?'

I wasn't sure how much familiarity I should show here –

how much interest would inspire him to continue without giving him reason to suspect I might be too formidable to be granted a hint of his secrets. But, in fact, my acquaintance with this branch of study was shallow. He was speaking of genetics, connected with anthropology only at the link of mutation and evolution, the point where the chains of two different sciences brushed together, invariably connected but pursuing separate paths.

I said: 'Not very much. I know that nucleic acid determines and transmits inherited characteristics, of course. The name is used for either of two compounds, DNA and RNA. I believe latest thinking is that the DNA acts as a template or mould which passes the genetic code on to the RNA before it leaves the nucleus.'

'That is roughly correct,' Hodson said.

'Very roughly, I'm afraid.'

'And what would result if the code were not transmitted correctly? If the template were bent, so to speak?'

'Mutation.'

'Hmmm. Such an ugly word for such a necessary and elemental aspect of evolution. Tell me, Brookes. What causes mutation?'

I wasn't sure what line he was taking.

'Radiation can be responsible.'

He made a quick gesture of dismissal.

'Forget that. What has been the cause of mutation since the beginning of life on this planet?'

'Who knows?'

'I do,' he said, very simply and quietly, so that it took me a moment for it to register.

'Understand what I say, Brookes. I know how it works and why it works and what conditions are necessary for it to work. I know the chemistry of mutation. I can make it work.'

I considered it. He watched me with bright eyes.

'You're telling me that you can cause mutation and predict the result beforehand?'

'Precisely.'

'You aren't talking of selective breeding?'

'I am talking of an isolated reproductive act.'

'But this is fantastic.'

'This is truth.'

His voice was soft and his eyes were hard. I saw how he was capable of inspiring such respect in Smyth. It would have been difficult to doubt him, in his presence.

'But – if you can do this – surely your work is complete – ready to be given to science?'

'The genetics are complete, yes. I can do, with a solitary organism's reproduction, what it takes generations for selective breeding to do – and do it far more accurately. But remember, I am not a geneticist. I'm an anthropologist. I have always maintained that the study of man's evolution could only be made properly through genetics – that basically it is a laboratory science. Now I have proved that, and I demand the right to apply my findings to my chosen field before giving them to the self-immured minds of the world. A selfish attitude, perhaps. But my attitude, nonetheless.'

I said nothing, although he seemed to be awaiting my comments. I was considering what he'd told me, and trying to judge the truth of the statements and his purpose in revealing them, knowing his tendency to jump to conclusions and cause a deliberate sensation. And Hodson was peering at me, perhaps judging me in his own way, balancing my comprehension and my credulity.

I don't know which way his judgement went but, at any rate, he stood up suddenly and impulsively.

'Would you like to see my laboratory?' he asked.

'I would.'

'Come on, then.'

I followed his broad back to the far end of the room. The beaded curtains moved, almost as though someone had been standing behind them and moved away at our approach, but there was no one there when we pushed through. The room beyond was narrow and dark, and opened into a third room which was also separated by curtains instead of a door. The house was larger than it appeared from without. At the back of this third room there was a wooden door. It was bolted but not locked. Hodson drew the bolt and when he opened the door I saw why the house had appeared to project from the cliff behind. It was the simplest, if not the most obvious, reason. It actually did. We stepped from the room into a cave of naked rock. The house, at this part, at least, had no back wall and the iron roof extended a foot or two under the roof of the cave, fitting snugly against it.

'One of the reasons I chose this location,' Hodson said. 'It was convenient to make use of the natural resources in constructing a building in this remote area. If the house were to collapse, my laboratory would still be secure.'

He took an electric torch from a wall holder and flooded the light before us. The passage was narrow and angular, a crack more than a cave, tapering at a rough point above our heads. The stone was damp and slimy with moss in the wash of light, and the air was heavy with decay. Hodson pointed the light on to the uneven floor and I followed him some ten yards along this aperture until it suddenly widened out on both sides. Hodson moved off and a moment later the place was lighted and a generator hummed. I looked in amazement at Hodson's extraordinary laboratory.

It was completely out of context, the contrast between chamber and contents startling. The room was no more than a natural vault in the rocks, an oval space with bare stone walls and arched roof, untouched and unchanged but for the stringing of lights at regular distances, so that the lighting was equal throughout this catacomb. There was no proper entranceway to the room, the narrow crevice through which we had passed simply widened out abruptly, forming a subterranean apartment carved from the mountain by some ancient upheaval of the earth. But in the centre of this cave had been established a modern and, as far as I could see, well-equipped, laboratory. The furnishings appeared much sturdier and more stable than those of the house, and on the various tables and cabinets were racks of test tubes and flasks and beakers of assorted shapes and sizes, empty and filled to various degrees. Files and folders were stacked here and there, just cluttered enough to suggest an efficient busyness. At the far side of the room there was a door fitted into the rock, the only alteration that seemed to have been made to the natural structure of the cave.

Hodson gestured with an open hand.

'This is where I work,' he said. 'The accumulation of years. I assure you this laboratory is as well equipped as any in the world, within the range of my work. Everything I need is here – all the equipment, plus the time.'

He walked to the nearest table and lifted a test-tube. Some blood-red fluid caught a sluggish reflection within the glass, and he held it up toward me like a beacon – a lighthouse of a man.

'The key to mankind,' he said. His voice was impressive, the dark fluid shifted hypnotically. 'The key to evolution is buried not in some Egyptian excavation, not in the remnants of ancient bones and fossils. The key to man lies within man, and here is where the locksmith will cut that key, and unlock that distant door.'

His voice echoed from the bare rock. I found it difficult to turn my eyes from the test-tube. A genius he may well have been, but he definitely had a flair for presenting his belief. I understood the furore and antagonism he had aroused, more by his manner than his theories.

I looked around a bit, not understanding much of what I saw, wanting to read his notes and calculations but fairly certain he would object to that. Hodson had moved back to the entrance, impatient to leave now that I'd seen the laboratory, not wanting me to see beyond a surface impression.

I paused at the door on the opposite side of the chamber. I had thought it wooden, but closer observation showed it to be metal, painted a dull green.

'More equipment beyond?' I asked.

I turned the handle. It was locked.

'Just a storeroom,' Hodson said. 'There's nothing of interest there. Come along. Dinner will be ready by now.'

It was curious, certainly, that a storeroom should be securely locked when the laboratory itself had no door, and when the entrance to the passageway was secured only by a key which hung readily available beside the door. But I didn't think it the proper time to comment on this. I followed Hodson back through the tunnel to the house.

A table had been set in the front room, where the initial conversation had taken place, and Anna served the food and then sat with us. The Indian was not present. Anna was still quite naked, and somehow this had ceased to be distracting. Her manner was so natural that even the absurd motions of placing her napkin over her bare thighs did not seem out of place; the paradox of the social graces and her natural state did not clash. The meal was foreign to me, spicy and aromatic with perhaps a hint of walnut flavouring. I asked Anna if she had prepared it, and she smiled artlessly and said she had, pleased when I complimented her and showing that modesty, false or otherwise, is a learned characteristic. Hodson was preoccupied with his thoughts again, eating quickly and without attention, and I chatted with Anna. She was completely charming. She knew virtually nothing outside the bounds of her existence in this isolated place, but this lack of knowledge was simple and beautiful. I understood full well what Hodson had meant when he'd suggested that, had he met a woman like this when he was young – was surprised to find my own thoughts moving along a similar line, thinking that if I had not met Susan —

I forced such thoughts to dissolve.

When the meal was finished, Anna began to clear the table.

'May I help?' I asked.

She looked blank.

'Why no, this is the work of the woman,' she said, and I wondered what pattern or code Hodson had followed in educating her, what course halfway between the natural and the artificial he had chosen as the best of both worlds, and whether convenience or emotion or ratiocination had guided him in that selection.

When the table had been cleared, Anna brought coffee and brandy and a humidor of excellent Havana cigars, set them before us and departed, a set routine that Hodson obviously kept to, despite his avowed denials of social custom and mores. It was like a dinner in a London drawing-room, magically transferred to this crude home, and seeming if anything more graceful for the transference. I felt peaceful and relaxed. The cigar smoke hung above us and the brandy lingered warmly within. I would have liked to carry on the conversation with this intriguing man, but he quite suddenly shifted the mood.

He regarded me over the rim of his brandy glass, and said, 'Well, now that you see I have no connexion with these rumours, you'll be impatient to get away and pursue your investigations along other lines, I assume.'

His tone left no doubts as to which of us was anxious for my departure. Now that his exuberance had been satisfied, he was disturbed again – a man of changing moods, fervour followed by depression – feeling, perhaps, that he'd once more fallen victim to his old fault, the paradox of talking too much and too soon, and regretting it directly after.

He looked at his watch.

'You'll have to stay the night, of course,' he said. 'Will you be able to find your way back?'

'I'm afraid not. I hate to be a bother, but —'

'Yes. Ah well, perhaps it's for the better. At least my location remains a secret. I mean no personal offence, but already you disrupt my work. The Indian assists me in certain ways and now he must take the time to guide you back through the mountains. I'll know better than to make that mistake again, however. It should have occurred to me before that I must instruct him to return alone from Ushuaia.' He smiled. 'I can think of few men who would disagree with the Indian, if it came to that.'

He said all this with no trace of personal ill will, as if discussing someone not present, and I could take no exception to his tone, although the words were harsh.

'The Indian may well be one of the most powerful men

alive,' he said. 'I've seen him do things, feats of strength, that defy belief . . . all the more so in that it never occurs to him how remarkable these actions are. He's saved my life on three separate occasions, at great danger to himself and without hesitation. Have you noticed the scar on his side?'

'I did, yes.'

'He suffered that in rescuing me.'

'In what manner?'

Hodson frowned briefly, perhaps because he was recalling an unpleasant situation.

'It happened in the Amazon. I was attacked by a cat – a jaguar. He came to my assistance at the last possible moment. I don't fear death, but I should hate to die before my work is completed.'

'I'd wondered about that scar. A jaguar, you say? Was the wound inflicted by fangs or claws?'

'I don't – it was a bit hectic, as you can well imagine. A blow of the front paw, I believe. But that was some time ago. Amazing to think that the Indian hasn't changed at all. He seems ageless. Invulnerable and invaluable to me, in such help that requires strength and endurance. He can go days without sleep or food under the most exhausting conditions.'

'I learned that well enough.'

'And you'll undoubtedly learn it again tomorrow,' he said, with a smile, and poured more brandy.

We talked for the rest of the evening, but I could not lead him back to his work, and it was still quite early when he suggested that we retire, mentioned once more that I would want to get an early start in the morning. I could hardly disagree, and he clapped for Anna to show me to my room. He was still seated at the table when I followed her through one of the curtained doors at the back and on to the small cell where I was to spend the night. It was a narrow room with a cot along one wall and no other furnishings. There was no electricity and Anna lighted a candle and began to make the cot into a bed. This was disrupting again, not at all like the natural accept- ance I'd felt at dinner, seeing her naked by candlelight, bend-

ing over a bed. The soft illumination played over the copper
tones of her flesh, holding my eyes on the shifting shadows as
they secreted and then moved on to reveal and highlight her
body. She moved. The shadows flowed and her flesh rippled.
Her firm breasts hung down like fruit ripe for the plucking,
tempting and succulent. I had to tell myself that it would be a
wicked thing to take advantage of her innocence, and think
very firmly of Susan, waiting for me in London. I think man is
naturally polygamous, although I don't know if this is necessarily a bad thing, and it took great resolution to force my
thoughts away from the obvious.

She straightened, smiling. The bed was ready.

'Will you require anything else?' she asked.

'Nothing, thank you.'

She nodded and left, and the room was stark and harsh with
her departure.

I crawled into my crude bed.

I didn't sleep well.

It was still early and, although my body ached and protested
from the rigours of the trek, my mind was active and alert.
The thought of starting out again early in the morning was
unpleasant, and I felt that very little had been accomplished
by my efforts. Perhaps Hodson would tell the Indian to set a
more leisurely pace, but I couldn't very well suggest this after
he'd already mentioned how inconvenient it would be to have
the Indian wasting time as my guide. It was a distasteful
thought, added to the futility of the journey.

Presently I began to drift towards sleep, my body overruling
my mind and drawing me into a state of half-consciousness,
half thinking and half dreaming. A vision of Susan occupied
my mind and then, as the dreams became more powerful than
the thoughts and my subconscious mind rejected the restric-
tions of my will, it became a vision of the splendid Anna which
I was unable or unwilling to reject. I yielded to this night-time
prowling of the id, the transformation of thought to dream.

I was asleep.

I awoke in instant terror . . .

The sound awakened me.

There was no gradual surfacing from slumber, I was fully conscious in that instant, and I knew it was no dream ... knew, even in that first moment, what the sound had been. Gregorio's haunted words flashed back to me – a sound like no man has ever heard – and I knew that this was that sound.

It was a cry, a deep rolling bellow, quavering at the end, a sound that only vocal cords could have made, but that no vocal cords I'd ever heard could possibly have made. It was indescribable and unforgettable, the tormented howl of a creature not in torment.

I lay, trembling and staring at the dark ceiling. The candle was out, and my fear was blacker than the room. It seemed impossible that a sound, any sound, could have rendered me helpless, and yet I was petrified. I've always considered myself as brave as the next man, but this sensation was far beyond human courage – beyond human conception. I wanted desperately to stay where I was, motionless and silent in the dark, but I knew I would never forgive such cowardice, and I forced myself to move, inch by agonizing inch, as though my bones grated harshly together.

My cigarette case and lighter were on the floor beside the cot, and I fumbled for the lighter and ignited the candle. Shadows leaped against the walls and I cringed away from their threatening shapes, waiting for reality to form. It was some seconds before I managed to stand up and pull my clothing over the ice and sweat of my skin. Then, holding the candle before me like a talisman to ward off evil, I moved to the door and pushed through the curtains.

The house was too quiet.

Surely no one could have slept through that sound, and yet there was no stir of awakening. It was as if everyone had been awake beforehand and anticipated the noise. It had been very near, loud and vibrating, as though echoing from close confines, and I thought of the cave behind the house; felt strangely certain the sound had come from there; moved quietly down the corridor to the front room and then through the second passage that led toward the cavern entrance. Although the sound was not repeated, the silence was terrifying in its own way, a silence formed from that sound or an effect of the sound. I was stiff with dread, my backbone tingling and my flesh rippling until it seemed that snakelike, I was trying to shed my skin. If all fear is emotional, this fear was primordial, linked more to instinct than conscious knowledge of danger. I wanted to locate the source of the sound, but the dread was far deeper than any conception of what I might find, a repulsion that lurked secretly within me in some atavistic remnants of the past, some hideous racial memory awakened.

I forced myself forwards, through the second room. The door opening within the cave was open, and the tunnel beyond was dark. Light showed at the end, where it widened into the chamber, but it failed to penetrate the passage, and stepping into the darkness was like plunging into cold liquid qualms of panic. I don't know what resolution drove me forwards, what reserves of willpower summoned the mechanical motions of advancing, but I held the candle before me and walked into the corridor.

The pale light circled before me, floating over the contorted rocks in evil designs, and wavering on to meet the electric light at the far end, fading against the great brilliance and recoiling over the stoves, over a bundle of rags that blocked my path.

Rags that moved.

I would have screamed, had my throat worked, but I was frozen into motionless silence as the rags shifted and took shape, and I found myself staring into a face, a face twisted and wrinkled and human, swathed in filthy shards, the eyes gleaming under the dark shelf of overhanging brow. It was a woman, ancient and bent and deformed. She had been coming toward me. Now she stopped and spread her arms wide, barring the way like some loathsome crucifix, the rags hanging from her elbows in folds that seemed part of her body, some membrane attaching her arms to her flanks.

She hissed, an exclamation, perhaps a word in some unknown language, rocking from side to side on crooked haunches, and another form loomed up behind her, brushed her aside and advanced on me. My heart stopped, then burst with a surge of blood that rocked my brain. I dropped the candle, and saw the Indian in the light that shot up from the floor, nostrils flaring and cheekbones casting oval shadows in the sockets of his eyes. His hand closed on my shoulder, the strenth unbelievable, as if those terrible fingers could have closed effortlessly through my bones. I fully expected to die at that moment.

The grip relaxed then. I was dimly aware that Hodson had shouted something from the laboratory; I heard a dull clang as the metal door beyond was closed. Then the Indian had turned me and was pushing me before him, back the way I'd come. I offered no resistance, and he was not unduly rough, although those hands could never be gentle. He walked behind me until we were back at my room, then pointed at the bed with all four fingers extended and stood in the doorway, bending beneath the frame, until I had crawled cringing on to the cot. When I turned he had left, the beaded curtains whispered his departure, and I collapsed in a limp reaction which it causes me no shame to recall.

It was some time before my mind was released from the emotions, and I was able to think. Then my thoughts came tumbling in disorder. What had caused that sound? What had taken place in the room beyond the laboratory? Who had the ancient crone been, what was her function, what would the Indian have done to me if Hodson had not shouted? Where was Anna? How on earth did this household fit together, what purpose did the members fulfil in whatever monstrous scheme was being conducted? I found no answers, and I don't suppose that I wanted those answers, that I was prepared to have such terrible knowledge etched on my mind, with my shoulder still burning from the dreadful clutch of the giant Indian, and that ghastly cry still vibrating in my memory.

Anna came to my room in the morning.

She acted as if nothing unusual had happened in the night,

and told me that breakfast was ready. I was still dressed, the
sweat dried on my clothing, but she didn't notice this, or
comment on it. I got up immediately and followed her to the
front room, where Hodson was already seated at the table. He
looked tired and drawn. I sat opposite him.

'Sleep well?' he asked.

I said nothing. Anna poured coffee from an earthenware jug.
Hodson's hands were steady enough as he drank.

'I found myself unable to sleep,' he said, casually. 'I often
get up in the middle of the night and do some work.'

'Work? What work?'

'I beg your pardon?' he said. His annoyance and surprise at
my tone seemed genuine.

'What on earth caused that cry in the night?'

Hodson pondered for a few moments, probably not deciding
what to tell me as much as whether he should answer at all,
rather to satisfy my curiosity or castigate my impertinence.

'Oh, you mean just before you came to the laboratory?'

'Obviously.'

'I wondered what brought you prowling about.'

'And I wonder what caused that sound?'

'I heard it,' he said. 'Yes, now that I think of it, it's small
wonder you should be curious. But it was merely the wind, you
know. You've heard how it howls higher up in the mountains?
Well, occasionally a blast finds a crevice in the rocks and
comes down through the cave. It startled me the first time I
heard it, too. I was tempted to find the fissure and have it
sealed, but of course it's necessary for proper ventilation.
Otherwise the laboratory would be as rank as the tunnel, you
see.'

'That was no wind.'

'No wind you've ever heard before, Brookes. But this is a
strange place, and that wind came from beyond where man has
ever ventured.'

I felt a slight doubt begin. I'd been positive before, but it
was just possible that Hodson was telling the truth. I had
noticed that the air in the laboratory was fresh, and couldn't

doubt there were actually openings in the rock. But the doubt remained slight, with the sound still recent in my memory.

'I'm sorry if the Indian alarmed you,' Hodson was saying. 'I've instructed him never to allow anyone in the laboratory without me, you understand. He was just performing his duties.'

'If you hadn't shouted —'

Hodson paused, his cup before his face.

'Would he have killed me?' I asked.

'For a scientist, you have a vivid imagination,' he said. He sipped from the cup. 'I'm no Frankenstein, you know. No mad scientist from a bad cinema film. Although, I must say, the mad scientists generally seem misunderstood by the clottish populace.'

'Who was the old woman?'

'If it's any concern of yours, she's an old servant. Not actually so old, but these people age rapidly. She's past her usefulness now, but I let her stay. She has nowhere else to go. Surely you don't see evil implications in an ageing old woman, do you?'

His expression was scornful and angered me.

'Very decent of you to allow her to remain,' I said. 'And to supply her with such extraordinary garments.'

His eyes reflected something that wasn't quite indignation.

'My affairs are my affairs,' he said. 'It's time for you to go, I believe. The Indian has your horse ready and is waiting for you.'

At the door, I said, 'I'm sorry for troubling you.'

Hodson shrugged. Anna was standing beside him.

'No matter,' he said. 'Perhaps it did me good to talk with someone. And good luck with your investigations.'

'Good-bye,' Anna said.

We shook hands solemnly, as she must have thought a parting required. She remained in the doorway after Hodson had gone back inside. The Indian had led the horses around to the front of the house, and I saw they were both nervous, stamping and shying. When I placed my foot in the stirrup, my mount sidestepped away and I had to hop after him on one foot, holding mane and cantel, before I was able to get into the saddle. The horse had been very placid before. The Indian slipped on to his own horse and led the way up the track. I looked back and waved to Anna. She raised a hand rather timidly, possibly not acquainted with this gesture of farewell. Then she vanished into the house.

Well, that is that, I thought, as we wound up the track from the narrow valley. But I noticed one more thing. On the incline to the north a prominence of shrub jutted down toward the basin, and as we drew above it I saw that a strip, perhaps a yard wide, seemed to be broken and flattened, running from the top of the hill nearly to the apex of this growth, and where the strip ended some loose brush and limbs seemed to be stacked in a small mound, as if concealing something. A vague form, greyish in colour, was just visible through this tangled pile. It appeared that something had been dragged down from the rim of the hill and hastily covered. I couldn't quite make out what it was. As we reached the top of the trail, and the land levelled out before us, I saw two dark shapes circling and starting a cautious descent, thick necks poised attentively, lowering their sharp beaks below arched wings. These repulsive carrion eaters sank slowly down towards the northern slope, and then the land shouldered up and I could see no more.

7

I must have looked in fine shape indeed, judging from Graham's expression when I halted the horse in front of his store, filthy and unshaven and brittle with exhaustion. I expect I looked no worse than I felt. The pace of the return journey had not been noticeably less than the first, and had followed too soon to allow my body to harden from that initial exertion. And that incredible Indian hadn't even paused before turning back. When finally we reached the hardened beginnings of the trail that led through the tablelands to Ushuaia, he'd pointed in that curious, four-fingered fashion, turned his horse sharply, and headed back into the hills.

Graham helped me to dismount.

'All right?' he asked.

'Yes. Just stiff and tired.'

'You look like a wounded bandit who's been running in front of a posse for a week,' he said.

I managed a smile, feeling the dirt crack along the creases of my face.

'Didn't expect you back so soon,' he said. He looped the reins over the post and we went into the building.

'Neither did I. I wasn't particularly welcome at Hodson's, I'm afraid.'

Graham frowned. Inhospitality is virtually unknown in frontier territories. He said, 'I always thought there was something queer about Hodson. What's he doing out there?'

'I honestly don't know.'

I began pacing back and forth over the wooden floor, loosening my muscles. The knots were firm. Graham called the boy to take my horse back to the stables.

'How far did you go?'

'God knows. How fast can a horse travel in those hills? We must have been actually riding more than twenty-four hours.'

'Yeah, that's right. God knows. But I'll bet that Indian covered the greatest possible distance in the time. It's amazing how these people find the shortest routes. Can't understand that Hodson, though.'

He reached behind the counter and came up with a bottle; he handed it to me and I drank from the neck. It was brandy, and it felt very good.

'Well, what now?' he asked.

'I don't know. First thing, I want to crawl into a hot bath. Then I'm going to sleep through until morning. I can't make any decisions in this state.'

'Good judge,' he said.

I thanked him for his help, told him I would see him the next day after deciding what further supplies or assistance I might need, and limped back to the hotel. The desk clerk raised a polite eyebrow when he saw the condition I was in, and I asked him to have the maid heat a bath. I think he concurred with that judgement, and he asked if I needed any help getting upstairs. I managed on my own, however, and as soon as I was in my room I stripped my grimy clothing off and put a bathrobe on, then sat down on the bed to wait for the bath to be readied. After a moment or two, I lay back and closed my eyes, just for a second.

I never heard the maid knock, and when I awoke it was morning . . .

I spent the day relaxing and writing two letters, seated at a table in the bar. Jones, despite his reluctance to follow in the paths of his fellow tourists, had succumbed to a chartered flight to Cape Horn, and there were no distractions, other than my own musings as to how he was getting along with the three widows, and an admission that I would rather have liked to see Cape Horn myself.

The first letter was to Smyth. I considered for some time before I began writing, and informed him in detail of my interviews with Gregorio and MacPherson and my visit to Hodson's, stressing, I fear, the devotion to duty which the latter entailed. I sketched the nature of Hodson's work briefly, from what the man had actually told me, and asked Smyth for his opinion of the possibilities of that, from general interest rather than in relation to my own investigations, and stressing that it was a theoretical point because Hodson would surely not welcome further concern on my part. I mentioned the Indian and Anna in terms, respectively, of awe and admiration, and was surprised to find how greatly Anna had impressed me. My conclusion was that I considered further probing warranted, despite Hodson's avowed disinterest and lack of connexion.

But I made no mention of that sound in the night.

Somehow, I found myself unable to express the feeling it had driven into me, and certainly there was no way to describe the sound itself, no comparisons whatsoever. And, now that I was back in the quiet hotel, I found myself almost willing to discount Hodson's connexion with the rumours. There seemed to be no connexion with his laboratory work, however advanced that might have been in its own right, and his explanation – the wind howling down the fissures – seemed reasonable enough, likely even, although it brought a chill to remember my certainty at the time. But it was far too subjective a feeling to symbolize by the written word, and I did not attempt it.

The second letter was to Susan. Before starting this, I re-read what I had written of Anna, and a sense of infidelity swept through me. I remembered how I had felt, watching her bend naked over the bed, with the candle light dancing over her flesh; how my loins had tightened with desire, and how close I had come to reaching out to her. I had never been unfaithful to Susan, and had never before felt the slightest urge or need, but there in the confines of that narrow cell, in that remote and forbidding land, I had struggled with an urgency so powerful —

Well. I had resisted, and I was very glad that I had, and I wrote to Susan with love.

8

My mind came back from that faraway place, through those eternal weeks. The waiter was taking the dishes away, concerned that we'd barely touched the food, but not mentioning it; aware that something was very wrong between us.

'Anything else, sir?' he asked, softly.

'A drink?'

'Yes. A strong drink,' Susan said.

Susan had never drunk very much. I ordered large brandies,

and she downed half of hers with the first swallow.

'I kept your letter,' she said, as if she had somehow followed my thoughts. 'The letter you wrote from Ushuaia. You still loved me when you wrote that, didn't you? Or was that a lie, too?'

'It was no lie. There is no lie, Susan. I love you now as much as then.'

'Yes, whatever changed your mind must have happened after you wrote. I know there was love in that letter.'

She drained the brandy.

'But I shan't ask you again.'

'Another?'

'Yes,' she said. She turned the empty glass in her hands. 'No, never mind. I want to leave, Arthur.'

'All right.'

I signalled to the waiter.

'I want to leave alone, Arthur,' Susan said.

'Susan. Darling —'

'Oh God. I can't stand this. I can't bear it. I'm going now.'

She stood up and walked quickly towards the entrance. I pushed my chair back and started to rise, then collapsed back on to the seat. The waiter stood beside the table and Susan was getting her coat at the counter.

'The bill, sir?' the waiter asked.

I shook my head.

'No. Not yet. I'll have another brandy.'

'Large, sir?'

'Yes,' I said.

I'd been drinking a large brandy the day that Gregorio came into the bar at the Albatross, too. It was the second day since my return from Hodson's, and I'd sent the boy from Graham's store to fetch Gregorio, feeling that it might be to my advantage to put my proposition to him here at the hotel, rather than at his shack – to talk to him on my own ground, removed from the realities of Gregorio's life.

He stood in the doorway, beside the boy. I nodded and the boy pointed to me and went back out. Gregorio walked down the bar and stood beside me.

'Oh, it is you,' he said. He didn't seem pleased. 'I didn't remember the name.' I had the impression that, had he remembered, he wouldn't have come.

'A drink?'

'Pisco,' he said, shrugging. The barman poured the grape alcohol into a large tumbler. Gregorio was in no hurry to drink, and his feet shifted nervously.

'I've been looking for your Bestia Hombre,' I said.

He nodded, expecting that. He lifted the glass.

'Pray God it doesn't look for you,' he said.

'Will you help me, Gregorio?'

'I? How is that possible?'

'I'd like you to take me to the place where you saw it.'

'No. I will not go there again.' It was more a statement of unalterable fact than an assertion of refusal. He took his blackened pipe out and began to fill it with some exotic mixture from a rubber pouch.

'I'll pay well.'

He looked balefully at me, struck a match and continued to regard me above the flame as he sucked the pipe into a haze of smoke. The contents blackened and curled above the bowl, and he pressed it back with a hardened thumb. A few shards escaped and drifted, smoking, to the floor.

'I need money,' he said. 'We all need money. But not to that place.'

'You needn't do anything else. Just guide me there. What danger could there be?'

'Danger? Who knows? Perhaps none. But that place is . . . it is not a good place. It has very bad memories. I am no longer young and no longer brave. The dog was brave.'

He shrugged once more.

'Well, could you show me on a map?'

'A map?'

I thought he hadn't understood the word.

'Mapa,' I said.

'Yes, I know this word. But what map? There is no map of that place. Not with detail.'

'Could you make a map?'

'Of no use to you. I have lived all my life here, and I am not young. I know the land. But to make a map – what is there to show on this map. It is rocks and trees and hills. How are they different? To me, perhaps, for I know them. But on the map it is the same.'

This was true, of course. It had been a thoughtless request. And, anyway, I needed a guide with me, a man who knew the land and, preferably, knew where Gregorio had seen the creature. And that was only Gregorio.

'I have already been out there,' I said.

'Yes.'

'I have heard the sound of the thing. Gregorio, I have heard it, and I know you told me the truth.'

His eyes were wide. I wanted to shock him.

'I heard it in the dark of night,' I said.

'And still you wish to find it?'

'Yes.'

'You are very brave, Señor. Braver than I.'

'That is because I know there will be no danger,' I said. 'I was frightened when I heard it, yes. But it is a living thing. It is no demon or spirit, whatever it is, it is alive, and we'll be well armed. It can't hurt us.' I tried to look confident, almost nonchalant, and Gregorio seemed to weaken slightly. He took the pipe from his mouth and drank, replaced the pipe and drew, cheeks hollowed and a deep line etched between his eyebrows.

'I would have a gun, too?' he asked.

I nodded. I don't honestly know if I had intended to carry a weapon, against my principles, but I do know I was relieved that Gregorio's reluctance made it necessary.

'I would like to kill it,' he said.

'Only in self defence —'

'I would very much like to avenge the dog, yes.' His jaw

tightened. 'But the dog is dead. It would not help the dog. It is my Spanish blood that has the desire for revenge.' He leaned against the bar with both hands, head down between his shoulders. His shoulderblades were sharp beneath the canvas poncho, and his thoughts were sharp beneath his furrowed brow.

'I would be very much afraid,' he said, without looking at me. The pipe bobbled in his teeth as he spoke.

'But you will show me?'

After a while he looked up.

'How much money will you pay me?' he asked.

But I knew that the money had very little to do with it.

We decided to leave in two days, which gave ample time to make preparations, and for me to recover from the physical effects of the last trek. Actually, I felt very well. I'd been exercising lightly since my return, so that my muscles hadn't stiffened much, and I felt that the exertion had hardened me sufficiently so that I didn't dread repeating the journey. Then too, this time I would be able to dictate the pace at which we travelled. Although I was eager to get to the area where Gregorio had seen the creature, I felt no need for haste now that definite arrangements were being made for departure, unlike the impatience I'd felt while waiting for Hodson's man to arrive without knowing when to expect him, when time and distance were unknown quantities. This time, we were able to plan accurately and take all the equipment and supplies necessary for a prolonged camp in the mountains.

Graham and Gregorio conferred on what we would need, and I left the decisions to them, with complete confidence in their judgements, hiring what I could and purchasing the rest according to their recommendations. For my own part, I bought only a change of clothing similar to what I'd worn on the first trek, and a pair of light sandals to alternate with the heavy boots. I'd paid so little attention to the rest that, on the night before our departure, I was surprised at the size of the pile that had accumulated.

We were taking two small Everest tents as well as sleeping

bags, groundsheets and blankets for warmth and shelter; a large amount of food both for ourselves and the horses, along with cooking utensils which fitted neatly together when not in use, and a double burner Butane stove which Gregorio considered an unbelievable luxury, without disdaining it; a complete first aid kit and a spade and axe, both of which were hinged and could be folded to simplify transport and packing, and an ample supply of pisco which did treble duty as sustenance, warmth and medicine, and which I found myself growing rather fond of at a few shillings a bottle. Stacked together, these supplies made a considerable mass in one corner of Graham's storeroom, but he assured me that everything could quite easily be distributed between two pack horses and our own mounts.

He had already arranged for the hire of the pack animals and the same horse I'd ridden before, which I'd suggested, feeling confident in its reliability, and in my own ability to control it. Gregorio intended to use his own horse, the grey gelding, and I added the hire fee for one horse to what I was paying him as a guide.

Graham was dealing with a customer while I made the gesture of checking the supplies. Gregorio stood behind me.

'Well, we certainly seem to have everything we could possibly need,' I said. 'You've been very thorough.'

Gregorio nodded, then frowned.

'What is it?'

'The guns?' he said.

I'd forgotten them, actually. I hesitated. I was afraid that Gregorio might do something rash out of hatred or fear or vengeance. But he was watching me expectantly, and I knew he couldn't be persuaded to go without a weapon. I didn't really blame him, either, and knew the idea of being able to defend ourselves would make us both feel better.

'Yes, I'll see about that now,' I said.

Graham had finished with the customer, and I went over to the counter and inquired about hiring guns. Gregorio followed, as if he wanted to make sure.

'I never thought of that,' Graham said. 'I didn't know you'd be needing guns.'

'I certainly trust we shan't.'

'Well, I don't hire guns myself. All my regular customers have their own guns, and the tourists who want to do any shooting usually make arrangements through their travel companies.'

Gregorio moved closer.

'There must be somewhere to hire them.'

'Oh yes. But why don't you borrow a couple from Gardiner?' Possibly he resented the idea of sending me to a competitor. 'Gardiner does some shooting and I know he has several spare guns. Want me to ask him?'

'I'll ask him,' I said. It seemed a good idea, and I was certain he wouldn't object. 'I'll go out to his place now.'

Gregorio moved back towards the supplies, satisfied I was making an effort, and I went out to the street and found a taxi to take me to Gardiner's.

He seemed pleased, as usual, to have company, and gave me a drink while we discussed my trip to Hodson's and I told him a little about my plans for the second journey. When I'd finished, he asked if there was anything he could do to assist me. It was just the opening I needed, but somehow I felt rather ridiculous about the guns.

As casually as I could, I said, 'I was wondering if I should take any weapons? What would you think?'

'Weapons?'

'Well, guns.'

'For sport or food or protection?'

'Protection, I guess,' I said, feeling foolish.

Gardiner smiled. 'So you've come to believe those rumours, have you?'

'I don't know. I recognize the possibility.'

He nodded thoughtfully, the smile gone.

'Might it be a good idea, anyway? There are foxes and such that might try to raid our supplies.'

'A damn good idea, if you ask me,' he said. 'No harm in being safe. And, I must say, these rumours are a bit hair-raising, no matter what it is that's been killing Mac's sheep.'

'What would you suggest I take?' I asked, feeling uncomfortable about asking a favour, and Gardiner saved me the necessity.

'I can lend you a gun, if you like,' he suggested.

'I'd appreciate that, if it's no inconvenience.'

'I've several spare guns. Not much to do these days but shoot, actually, and guns accumulate the same as golf clubs or tennis racquets or darts – whatever your game is, there's always a new piece of equipment that strikes your fancy. But I'm wondering what would be best for you? It's hard to decide when you have no idea what you might have to shoot.' He seemed completely serious in considering this. 'Shotgun or rifle, which would you prefer?'

'I'd be more comfortable with a shotgun, I think. But if you can spare two, Gregorio could carry the rifle.'

'Sure. That solves that problem. Gregorio will probably be happier with a gun, too.'

'Yes. He believes what he saw, whether I do or not.'

Gardiner refilled our glasses and left the room; he returned in a moment with the firearms and handed me the shotgun. It was a superb gun, matched to the one hanging on the wall, hand engraved by some craftsman in Bilbao.

'Double twelve bore,' he said. 'Full choke on the left.'

I admired the workmanship for a moment, then threw it into aim. I was roughly the same size as Gardiner and the balance suited me well.

'A splendid gun. This will do me.'

'I suppose Gregorio can use this all right,' he said, handing me the rifle. It was a .303 Savage, the lever action feather-weight model, light and efficient in rough, wooded country where a longer rifle might be cumbersome. 'It hits hard and it's fast,' Gardiner said. He looked at me gravely. I suppose he'd sensed something of my nervousness, and he was quite serious when he said, 'Just in case.'

'Yes. Just on the off chance, eh?'

'I'll give you cartridges and shells before you leave.'

'I'll pay you, of course.'

He gestured.

'On the museum, of course.'

'Oh, well, all right then. Better yet, have Smyth send me half a dozen bottles of that fine brandy he keeps.'

'Certainly,' I said.

I'd never known that Smyth kept brandy, fine or otherwise. There were many things I didn't know.

Gregorio was sitting on the front steps at Graham's when I got out of the taxi with the guns. He nodded appreciatively and I handed him the rifle. He worked the lever a few times, then threw it to his shoulder in quick aim. I could see he'd used a rifle before. He nodded again, satisfied.

'This is good. I will carry this?'

'That's right. But, Gregorio, you must promise me that you won't use it unless it's absolutely necessary.'

'Necessary?'

'To our safety.'

He smiled. His teeth flashed.

'Yes, I will promise that,' he said. 'But, if we find this thing, I think it will be most necessary . . .'

9

We left early in the morning. It was raining and the dark clouds were torn by wind, strung long across the sky. Gregorio led the pack horses and I rode beside him, just stiff enough so that my muscles welcomed further exertion. Gregorio rode much the same as the Indian, although he used a saddle and boots, slumped slightly forward and relaxed. We both had our hoods pulled up against the rain and didn't speak much. I was concentrating on our route, and knew that we were following the same trail the Indian had taken from town, apparently the shortest or the only trail to the hills, such as it was. I was able to spot several landmarks I'd passed before, unusual rock formations and abnormally formed trees, the same impossible perch from which, perhaps, the same placid wild sheep observed our passage. We travelled slowly and steadily, and stopped for lunch before we'd reached the foothills; we rested for a few minutes and then pressed on again. Gregorio had lighted his pipe and the battered bowl jutted from his cowl, spluttering as the rain damped the burning mixture. The sky was dark, the weather foul. Where the low clouds were shredded by the wind darker clouds covered the gap from above. It looked as if it might rain for days.

When we reached the foothills and began to climb, everything seemed familiar, unlike the outstanding landmarks of the rising tableland, and I realized this was because everything was the same, curious and unusual formations repeated many times over until they became commonplace. I had no idea now whether we were still following the path the Indian had taken. Gregorio undoubtedly knew the land, but lacked the Indian's infallible sense of direction or familiarity, and he had to stop from time to time to get his bearings, relying on a visual knowledge which the Indian hadn't needed. We made frequent mistakes, and had to turn or backtrack, but they were not serious and our progress wasn't greatly hindered. Several times we stopped to stretch and sample the grape alcohol. The rain continued and it grew colder; the reins were slippery and the damp began to seep through my windbreaker, adding the unpleasant sensation and scent of wet wool to my discomfort. I was quite satisfied when Gregorio suggested we stop for the night, although I knew we had not made nearly as much progress as I'd made on the first day following the Indian.

We made a campfire, not bothering with the Butane stove or the tents until we'd reached a more permanent camping place, but sheltering against the rocks in our sleeping bags, talking for a while and then lapsing into silence. Gregorio's pipe glowed for a while longer and then we slept.

It was still raining in the morning. The fire was out and we had to relight it to make coffee. We ate our breakfast from tins while the horses watched with drooping ears. Progress was slower on this second day, as we climbed higher and the forest thickened around us. It was necessary to move in single file now, and I dropped to the back of the line. We had been travelling for several hours when we came to a stream. It was impossible to tell if this was the same stream I'd crossed behind the Indian, when I'd noticed that scar on his side, but if it was the same water, we had certainly come to it at a different place. The banks were shallow and we had no trouble fording it. I thought it was probably the same stream, but that we were farther to the north. On the opposite bank the land rose more sharply, and I began to anticipate reaching the top of the range – the same distance, roughly, as I'd made in the first long haul of some twelve or thirteen hours behind the Indian. But as we continued to rise higher and the land did not begin to level off, it strengthened my belief that our path lay farther north, where the mountain range extended towards the Pacific. Either that, or we were travelling much slower and more circuitously than I hoped.

In the late afternoon we came to the highest point of this slope, and the land lay below us on all sides. There were further mountains to the west, hazy and unreal in the rain. I asked how far we'd come and Gregorio told me we were more than halfway there. This was encouraging, but inspired no great desire to press on more rapidly. We went on a few miles beyond the top, to gain the shelter of the trees and hills, and made our second camp.

Sitting beside the fire, after dinner, Gregorio broke open the box of cartridges and silently began to load his rifle. He put the safety catch on but kept the gun beside him. The shotgun was in my pack, stock and barrels separated and carefully wrapped. I felt no urge to get it out. My foreboding had diminished, and the land no longer seemed so wild and savage on this second trek, at a slower pace and with a guide to whom

I could speak. But I thought Gregorio might prefer me to be armed.

'Shall I get my gun out?' I asked.

He shrugged. 'We are not very close,' he said. 'It is just that I am nervous. I have never before been in the mountains without a dog to awaken me if there is danger. I left my dog with a friend . . .'

I wondered if he still had the same dog that had fled when El Rojo died. But I didn't ask him.

We descended gradually thoughout the morning of the third day. The rain had slackened somewhat, although the sky remained dark, gunmetal streaked with black. Progress was good and, although the land still lay below us north and south, looking back I could see we had come a considerable distance from the peaks. The land was fairly open and I was able to ride abreast of Gregorio, but he seemed in a solemn mood. He had the rifle slung across his back and looked like a Hollywood Hemingway bandit. We stopped late for lunch, and he didn't seem interested in the food but drank rather more pisco than usual to wash it down, then forfeited his after-lunch pipe in his impatience to get under way again.

A mile or so from where we had halted, he turned from the obvious flat route and led the way along an inclining shelf towards the north. Trees grew in a curiously straight line on our right, their limbs drooping wearily under the weight of hanging moss and pressing rain, and the ridge on our left dropped away sharply in layered rock. Presently, the incline became more gradual and then disappeared as the land rose to meet it in a triangle. I realized it had been a long canyon, and we had come to the end of it. Gregorio pushed his hood back, and the wind rippled his stiff hair. He was looking about, alert and concerned, and I wondered if we were lost.

Then he reined up, slipped the rifle from his back and held it across the pommel. The grey gelding pawed the ground.

'What is it?' I asked.

'We are there.'

'Where?'

He pointed towards the trees at the head of the canyon.

'That is where I saw it,' he said.

I nodded and dismounted. Gregorio looked down at me for a moment, then swung from the saddle.

'Will you show me?' I asked.

'I came here. I am not very brave about this, but neither am I a coward. I will show you.'

He looked very Spanish suddenly, arrogant and proud. We tied the horses to a leaning tree and walked towards the trees. I remembered the darkness and silence he'd told me about, but didn't feel that sensation. It didn't seem a frightening place. Gregorio pushed through the brush, the short rifle held before him, and I followed. The trees inclined towards us and we were in an open glade. There was nothing there. Gregorio moved across the space, his boots sinking into the soft earth, head lowered and moving from side to side.

Suddenly he stopped very quickly. I came up beside him. His knuckles were white on the rifle, his teeth were white as he drew his lips back, and when he moved the toe of his boot I saw something else flash white on the ground. I knelt, and felt a sudden beat of sympathetic pain. It was the broken skull of a dog. A brave dog.

I wanted to say something, but one doesn't express those things. Gregorio stared at the skull for a moment, stone faced, and then he shrugged.

'It is done,' he said.

There was nothing else there. He walked silently back to the horses.

10

We made our permanent camp some distance from that glade. That was our focal point and I didn't want to go too far from it, but Gregorio wouldn't have wanted to be too close to the scene so horrible in his memory, although there was certainly nothing there now. I'd searched methodically for footprints or patches of hair that might have been torn out on the thorns, but found nothing except a few more bones, scattered and picked clean. The scavengers had made a thorough job of their grisly feast.

Physically, the spot where we made camp was far more gloomy than the glade. Gregorio had chosen it for maximum shelter and convenience rather than scenic grandeur, although there was a certain unreal and eerie enchantment about the place. A brooding, timeless, unchanging mood clung to the rocks and trees, a smell of arrested decay that had begun but would go no further, as though a primordial swamp had been suddenly frozen for eternity.

It was an area enclosed by a rough oval of rocks and trees a dozen yards wide at the narrowest segment of the ring. The rocks were of all shapes and sizes, from boulders to stones, and the trees grew from all angles between them and around them, twisting to conform with the immovable rocks and bowing away from the constant winds. Several trees had grown together, joining at the trunks and limbs while boulders separated their roots; others had split around narrower rocks so that two trees shared the same roots. The stones were covered with slimy moss and fungus and sallow creepers dripped from the limbs.

I held the horses while Gregorio scrambled over the rocks, vanishing behind a curtain of swaying vines. He returned shortly, satisfied that the interior of that oval would be the ideal place to make our camp. It was enclosed from the wind, the trees arched into a roof overhead, and best of all a narrow stream ran through the space, appearing in a spurt of fresh water from between the rocks.

It was difficult to get the horses inside. They were reluctant to cross the barrier of rock and we had to lead them one at a time, clattering and sliding, but once they were inside they were safe and we didn't have to worry about them. They wouldn't cross the rocks voluntarily and it eliminated the need to tie or hobble them, as well as the effort of carrying water from the stream across the treacherous footing, as would have been necessary had we left them outside.

I erected the tents while Gregorio fashioned an interior barrier of rock and dead trees to keep the horses out of the living quarters of our strange dwelling, and used the folding axe to hollow a log into a feeding trough. Then I set up the stove and attached the Butane bottle while he built a circle of rocks in front of the tents to serve as a fireplace. The stove was adequate for cooking, but we needed a fire for warmth and light. Together we unpacked the rest of the supplies and covered them with a tarpaulin. Our camp was made, crude but adequate, and it was time to decide what the next step should be. I lit a cigarette and considered the prospects. Gregorio was gathering whatever dry wood he could find. Now that the destination had been reached, I felt a sense of futility. We were here, but had anything other than distance been accomplished? I don't know what spectacular clue I'd hoped to find but there had been nothing, no sign of the creature's presence in the area and no reason to suppose he was still there. All I could do was wait and observe and hope, and that seemed a passive and remote approach. I decided to confer with Gregorio and waited while he used a chemical fire lighter to start the camp fire, and brought water for coffee.

The smell of coffee boiling in the open air is sufficient to raise the lowest spirits, and the prospect of lacing it with grape alcohol was even better. Gregorio seemed to have shaken off his depression by the time we sat huddled at the fire, tin cups steaming in the damp air. I felt peaceful again. It was the end of the day, but nightfall was not a definite thing under that overcast sky. The raindrops battered at the fuscous forest surrounding us, seeking entrance through the foliage and falling like moths to the firelight. It was dark and sombre, a scene from a nightmare world. The little stream splattered from the rocks in peaceful contrast to the wind calling overhead, and the pungent odour of Gregorio's pipe drifted sharply through the scent of sodden vegetation and mouldy earth.

Presently, feeling that I should do something constructive, I took out my map case and unfolded the best map obtainable of the area. It was sadly lacking in detail, with frequent gaps, indicating nothing more than approximate altitude. I asked Gregorio where we were, and he frowned over the map. A raindrop bounced heavily from the Straits of Magellan.

'Here. Somewhere here.'

He stuck a forefinger in the centre of one of the blank areas. It told me nothing except that we were over 5,000 feet above sea level.

'Well, are there any landmarks, anything to get an approximate bearing from?'

Gregorio thought for a moment, his finger moving over the map. 'MacPherson's ranch is nearest,' he said. His finger strayed northwards a vague distance but remained within the confines of the blank space. 'Somewhere here. It was there I was travelling when I looked for work. When I saw it.'

That was encouraging, and I kicked myself mentally for not finding out sooner where MacPherson's place was. The creature had been there several times, at least once since Gregorio had seen it, and this knowledge increased my hope that it still frequented this area. I modified my self-castigation by realizing I couldn't have found MacPherson's on this map, anyway, and hadn't known Gregorio was headed there, but decided I'd better tie up the other possibility into this framework.

'Do you know where Hodson's is?'

Gregorio shook his head. 'I don't know that name. Is it a ranch?'

'No. Just a house. In a valley.'

He smiled. 'There are many valleys,' he said. 'I know of no house. Not north, I think. I know what is north from here, that is where I sometimes work.'

I folded the map carefully and slid it back in the case.

'How shall I go about finding the creature?'

He shrugged, looking into the fire. The light danced off his face like sunbeams off granite.

'Wait,' he said. 'You must wait.'

'But why should it come here?'

'Perhaps for two reasons,' he said. He was smiling again, but it was a strange, tight smile. 'One is the water.' He nodded towards the stream. 'It is the only water to drink on this side of the mountain. There are small streams that come and go and ponds that grow stagnant, but this is the only constant fresh water in some miles. It begins only a little way from here, and it ends just beyond. So, if this thing must drink, I think it will drink near here.'

This revelation delighted me, although I felt very much the amateur for not thinking of such a simple aspect of the search, and I was grateful for Gregorio's good sense. He was still smiling into the fire.

'And the other reason?' I asked.

'Because we are here,' he said.

It took a moment to understand what he meant. The fire was hot on my face, but a definite chill inched up my spine. Gregorio stood up and walked over to the supplies and packs, then returned with the shotgun and handed it to me. I saw his point. I bolted it together and kept it in my tent.

In the morning I set out to trace the stream to its source. Gregorio assured me it wasn't far, and that it emerged from a subterranean course through the mountains. I wore my heavy boots for scrambling over rocks and carried the shotgun. Gregorio volunteered to accompany me, but I didn't think it necessary since I was going to follow the stream and couldn't very well become lost since I could easily follow it back again.

The stream burst into the camp in a miniature waterfall, tumbling from a narrow opening in the rocks and falling a few inches with comical fury, a Niagara in the insect world. It was impossible to follow the winding stream around and under the rocks but that wasn't necessary. I crossed the barrier at the

easiest point and walked back along the perimeter until I came
to the spot where the water flowed into the circle. It was just a
shallow flow there, and I saw that it must have been com-
pressed and confined as it ventured through the rocks, to break
out in such Lilliputian ferocity at the other side. But on this
open ground it wandered through marshland with little direction, and it wasn't easy to follow its main course. Several times
I found that I'd gone a few yards along a side branch which
diminished and then vanished, seeping into the ground. There
was still no danger of losing my way, however, since I was moving upwards and could still see the trees surrounding the camp,
and as I walked farther the stream became wider and deeper.

I had been walking for ten or fifteen minutes when I heard
the rumbling ahead, and knew I must be approaching the
source. I was almost at the crest of the hill, and behind it a
high cliff towered against the sky. The stream was much larger
here, and when I came to the top I saw the waterfall, still
above me on the next hill. It was an exact replica of the
cascade in the camp, magnified many times over. The water
surged from a long gash in the cliff and pounded down, defy-
ing the wind, in a torrent at the foot of the unassailable rock
wall. The avalanche had worn the land away and formed a
turbid pool at the base of the cataract, and this in turn spilled
the overflow out to form the stream.

I hurried on until I was standing beside the pool. The spray
dashed over me and the sound roared in my ears. It was a
natural waterhole which any large animal would use in preference to the shallow stream, and I immediately saw traces of
those animals. I recognized the tracks of fox, muskrat and wild
sheep, and saw various other unidentifiable prints.

I moved around the bank to the other side.

And there, quite distinctly, I found a print that was almost
human. I stared at it for some time, hardly believing I'd discovered it so easily and so soon. But there it was. It wasn't
quite the print of a barefoot man. The toes were too long and
the big toe was set at a wider angle than normal. But it was
without doubt the footprint of a primate, and a large primate

at that. My heart pounding, I searched for further evidence, but there was only the one print. From that point, the creature that made it could have easily leaped to the nearest rocks, however, and it was all the evidence I needed to convince me I was in the right place, and that all I needed now was patience. If I waited, concealed near the waterhole, sooner or later the creature would appear.

But that suddenly posed another problem, one I'd been deliberately ignoring until the time came. If and when I did find the creature, what would I do? Or what would it do? My problem was based on not knowing what it was, whether it was man or beast or both. If there was any chance it was a man, I couldn't very well trap it or use force to capture it. It was a tricky moral judgement, and one I was hardly qualified to make before I'd seen it, and decided, tentatively at least, what it might be.

I returned to the camp, excited and anxious to tell Gregorio what I'd found. As I slid down from the rocks, I thought for a second that he wasn't there, and then I saw him by the horses. He had the rifle in his hands, pointing at the ground, but I had seen a blur of motion from the side of my eye, and wondered if he'd been waiting with the rifle aimed at the sound of my approach. Once again I felt a foreboding that he might act rashly; I knew, without doubt, that if it had been the creature that had just scrambled into the camp, Gregorio would have used his weapon with no hesitation.

I didn't tell him about the footprint. I told him I'd been to the waterhole, however, and that I intended to wait there in concealment.

'When will you wait?' he asked.

'As soon as possible. Tonight.'

'At night?' he asked, his tone not quite incredulous – more as though he couldn't comprehend such a thing than that he disagreed with it.

'I think the chance of seeing it would be better at night. And it will certainly be easier to conceal myself in the dark.'

'Yes. Those things are true,' he said, as if other things were

also true. But he offered no discouragement, in the same way
that one doesn't argue with a madman.

11

There was a moon above the clouds and long shadows drifted
across the land in skeletal fingers. By day that desolate cataract had been eerie enough, but in the moonlight the rocks
seemed to take on a life of their own, grotesquely carved
monsters that writhed and rolled in confused contortions, and
would have been more in place on that moon which lighted
them than on earth.

I lay face down in the forest, watching the water leap in
silver spray from the pool. The shotgun was beside me and I
kept one hand on the stock, the other on my electric torch. I
lay very still, hardly daring to breathe, conscious of the soft
ground and wet grass, the night noises cutting through the dull
roar of the water, and my own heartbeats. I had no way of
knowing how long I'd been there. My watch had a luminous
dial, and I'd left it back at the camp, taking no chances with
my concealment.

A sudden sound stiffened me. There was a scurrying in the
brush beside me as some small creature passed by, not a dozen
feet from my right hand, and emerged beside the pool a
moment later. I relaxed, letting my breath out quietly. It was a
fox, only a fox. It looked about, cautious and alert, and then
began to drink. An owl peered down from a nearby tree, then
turned round yellow eyes away, seeking a less formidable
meal. I judged it to be about three o'clock and my eyes were
heavy. I was about to concede that my first night's vigil would
be ended without results, although I intended to stay there
until dawn. A large cloud spun out across the moon, black with
frosted edges, and all the long shadows merged over the pool.
Then, whipped on by the wind, the cloud disintegrated and
the light glided back.

I was instantly alert.

The fox had stopped drinking. It stood, poised and tense, pointed ears quivering. I had heard nothing, and felt certain I'd made no sound, but there was something in the animal's bearing that implied caution or fear. The owl had vanished, the fox stood silhouetted against the waterfall for several minutes. Then suddenly it darted to the side, toward the undergrowth, halted abruptly and changed course. There was a louder stir in the trees as the fox disappeared. I rolled to my side, trying to follow the animal's flight without using the torch. Just above the spot where it had gone into the brush, a tree limb swayed, a heavy limb, moving as though it had just been relieved of a weight.

I pushed the shotgun out in front of me, thinking even as I did how I'd feared Gregorio might act rashly, and how that fear could well be extended to myself. And then there was no time for thought.

The limb moved again, bending farther down and slowly rising until it merged with the limb above at one wide point. The point moved toward the trunk, blocking the light. There was something on that limb, something heavy and large, crouching. Then it was gone, the limb swayed, unburdened, and something moved through the dark trees, away from the clearing. The sound grew faint, and left only the wind and water to throb against the silence.

I did nothing. For a long while I lay perfectly still, waiting, hoping it would return and, at the same time, feeling relief that it had gone. Whatever it was, it had arrived with a stealth that had defeated my senses; I'd heard nothing and seen nothing, and was quite aware that it could just as easily have been in the tree above me. I rolled on to my back and looked upwards at the thought. But the tree was empty, the barren limbs crossed against the sky, and whatever had come, had gone. I didn't go after it.

Dawn came damp and cold. I got to my feet and stamped, then stretched, feeling a stiffness far more unpleasant than that

caused by exertion. I lighted a cigarette and walked out of the
trees. I could see the marks the fox had left beside the pool,
and bent down to scoop some water and drink; I splashed my
face and washed my hands. The second part of my vigil had
passed very rapidly, and I can't begin to recall the inter-
mingled profusion of thoughts that had occupied my mind.

Then I walked back along the route the fox had taken to the
trees, looking at the ground and not knowing what I expected
to find. A patch of undergrowth seemed to have been broken
and I leaned over it. There was nothing on the ground. As I
straightened up a drop hit me on the cheek, too heavy for rain,
and when I wiped it my hand came away red. I thought I'd cut
myself on a branch, and rubbed my cheek, then took my hand
away and held it out, palm upwards, to see if there was blood.
There wasn't.

And then, as I was watching, there was. A drop fell directly
into my palm, thick and red.

I jerked back and looked up, but the tree was empty. The
blood was dripping, slowly, from a small dark blot on the
lowest limb. I couldn't quite make out what it was, although I
felt a cold certainty that I knew. I broke a branch from the
thicket and reached up, lifted the object and let it fall to the
ground. I felt sick. It was the hindquarters of a fox, blood-
matted tail attached, torn away from the rest of the body.

I searched, but not too thoroughly, and I didn't find the rest.

Gregorio was squatting by the fire. He held a mug of coffee
out to me as I walked over from the rocks. My hand shook as I
drank and he remarked on how pale I was. It wasn't surpris-
ing. I'd spent a night without shelter on the cold, damp
ground. I took the coffee into my tent and changed into dry
clothing. I felt very cold now and drew a blanket over my
shoulders, lighted a cigarette but found that it tasted foul and
stubbed it out. Gregorio pulled the flap back and handed me a
bottle of pisco. He seemed to want to talk, but saw I didn't
feel like it. He didn't ask if I'd discovered anything, assuming
perhaps that I would have mentioned it or, possibly, that I

wouldn't mention it anyway. I drank the pisco and coffee alternately, my mind dull. The rain was smacking against the canvas without rhythm, a drop, a pause, two drops, three drops, another pause, and I found myself concentrating on the irregular tempo, a form of self-imposed Chinese water torture subconsciously devised to occupy my mind and avoid making conclusions and decisions, I shook my head, driving the stupor away and forcing my mind back into focus.

There had been something in that tree. That was one certainty, perhaps the only one. It had seemed large and bulky but the moonlight was tricky and I couldn't be sure of that. Just something. A large bird? I knew better and wondered why I was seeking alternatives to what I should have welcomed. I knew damn well what it had been, what I should have been overjoyed to know, and no amount of sceptical ratiocination was going to change that knowledge. Even had I logically thought differently, I still would have believed with the force of emotion.

I drank some more pisco and followed my thoughts.

Whatever it had been, it was powerful enough to tear that unfortunate fox apart. There were no marks of fang or claw, the fox hadn't been cut or bitten apart. It had been pulled in two with enormous strength. There had been no sound, save the rustling of the trees, no death howl or struggle. Either the fox had been stifled or destroyed so quickly that it could make no cry.

That struck a discord somewhere. I remembered the terrible sound I'd heard from Hodson's laboratory, and the sound, the same sound I felt sure, that the creature had made after it killed El Rojo. Why had it been silent last night? Had it heard me, detected my presence in some way and been frightened off? Or was a fox too insignificant a victim to warrant a victory cry? If it had sensed my presence, would it return? I might have missed my only opportunity. Why hadn't I used my torch? Was it caution or fear or . . .

Gregorio was shaking me.

I opened my eyes and was startled to realize I'd been half-

onscious, between thought and nightmare. My teeth were
licking together, my stomach turned over, my forehead was
urning. Fever laced me. Gregorio put his long, delicate hand
n my brow and nodded thoughtfully. His concerned face
rew near and then receded, swelled like a balloon and then
hrunk away again. I observed everything through a haze, an
nequal fog that parted on reality and then closed over again. I
vas only dimly aware of Gregorio's strong hands as he helped
ne into my sleeping bag, and then quite distinctly knew I was
aking two of the small white pills Graham had recommended,
ould feel their roundness in my throat and taste the bitterness
n my tongue. Reality paled once more, and yet my mind was
lert on a different level and I wondered with lucid objective-
ess whether I'd fallen prey to some exotic fever or merely
uccumbed to the wet cold of the night. Then I fell into dis-
irbed sleep.

When I awoke it was evening. The campfire turned the can-
as burnished gold. I watched the rough texture glow, aware
f the minute details of colour and grain on that clear, dis-
iterested level of consciousness. Presently the flap parted and
iregorio looked in.

'Feel better?' he asked.

'I don't know.' I didn't. 'What's wrong with me?'

'Fever. Chill. Who knows? Not serious, I think. You must
est and be warm for a few days.'

'What time is it?'

'I have no clock,' he said.

My own watch was on the crate I'd used as a table. I
odded towards it and Gregorio handed it to me. It was ten
'clock.

'I intended to go back to the waterhole tonight.'

He shrugged.

'That is not possible now.'

'No, I guess not,' I said. I felt relieved about it. After I was
eling well would be time enough; I would be unable to
bserve properly in this weakened condition and would un-
oubtedly become more seriously ill. And, perhaps feeling a

need for more justification than my own physical failure, I told
myself that the creature might well have sensed my presence
and be wary. It was far wiser to wait.

I took two more pills, drank a glass of water, and slept more
soundly.

I felt better in the morning. I still had a slight fever, but my
head was clear, the curious dichotomy of muddled reality and
sharply focused details had ceased. I was able to walk around a
bit in the afternoon and force down some food in the evening,
and decided I had fallen to a chill rather than some disease.
But I was still weak and dizzy, and there was no question of
returning to the vigil that night. Gregorio saw that the delay
disturbed me.

'I could keep watch,' he said, dubiously.

'No. That wouldn't do any good. I'll have to see this creature myself; you've already seen it.'

'That is so,' he said, and celebrated his reprieve with a mug
of pisco.

I went to bed early and read, but found the strain of the
kerosene lantern painful, the words blurred. I turned the light
out and closed my eyes. I didn't feel sleepy, but sleep crept
over me in modulated waves. I remember feeling annoyed that
I was wasting this opportunity, and blaming my weakness for
hindering the investigation; telling myself that I had to find
the creature while it was in the area, that there might never be
another chance to find it. I was determined to return to the
waterhole the next night.

There was no need. It found us.

12

I was awake and something was snarling outside the tent. It
was the second time I'd been awakened by a sound in the night,
but this time I didn't hesitate – this snarling did not petrify

me as that other terrible cry. I slid from the sleeping bag and grabbed the shotgun. My eyes felt too large for their sockets, my mouth was dry. The snarl came again and I could hear the horses screaming. I pushed the flap open and let the gun precede me from the tent. The fire was burning low, and it was dark beyond. Gregorio came from his tent standing straight, the rifle at his shoulder, his eyes wild in the glow of the fire. He turned toward the horses.

The horses had gone mad. They were frantically milling about their enclosure. I moved to the side, to get a line of vision beyond the fire, and one of the horses leaped the rocks Gregorio had piled up. It was the grey. It charged towards me blindly and I flung myself to the side, heard the horse tear into my tent, saw the canvas flapping as I scrambled to my feet again. Another horse had attempted to leap the wide outer barrier and I heard its hooves clattering desperately for a footing, then saw it go down between the rocks, struggling to rise again. The other two horses were running in a mad circle around the enclosure, one after the other, following the circle. The second horse flashed past and I could see into the centre of the corral.

Something crouched there.

The firelight barely reach it, outlining it dimly against the barrier. It stood on four legs, but the shoulders were higher than the haunches, its weight on the hindquarters as it circled, turning with the horses. As I watched, it drew its arms upwards and coiled.

'Something's in with the horses!' I cried.

And it moved. One arm swept out wide, hooking at a horse's flank. The horse reared, forelegs pawing the air as it rose, rose too high and toppled over backwards. It blocked the creature from my sight. I had the shotgun up and, man or beast, I would have fired. But I couldn't shoot without hitting the horse. Gregorio was frozen in position, the rifle levelled, his face grotesque. The horse flailed the air, fighting to get up, but the creature was on it, rending and tearing, its snarls muffled against the horse's flesh.

The shotgun boomed. It sounded unbelievably loud to my inflamed senses. I had discharged it into the air, whether by accident or design or instinct I don't know, and the hollow blast bounced from the surrounding rocks as the pellets laced through the trees.

The horse was up, bucking and rearing, and the creature turned toward me, squat and square, poised motionless for an instant. Then its long arms swung, knuckles brushing the ground, and I brought the shotgun down; for a moment I was looking at the creature down the barrels, my finger on the second trigger. I could have shot it then, but I was looking at its eyes. And it looked back at me, savage and fierce but also curious and startled by the sound. I couldn't pull the trigger. The creature wheeled about, its great bulk pivoting with amazing speed, and moved toward the rock barrier. I followed it with the gun; saw it leap into the shadows; heard the report of Gregorio's .303, sharp and crackling in contrast to the shotgun.

The creature went down, howling, twisting in pain. Then it lunged up again. Gregorio worked the lever, the spent shell sparkled, spinning through the firelight. The creature was in the trees when he fired again, and I heard the slug smack against solid rock. We looked at each other. The creature was gone.

Gregorio was holding the grey, one arm around its neck. He spoke softly and the horse lowered his head, trembling. The horse that had been attacked was dashing about the corral, white foam pouring from his mouth, lips curled back from square teeth. A great hunk had been torn from its flank and long gashes were open over its ribs. I saw that it was my horse, the one I'd ridden and become attached to, and felt my jaws tighten.

I moved back to the wreckage of my tent. The poles were snapped, the canvas spread over the ground. I found my trousers amidst the debris and pulled them on. The horse that had fallen on the barrier was still struggling to rise, wedged between two smooth boulders, whimpering in pain.

'Now you have seen it,' Gregorio said.

I nodded.

'That was how the dog died,' he said, with far more sadness than hatred. The grey's head came up, ears pricked, and he whispered soothingly. The fourth horse moved toward him uncertainly, head turned, looking at his injured companion. I pulled the canvas from our supplies and found the box of shotgun shells, broke the gun open and reloaded the right barrel, then stuffed shells in the pockets of my windbreaker. I felt no fear now. Action had dispensed with dread. I felt determined and angry, and had no doubts that I'd use the gun if I had to. I knew that, whatever the creature was, it was not human enough to command human rights. I was not much of a scientist at that moment, but perhaps more a man. The smell of gunpowder was sharp on the thick air, a few leaves fluttered down from the blasted branches overhead. I walked over to Gregorio.

'You will go after it?' he asked.

'Yes.'

'It is wounded.'

I nodded. Gregorio had hit it once, and there are few animals a .303 won't bring down. I had no doubts that I could find it now.

'Someone should stay with the horses,' Gregorio said.

'Yes. You must stay.'

'It may be waiting for you.'

'I'll be all right.'

Gregorio regarded me with Indian eyes. He wanted to be brave, and he was brave. The grey gelding was still trembling under his arm and he nodded. That was right, someone had to stay with the horses. But he lowered his head and didn't watch me leave the camp.

I could hear the horse screaming in the rocks behind me. When I'd passed, he turned a wide eye upwards. His foreleg was snapped and he was lodged helplessly, looking for help we

could not give. I called Gregorio and went on. The crack of his
rifle came through the trees and the horse stopped screaming. I
felt a cruel satisfaction when I found a smear of blood marking
the creature's passage. It was large and dark in the light from
my electric torch, and I didn't think he'd be moving very fast.

He wasn't. When I had crossed the rocks I saw him lurching
up the hill that led to the waterfall. When he'd attacked the
horse, he had uncoiled like a steel spring, fast and fluid, but he
moved with a rolling, drunken gait now. His legs were short
and crooked and he used his long arms for support as he ran.
Perhaps his peculiar gait was not suited to travelling on open
ground at the best of times, and the bullet had taken its toll of
his strength.

I moved to the right, towards the trees, so that I would be
able to cut off any attempt to disappear into the bush where he
could move so much more silently and faster than I. But he
didn't attempt that. He was following a straight course up the
hill, as though not merely fleeing but moving towards a
definite destination. I had the torch in my left hand and the
shotgun cradled on my right arm. There was no need for
stealth or caution as long as I kept him in sight, and I followed
quickly. He was only three or four hundred yards in front of
me, and I drew closer without great effort.

He reached the top of the hill and paused, then turned and
looked back at me. He was silhouetted against the sky and his
eyes gathered the moonlight. I knew he had the vision of a
night animal, and was thankful for my torch. He watched me
for a few seconds, his heavy head turning from side to side,
then wheeled and vanished over the crest. I began to run,
wanting to keep him in sight, but not worried. I was familiar
with this terrain, and knew that the second hill stretched on for
a long distance, that he couldn't possibly ascend it before I was
over the first hill. I was breathing hard now, the soft earth
sucking at my boots and slipping from under me, but I ran on
and topped the rise.

The creature was not in sight. There was a small pool of
blood where he had paused and looked back, and a few scat-

tered dark patches beyond, heading toward the waterfall. But he had vanished. The far hill stretched away, smooth and rolling, with no concealment. The trees to the right had been in sight as I climbed. Behind the waterfall, the cliff rose sheer and unscalable. There was nowhere he could have gone except to the waterfall, and I moved down, walking slowly and cautiously now, my thumb on the torch switch and my finger on the triggers.

I came to the soft mud surrounding the pool and switched the torch on. A point of light reflected back from the cliff and I tensed, thinking it was those night-creature eyes, but it was only a smooth stone, polished by the waterfall. The beam played over the reeds and found nothing; then, at my feet, I found his prints. They were distinct and deep, moisture just beginning to seep in, the feet with wide angled toes and the impressions of his knuckles on either side. The tracks moved to the edge of the pool. I turned the light on the water, but the broken surface revealed nothing. Very slowly, I walked around the bank to the far side and inspected the ground. There were no prints emerging from there. The creature had gone into the pool and had not come out. And yet, it was not in the water. There could be only one explanation, and I let the light flood over the tumbling cataract. The cliff was perpendicular, grey stone, the water sparkled down, and there, just where they met, a narrow rim of blackness defied illumination.

I walked up to the cliff, the water lapping at my feet, the gun level at my hip, and there I found the cave. It opened behind the waterfall, an aperture some three feet high, completely hidden in the light of day unless one stood against the cliff face. The pool was slightly higher than the cave floor, and the water ran inwards, several inches deep. There was a smear of red against the angle of rock.

I had found far more than the creature's waterhole, when I'd come to this cascade. I'd found its home.

Did it take a greater courage than I'd ever known I possessed to enter that black cavern, or were my senses and emotions too numbed with fever and excitement to feel fear? I know that I went into the Stygian darkness without hesitation, and that I felt very little at all. I simply did it, without thought or doubt. The only sensation I was conscious of was the water rivetting my neck and back as I stopped under it, and then I was kneeling in the cave. The floor rose and the water penetrated only for a few yards. I shone the torch before me. It flowed well into the tunnel, but the blackness stretched on in the distance. It seemed interminable, and I had the sudden fear that it emerged again at some point and that the creature would escape me. The thought forced me on. I had to crawl for a few yards and then found it high enough to stand, crouching. It was narrow, my arms brushed against the sides, and it was straight. There was little danger. I had the torch and the gun and the creature could only come at me from the front. If I was forced to kill it, I would be able to. I didn't want to, however. My anger at seeing my horse's agony had lessened, I was more the scientist than the hunter once more. I determined that I would make every effort not to kill it; if I was forced to fire, my first blast would be aimed at its legs. But perhaps it was already dying, had crawled home to suffer its death throes alone. If that were true, it seemed brutal to pursue it, but there was no way to know, and I moved forward following the beam of light.

The walls were slimy with greenish moss, cracked with numerous narrow fissures where the mountain had moved in ages past. It was very quiet. My heavy soled boots made no sound on the stone, and the drops of blood underfoot became fewer and farther apart. The cave widened gradually as I moved into the depths, fantastic formations of broken rock emerged from the walls, pillars and trellises jutted up and hung down from floor and ceiling. I approached them warily, but there was nothing waiting behind. The tunnel continued to follow a straight course and it seemed I'd been walking a long time.

And then the light hit rock ahead, spreading out fluidly to both sides. I thought for an instant that I had come to a dead end, and then saw that the tunnel turned at right angles, a natural geometric angle following a fault in the solid stone. I approached the turning very slowly. If the creature were waiting for me, it would be here.

I stopped a few feet from the turn; held the torch under the stock so that I had both hands on the gun and the light followed the line of the barrels, took a deep breath, braced myself, and stepped out wide of the corner in one long stride.

I stopped dead.

The creature was not waiting there. There was nothing there. Nothing but a green metal door ...

The door swung open, heavy on its hinges. Hubert Hodson said: 'I expect you'd better come in.'

13

Hodson took the shotgun from me. I was too staggered to resist. I realized I'd passed completely under the mountain, and that we had inadvertently made our camp directly opposite Hodson's house, separated by the unscalable cliff but connected via the tunnel through the rock; that the door he'd claimed led to a storeroom actually opened into the tunnel. I followed Hodson through the door, expecting to enter the laboratory, but in that respect I was wrong. There was a connecting chamber between, a small poorly lighted room with another green door in the opposite wall. That door was open and I could see the brightly illuminated laboratory beyond. Hodson closed the door behind us and turned the key. Heavy tumblers fell into place. He pushed me ahead of him, towards the laboratory.

A low snarl sounded beside me. I wheeled about, pushing Hodson's hand from my shoulder, tensed and then froze. The creature was in that room. It crouched in the corner, behind heavy steel bars, watching me with comprehension and hatred. All the details instantly impressed themselves on my con-

sciousness as a whole, a single, startling tableau. The bars
fitted into the wall on one side, and were hinged so that they
could be swung open and closed again, forming a cage with
three solid rock walls. The creature was in the cage, only a few
feet from me, a grotesque caricature of man. Its chest was
rounded, its shoulders stooped and heavy, its arms long. Short,
coarse hair bristled on its body, but its face was smooth and
brown, wide nostrils flaring and small eyes burning beneath a
thick, ridged brow. I saw a dark, damp patch on its side, a few
spatters of blood on the floor, and standing between us, one
hand on the bars, stood the old crone. She had turned to look
at me, and her eyes glowed with malevolence, with a hatred
more intense and inhuman than that of the creature itself.

The creature lunged at me. One huge hand tore at the bars
and the steel sang with vibration. I started to shout a warning
to the old woman, but it was not after her. It ignored her. It
reached out, groping for me through the bars, snarling with
broad lips drawn back. I backed away and Hodson touched my
shoulder.

'Come. We mustn't stay here. He knows you injured him
and I wouldn't trust even those steel bars if he goes berserk.'

'The old woman —'

'She will be all right,' he said.

He pushed me toward the laboratory. The snarling became
less violent and I heard the old woman speaking in some
strange language — speaking to the creature. And the second
metal door clanged shut behind us.

Hodson took me to the front room, motioned to a chair and
began searching through a drawer. I saw him slip a hypo-
dermic needle in his pocket.

'You aren't going to use that on it?' I asked.

He nodded and brought out a large box of medicinal supplies.

'A tranquillizer,' he said.

'But it'll tear you apart if you get near.'

'The woman can manage it,' he said. 'Wait here. I'll be back when I've repaired the damage you've done.' He went back through the curtains. I sat down and waited.

Hodson returned, his shirt sleeves rolled up, poured two large drinks and handed me one.

'It wasn't a serious wound,' he said. 'He will live.'

I nodded. Hodson sat down opposite me. The drink tasted strange on my dry tongue, and my fever was returning. There were so many things I wanted to ask, but I waited for Hodson to speak first.

'So this is the proper study of man? To shoot man?'

'Is it man?'

'Assuredly.'

'It attacked my camp. It was killing one of the horses. We had no choice.'

He nodded.

'Quite so,' he said. 'That is man's nature. To kill and to have no choice.' He shook his head wearily, then suddenly laughed.

'Well, you've found my secret. Now what?'

'I don't know. It's still a secret. I'd like a chance to examine the creature.'

'No. That isn't possible.'

'You've already examined it completely, I suppose?'

'Physically?' He shrugged. 'I'm more interested in studying his behaviour. That's why I've allowed him to run wild and unrestricted.'

'And yet it returns here? It comes back to a cage of its own choice?'

He laughed again.

'I told you. It is man's nature to have no choice. It returns because it is man, and man goes home. That is a basic instinct. Territorial possessiveness.'

'You're certain it is human?'

'Hominid. Yes. Absolutely.'

'Will you tell me about it?'

'It's a bit late for secrets.'

'How can you be sure it's human? Hominid? As opposed,

say, to some new form of ape? What is the definition, what criteria are you using?'

'Criteria? There is so much you fail to understand. There is only one definition of man. I used the absolute criteria.'

I waited, but he didn't clarify. He sipped his drink; he seemed to be waiting for my questions.

'You discovered it here, I take it?'

'In a sense, yes.'

'How long have you known about it?'

'For a generation.'

'Are there others?'

'Not at the moment.'

This was telling me nothing. I said: 'Why have you waited so long, why keep this secret? What have you gained by your silence?'

'Time. I told you once before. Time is essential. I'm studying him as a man, not as a curiosity. Naturally I had to have time for him to mature. Who can gauge man's behaviour by studying a child?'

'Then you found it when it was very young?'

'Yes. Very young indeed.'

He smiled strangely.

'And when did you determine it was human?'

'Before I . . . found him.'

'You aren't making sense,' I said. 'Why give me riddles at this stage? What is your definition of man?'

'I need no definition,' he said. He was enjoying this. He wanted to tell me, his irrestible urge to dumbfound his fellow scientists returned, his countenance livened.

'I didn't exactly discover him, you see,' he said. 'I know he is man because I created him.'

He regarded me through a long silence.

'You mean it's a mutation?'

'A very special form of mutation. It is not a variation, but a regression. What little I told you on your last uninvited visit was true, but it wasn't all the truth. I told you I'd discovered how to control mutation, but this went much further. In

mastering mutation, I found it was the key to cellular memory
– that the law of mutation be applied to unlock the forgotten
replications.'

He finished his drink. His face was flushed.

'You see, cells forget. That is why we grow old, for instance.
Our cells forget how to replicate youth. But this knowledge,
although forgotten, is still there, in the same way that things a
man forgets exist in his subconscious mind. Exactly the same,
on a different level. And as subconscious knowledge can be
remembered under hypnosis, so the cells can be induced to
remember by chemical treatment. And this, Brookes, is the
very root of life. It may, among other things, be the key to
immortality. We can teach our cells not to forget the replication of youth.' He shrugged. 'But man, as he is, isn't worthy of
immortality, and I'm not interested in giving it to him. It will
come. I am interested in man's evolution, and I've applied my
knowledge in that field. I am the first and only man who has
seen evolution as it occurs. Brookes, I am the creator of my
ancestor!'

There was more than enthusiasm in his face. There was
something akin to madness.

'But how —'

'Don't you understand yet? I treated the parents, chemic-
ally affecting their genes so that they carried a recessed
heredity. The offspring, the creature you have seen, is regressed back through aeons of time – carries the traits our cells
have long since forgotten. I could possibly have taken it even
further, back to the first forms of life, the single cellular
creatures that existed in the dawn of life. But that, too, is of no
interest to me. I limit myself to man.'

He took my glass, crossed the room and refilled it.

'How do you classify this creature?' I asked.

He sat down again, frowning.

'I'm not sure. The ancestor of a branch of modern man. Not
our branch, perhaps, but a parallel line. Man as he may have
been ten million years ago. Or five million years. Time is
essential but indefinite.'

'And it was actually born of parents living today?'

'The father is dead. I'm afraid that his offspring – or his ancestor, whichever you prefer – tore his throat out several years ago.' He said this with clinical detachment. 'The mother – did you wonder why the old woman could control it? Why it came back here when it was hurt? She is the mother.'

After a while I said, 'Good God.'

'Shocked or surprised?' Hodson asked.

'Surely it can't be right to create something so unnatural?'

He stared scornfully at me.

'Are you a scientist? Or a moralist? Surely, you know that science is all that matters. What does that old crone matter? What are a few dead sheep? Or a few dead men, for that matter? I have seen the behaviour of one of man's ancestors, and isn't that worth any amount of suffering?' He was talking rapidly, gesturing with both hands, his eyes boring into me.

'And the further possibilities are countless. Perhaps, with time to work in peace, I will learn to reverse the process. Even that. Perhaps I will be able to progress cellular memory. To sidestep evolution. The knowledge must already be there, the cells simply haven't learned it yet; they learn it gradually as they forget the old knowledge. But it's there, Brookes. It was there when the first life crawled out of the sea. The future and the past, side by side. Think of it! To create man as he will be a million years from now!'

I was in two minds, on two levels. I didn't know whether to believe him or not on the superficial scale, but deeper, where I couldn't help but believe, magnetized by his voice, my reactions were divided again. The fact, and the possibilities, were wonderful beyond comprehension, but the details were appalling, the use of human beings in this experiment grotesque. To think of a living woman giving birth to that monstrosity in the cage was abhorrent. Perhaps, in some ways, I was a moralist, and certainly scientific interest struggled against a surge of repulsion.

'Think of it!' Hodson repeated, his eyes turned inwards

now as he thought of it himself. His knuckles were white, tightening on his glass. He had been profoundly affected by this opportunity to speak of his discoveries, the overpowering urge to break the silence of twenty years. We had been talking for some time. A grey early light blocked the window; a bird was singing outside. In the surrounding hills day was breaking, day creatures awoke and night creatures slunk back to their warrens and dens, following the ways of nature, oblivious to the ways of science. But science was overtaking nature. I lighted a cigarette and drew the harsh smoke deeply into my lungs. I knew it wasn't a good thing, and it went far deeper than outraged morality.

'It can't be right, Hodson. Preying on these primitive people who don't understand what you are doing to them. That old woman —'

Surprisingly, he nodded in agreement. But not for the same reasons.

'Yes, that was a mistake. I'd misjudged the potency of my process and, more important and less forgivable, I failed to consider the theory of parallel evolution. This creature wasn't my first attempt, but it was the first to survive. The others didn't bear up to the strain, although the post-mortems proved most enlightening. But we learn from our blunders, and I have at least proved that all modern man did not descend from the same common ancestor. I suppose that was a worthwhile discovery. Evolution in the New World, at least in this part of South America, developed without connexion to the rest of the world and, more surprisingly, at a different time in history.' He had been talking softly, rather wearily, but now his oratorical tone returned, his eyes lighted once more.

'Twenty million years ago, sometime in the late Cenozoic era, and somewhere in Asia, the ancient primates divided into two branches. One branch led to modern apes, the other to creatures which became increasingly human. One million years ago, these creatures became *homo*. Forty thousand years ago, they became *sapiens*. And they are our ancestors, Brookes. Yours and mine. But these men did not come to the part of the

world. The same process of division occurred here, in much
the same way and for much the same reason, but countless ages
later in pre-history. The humans who developed here, like the
New World monkeys, were different in many respects. Less
advanced on the hereditary scale, because they emerged at a
later point, and had to survive harsher conditions in some
respects. The climate was the greatest factor responsible for
the differences. The hominids developed in relation to this
hostile climate, they became much tougher and resistant to
extremes, able to exist naked in freezing wind and water. In
that way they advanced faster, beyond our branch. But there
were fewer natural enemies here, they were the predominant
life form, and survival was gauged only against nature. While
our branch of mankind developed tools, thumbs, uncurved
spines, vocal cords and, finally, superior brains to enable them
to exist against the powerful predators, these people had no
need to advance along similar lines. Quite naturally, they did
not. The physically stronger lived to breed and pass on those
traits, while the intelligent, with no advantages in survival,
succumbed to the evolutionary laws and advanced at a much
slower rate. These creatures were as different from their Asian
and European counterparts as llamas from camels, capuchin
from rhesus.

'Who knows? Perhaps this branch was superior; given time
they might well have developed into supermen. But they
didn't have that time. Our branch had a head start and
developed too quickly. We became travellers. We ventured
down here from the north and the natives could not survive
against us, or beside us. They died out. Perhaps we killed
them, perhaps we brought disease unknown to them, perhaps
our superior brains succeeded in acquiring all the available
food. At any rate, they did not survive. But there was some
interbreeding. That was selective and the offspring retained
the qualities of both branches – the mind of one, the strength
of the other. They were remarkably adaptable to life. The
native branch ceased to exist, but the crossbreeds survived
alongside the new branch. God knows how long ago this cross-

breeding took place, perhaps fifty thousand years. They were still here when Darwin came, I know that. But, little by little, the native traits had weakened in the individuals. Although they may have been predominant at first, they were bred out by sheer weight of numbers, until only the odd throwback possessed them.'

He paused, choosing his words, while I waited in dumb fascination.

'The old woman is one of those atavisms, as far as I know the last and only living human to bear a prepotency of the vanishing characteristics. That was why I selected her for my experiment. Her genes were closer to the past, the memory was not buried so deeply, and the ancient traits were predominant. That was why I selected her, and that was where I blundered.

'Do you begin to understand?' he asked.

Behind him, the window had silvered as the sun began to slant down the hills. I was burning with fever, and a different fever had set my mind alight. I nodded.

'The experiment succeeded too well,' he continued. 'The result – you have seen the result. It is human, because it was born of woman, but it is not human as we know the word. It is fascinating and fabulous, certainly the living ancestor of an extinct branch of mankind, but not our ancestor. Not yours or mine and only partially the old woman's. And thus it is a dead end, a creature whose offspring are already extinct. There is much to be gained by studying it, but little to be learned of man. I have formulated the theoretical descent of a being that no longer exists, but it is not much different to tracing the remote ancestry of the passenger pigeon or the dodo. You can understand the frustration of that?'

'But my God, what an opportunity —'

'Perhaps. But it is not my field. I will give it to the world when I have applied it to my own pursuits. Another experiment, eliminating the error. If only I can live long enough to see it through. With what I have already learned from this creature – from watching it grow and mature, with strictly clinical interest —' His mind seemed to be wandering now, his thoughts confused, divided between acquired knowledge and the further knowledge he anticipated. 'It killed its father when it was twelve years old. It developed much more rapidly than man. I judge its lifespan to be a mere thirty years, certainly not more. But it will not grow old. This branch could not survive an old age, it will retain its physical powers until it has attained its normal lifespan and then it will die. And with it will die its genus. Perhaps the post-mortem will be interesting. The study of its life has been frustrating. It can't speak. It has vocal cords but they aren't capable of mastering more than bestial sounds. That was the greatest disappointment. Think of being able to converse, in your own language, with pre-historic man! It's cranial capacity is about 1,550 cubic centimetres – roughly the average of Neanderthal man, but its brain is relatively free of convolutions. Its branch did not need a mind, it needed strength and endurance. Did you see its eyes glow in the dark? The inner wall of the eye is coated with guanin, like most night creatures. Perhaps that is more valuable than thought to the creature. It hardly thinks at all. It feels, it acts by instinct. Its basic instinct seems to be to kill. Only the old woman has any control over it now. The Indian used to manage it by his great strength, but soon it became too powerful and vicious even for him to handle. It attacked me one day. That was where the Indian acquired that scar, of course. He saved my life, but even he fears it now. Only the old crone – it shows the basic instinct of motherlove – it killed its father, but obeys its mother without needing to understand her ...'

I shuddered. There was something terrible in this regard of a beast for a human, and even more terrible knowing that the pitiful old woman regarded that monstrous creation as her child. I wondered, with absolute horror, if she had given it a name. I closed my eyes, uselessly. The horror was behind them.

Hodson stood up and took my glass. He brought it back refilled and I took a long swallow.

'You intend to continue this experiment? To create another creature like that?'

'Of course. Not like that, however. The next one must be our ancestor. The same process, with parents of our branch of mankind. It is only necessary to treat the male, although the regressed mutation occurs in the female. The Indian might be an ideal specimen, in fact.'

'You can't,' I said.

Hodson's eyes widened, amused.

'It's fiendish!'

'Ah, the moralist again. Do you consider the creature evil? Brookes, if you had been born a million years in the future – how would your behaviour seem to the men of that distant time?'

'I don't know,' I said, very slowly. I had trouble forming the words. Something seemed to weigh my tongue down, and the same weight pressed on my eyes. Hodson's eyes burned at me, and then they began to dull. The fire had left him, extinguished in his revelations, and he became solemn, perhaps knowing he had once again succumbed to his old fault; he had told me too much.

'Do you believe me?' he asked, smiling.

'I don't know,' I repeated. I moved my head from side to side. It swivelled beneath a great burden, my neck faltered under the heaviness and my head dropped. I was staring at the floor. I could hear Hodson speaking, far away.

'It wouldn't have taken much imagination to think of these things,' he said. 'But it would have taken fantastic discoveries to actually do them. Perhaps I have merely been toying with you, Brookes. You know how I have always taken pleasure in shocking people. Perhaps this is all simply a hoax, eh? What do you think, moralist? Have I been deceiving you?'

I tried to shake my head again. It hung down, lower, my knees seemed to be rising to meet my face. The chair receded from under me. I fought under this enormous gravity, struggled upwards and stood before Hodson. He was still smiling. The room whirled and spun, his face was the only fixed point in my focus, my eyes were held on his grinning teeth.

'You're not well, Brookes?' he asked.

'I ... dizzy ... I ...'

The empty glass was still in my hand. I looked at it, saw the points of light reflected along the rim; saw the tiny flakes of white powder in the bottom ... Saw nothing.

14

I floated back through planes of awareness and Hodson's face floated over me, lighted from beneath with weird effect. I wondered, vaguely, why he had stopped grinning, then realized I was no longer in the front room, that I'd been unconscious for some time. I was dressed, but my boots were off. They were on the floor beside the candle that shot dancing light upwards, sweeping Hodson's countenance and fading out weakly in the corners of the room. It was the room I'd slept in on my last stay, and I was lying on my back on the cot.

'Ah. You are awake,' Hodson said.

I blinked. I felt all right.

'What happened to me?'

'You fainted. You have a fever, apparently you've been ill. I didn't realize that, or I wouldn't have deliberately shocked you so outrageously. I'm sorry.'

'That drink – you drugged me.'

'Nonsense. You simply fainted. In your feverish state my little amusement was too much for you. Your perceptions were inflamed. Why, for a few minutes, I believe you actually thought it was the truth.'

'You told me ... those things ...'

'Were all pure fabrication. Oh, there was a basis in fact; I have indeed experimented along those lines, but without success. I'm afraid I simply couldn't resist the opportunity to – pull your leg shall we say? Of course, had you been thinking clearly you would have seen the impossibility of such a tale.'

'But I saw the creature.'

'An ape. I assure you it was merely an ape. A curious cross-breeding of Old and New World primates, resulting from one of my experiments in controlled mutation. Unsuccessful, from my point of view, actually, since it's merely a hybrid, not actually a mutation – far less a regression.' He chuckled at the absurdity of such a concept.

'I don't believe you.'

Hodson shrugged.

'As you like. Your opinions cease to interest me, now that I've had my little game.'

'Will you allow me to examine it then? There can be no harm in that, if it's just an ape.'

'That, I regret to say, is impossible. The wound you inflicted upon it was more serious than it appeared. There were internal complications and my surgical skill is paltry. I'm afraid that the ape has expired.'

'An examination of the body will satisfy me.'

'I have no desire to satisfy you. If it weren't for you, the ape would still be alive. At any rate, the remains have already been dissected and disposed of.'

'Already?'

'You have been sleeping for —' he regarded his watch, 'some ten hours. Sufficient time to derive whatever scientific benefit can be found in examining a deceased hybrid. You may see my notes, if you like.'

'Everything you told me was a lie?'

'Not a lie. What is a lie? A study in man's gullibility, perhaps. An objective observation of the effect of the absurd upon the credulous. You have undoubtedly heard how I used to enjoy shocking people with unfounded theories? My pleasure was not so much in the outraged reception of my statements, as in observing a man's reaction afterwards. This, in its way, was also a study of mankind. And that, Brookes, is my field, in all its manifold aspects.'

I shook my head. It should have been so much easier to believe him now than it had been before. But, somehow, I couldn't quite do so. His tone lacked that enthusiasm and excitement it had carried before – an enthusiasm derived from success and pride in his accomplishments. And yet, I had not been thinking clearly, I'd been feverish and weak and susceptible to suggestion, and Hodson was a master of deliberate deception. I tried to reason, but my thoughts came helter skelter, my mind whirled, touching on valid points and then spinning on before I could follow a line of reasoning.

'Rest now,' Hodson said, far away again. 'You'll be able to laugh at yourself in the morning.'

He took the candle with him. The room was black, and a sympathetic blackness began to nudge me towards sleep, a blank space growing larger in my brain.

The light had returned when I opened my eyes again.

Anna stood beside the bed, holding the candle. The curtains swayed behind her, the house was very quiet. She smiled down at me, looking concerned.

'You are all right?' she asked.

I nodded.

'I was worried for you.'

She hovered over me uncertainly. She wasn't embarrassed, because she knew nothing of propriety or shame, but she seemed undecided.

'May I sit beside you?' she asked.

'Of course.'

I slid over. Anna sat on the edge of the cot. I was still wearing my shirt and trousers and she was still naked. She curled one leg beneath her and placed the candle on the floor, stared at it for a moment and then moved it a few needless inches. Her smile was shy, although she did not know what shyness was. She placed a cool hand on my brow. My fever seemed to have left me now, but that cool palm felt very good and I placed my hand over hers. She leaned slightly toward me and her firm breast brushed against my forearm. I remembered how much I had wanted her the last time we were together in this little cell; realized that desire was stronger now than before; wondered if she knew, if she understood, if she had come to me because she felt the same way.

'I don't disturb you?' she asked.

'You do. Very much.'

'Shall I leave?'

'No. Stay here.'

It wasn't the playful teasing of a woman, she meant exactly what she said, honest and artless.

'You are not yet well —'

I moved my hand to her hip. Her flesh was silken warmth, her hair so black it seemed a hole in space, falling over her shoulders and absorbing the candlelight completely, without gloss or shine. My hand moved, stroking her thigh, and my mind avoided all thoughts of right and wrong.

'Shall I lie down?' she asked.

I pulled her to me and the length of our bodies pressed together. I could feel her smooth heat through my rough clothing, and her lips parted willingly against my mouth.

'I don't know how to do it,' she said.

'You've never made love?'

'No. You will show me how?'

'Do you want me to?'

'Very much,' she said. Her arms clung to me, timidly but firmly. I shifted, rising above her, and she lay back, watching and waiting for me. Her passion showed only in her eyes, and was all the more inspiring because she did not know the accepted motions of manifesting desire.

'Really? You never have?' I asked.

My hand moved on her gently.

'Never. There has been no one to teach me.'

It cut sharply through my fascination. She hadn't come because she wanted me, but simply because I was the first man available to her. My hand stopped moving on her flat belly, she frowned, looking into my face.

'What is wrong?' she asked.

Another thought was toying with the edge of perception, a vague uneasiness that had seized its foothold in that moment of diminished desire. I wasn't quite sure what it was . . .

'Does Hodson know you've come to me?' I asked.

'Yes.'

'He doesn't mind?'

'Why should he mind?'

'I don't — Anna, when I was unconscious – did Hodson do anything to me?'

'He fixed you. Made you well.'

'What did he do?'

My heart was thundering, pumping icebergs through my arteries.

'What is wrong? Why have you stopped loving me?'

'What did he do?'

'I don't know. He made you well. He took you to his laboratory and fixed you so that you would be all right for me to come to . . .'

She said this as though it were the most natural thing in the world. The icebergs melted in my blood.

'Why have you stopped?' she asked. 'Am I no good for making love?'

My mind erupted in horror.

I stood beside the bed, my boots in my hand. I didn't remember getting up. Anna was staring at me, hurt and disappointed, unable to understand how she had failed – a child punished without reason. But what reason could I give her? She was of a different world and there was nothing I could say. My breath came hard, but not with desire now. I wanted only one thing, to escape from that fiendish place, and Anna's graceful body had become loathsome to me.

I moved to the door. Anna watched me all the while. I couldn't even say farewell to her, couldn't even beg her not to give the alarm. She was still staring as I passed through the curtains and they closed between us. It was more than those curtains that stood between us. I went down the hallway to the front room. The house was silent, Anna made no sound behind me. The front room was empty and I moved quietly on bare feet. I didn't know what Hodson would resort to if he found me, didn't know if he would force me to stay, even if he might not kill me. But I felt no fear of this. The numb horror of the situation was too great to share its place with any other emotion, too great to be realized; and my mind froze in self-preservation.

I crossed the room and went out of the door, started walking calmly across the narrow basin of the valley, almost sluggish in my determination. The night was black and cold, my body felt like a heated rod passing through the absolute zero of space, my course preordained and no friction to halt me. The ground rose and I began an angled ascent of the hills; I noticed objectively that I was climbing the same hill where the vultures had dropped down to feast the last time I departed from Hodson's. But this made no impression. Everything was external, my breath hung before me and the clouded sky was low, blanketing the hills as I climbed up to meet it.

My thoughts were superficial and purely functional, my mind rejecting the horror of the situation and concentrating on the task at hand, plotting the logical course. I had to ascend the hills, keeping in a north-eastern direction which would bring me out east of the sheer cliffs which housed the tunnel, then descend the opposite side towards the north-west, compensating for the angle and coming out somewhere near the waterfall. The high, unscalable cliffs would be visible for miles as I walked down, and I felt certain I could find them, and find the camp in relation to them. I told myself I was safe now; there was no way that Hodson could find me.

Halfway up the incline I paused to catch my breath and realized I still carried my boots in my hand. I sat down and pulled them on, looking back toward the house as I tied the laces. The house was dark and quiet. Perhaps Anna was still waiting and wondering in that little room, or perhaps Hodson knew that pursuit would prove futile. The night was very dark, and there was no way he could follow me over that rocky land. Even the extraordinary Indian would not be able to track a man at night through such terrain. Hodson had no dog to follow by scent, no way to know what direction I'd fled in, no way to —

My fingers snapped the laces.

There was one way.

There was one being behind me with the senses and instincts of the hunting carnivore – one creature capable of silently tracking me through the blackest night – one creature whose eyes glowed with night vision and seethed with hatred —

I ran, mad with fear.

I ran. The broken laces slapped at my ankle, loose stones slid beneath my feet, trees loomed up suddenly before me and I crashed through in wild flight. I stumbled and fell, leaped up to fall again, banging against rocks and trees, tearing my fingernails at the roots as I heaved myself over boulders and caught at sapling limbs, crushing my shins and elbows without feeling pain. My mind was outside my body; I watched myself scramble through dark confusion; saw my forehead collide solidly with a rocky overhang and a line of blood seep down my temple; saw my balance tilt as I overstepped a ridge and tumbled down, legs still churning – and, all the time, apart from my body, my mind screamed that Hodson would have no qualms, that Hodson had no regard for human life, that Hodson would release the creature —

And then my mind was back inside my throbbing head, and I leaned exhausted against a mangled tree at the top of the mountain. I'd run for hours and for miles, or for minutes and for yards, it was all the same. My chest heaved so violently that it seemed the tree was vibrating and the land was running beneath my feet. I looked back. All the trees were vibrating. A razorback of land humped up in the centre and crumbled at the edges, a solid wave of earth skimmed over the rock toward me, uprooting brush and trees in its wake, and the earth itself groaned in agony. Far away a deep rumble sounded for a moment, and then died out. The movement ceased and the moaning faded. The land looked different, the contours shifted and altered, but the same wind cried above and the same blood pounded through my bursting veins.

15

Gregorio found me in the morning.

I was still walking, following some natural instinct toward the camp, the long night a blurred memory behind me, highlights and shadows in contorted chiaroscuro and strained awareness. My panic had left with the dawn, I was walking on calmly and steadily, placing one foot before the other in studied concentration. From time to time I looked up, but I couldn't see the cliffs; lowered my head and watched my feet; noticed that the broken lace was still flaying at my ankle but didn't think to tie it. Then I looked up again and there was Gregorio. He was on the grey, staring at me, his mouth open, and I saw him through the red-rimmed frame of hollow eyes.

He moved forward on the horse and I leaned against his knee.

'Thank God,' he said.

He swung from the saddle.

'How did you find me?' I asked.

'I rode this way. I didn't know. I thought that I had killed you.'

That made no sense, but I didn't want sense. I collapsed against him.

I was in Gregorio's tent. My own tent was still spread over the ground. Gregorio gave me a tin mug of water and I gulped it down, feeling it trickle over my chin.

'You are all right now?'

'Yes.'

'I thought that I killed you.'

'I don't understand. How —'

'When you did not return in the morning – when it was light

– I followed your tracks. And the tracks of the creature. I followed to the waterhole and saw where you had gone into the cave behind the water. There were no tracks coming out. I called to you and there was no answer. I did not dare to enter and I returned to the camp. But I felt very bad because of this. I waited all day and felt bad because I had not gone in the cave. I drank pisco and waited and when it was night again and the pisco was gone I was not so afraid. I went back to the waterfall, pretending that I was brave and that it was shameful I had not gone into the cave. I called again and then I went past the water and stood inside the tunnel. I stood in the entrance but I had no courage to go farther. I could not see the sky and I had no torch. I called more but there were only echoes. I thought you were dead. Then I thought that perhaps you were injured and were too far away to hear me call, and so I fired the rifle three times so that you would hear.'

He paused, his hands moving expressively and frowned as he sought the words.

'The noise of the gun and the echoes – they caused something. The noise inside the mountain. It caused the mountain to move. I ran out just in time. I saw the cave close, the rocks came together and the cliffs moved backwards so that the top slid down. But it slid on the other side, not on me. I thought you were inside, maybe you were injured, and that I had buried you. Thank God it was not so.'

I nodded. 'The vibrations. There were faults in the rock. I felt the mountain move last night, but I thought it was my imagination. Did it move very far?'

'I think far. I could not tell, it moved on the other side. To the south.'

'Perhaps it is just as well,' I said.

'If the creature was inside —' Gregorio began.

'Perhaps there are things that man should not know,' I told him. And then I suddenly understood the full import of that, the full extent of what I did not know. Hodson's words sounded in my mind . . .

'*It is only necessary to treat the male . . .*'

Gregorio looked at me with concern. He thought I was sick again, because I was very pale.

Two days later I was well – as well as I will ever be. We rode back along the path of my flight, in the early morning. My horse was as placid as ever, despite the gruesome wound on its flank. It was a good horse, and I was glad it had survived. Gregorio was curious as to why I should insist on this journey, but there was nothing I could tell him. There was nothing I could tell anyone, and when we rode over the top of the hills my last hopes vanished. It was what I had expected, what I had known with terrible anticipation.

The narrow valley was no longer there. The sheer cliffs at the apex had slid back at a gentler angle, forming the Tarpeian Rock from which my hopes were hurled to their death, and the base spread out in broken rock and upheaved earth in a shallow triangle where the valley had been. There was no sign whatsoever of Hodson's house or the cave beyond. I looked down from the hills, but hadn't the heart to descend. There was nothing to be found amidst that wreckage that would help me, no way to discover which of Hodson's stories had been deception. After all, it might have been an ape . . .

It might have been. Perhaps he had done nothing to me in that laboratory. Perhaps.

There was only one way to tell, and the method was too horrible to contemplate; it shared a common path with madness.

'Shall we go down?' Gregorio asked.

I had a fleeting thought of Anna, innocent and helpless within the framework Hodson had built around her life, buried somewhere beneath those countless tons of stone. Had she still been waiting in my bed? It didn't seem to matter. I had no sorrow to spare.

'Shall we go down?' Gregorio asked again.

'It won't be necessary.'

'This is all you wished to look for?'

'This is all there is, my friend.'

Gregorio blinked. He didn't understand. We rode back toward the camp, and he watched me nervously, wondering why I would not look at him. But it had nothing to do with him.

It was raining, but there was sunlight above the clouds. A flock of geese passed overhead, flying in precise formation toward the horizon, following a call they did not understand. Birds were singing in the trees and small animals avoided our path. The world was moving on at its own slow pace, with its own inexorable momentum, and nature avoided us and ignored us. Perhaps, for a few moments while the land was rumbling, nature had acted in outrage and defence, but now it was quiet once more; now it would survive.

We broke camp and headed back to Ushuaia.

There was a letter from Susan waiting at the hotel, telling how much she loved me, and Jones told me how Cape Horn looked from the air . . .

The restaurant was closing.

The late diners had departed, the waiters had gathered in the corner, waiting for me to leave. Susan had gone. My glass was empty and I was alone. I signalled and the waiter came over quickly with the bill. He thought I was drunk. I over-tipped him and went out to the street. It was late; only a few people hurried past. They were strangers, and I was a stranger. I began walking home, slowly and thoughtfully, accompanied by whatever horror I may, or may not, bear in my loins. I will never know.

There are some things it is better not to know.

Ghost & Horror in Pan

Occult & Supernatural

Richard Cavendish
THE BLACK ARTS   40p

Frank Edwards
STRANGE PEOPLE   20p

Muriel Grey
THE BOOK OF DREAMS   30p

Rosalind Heywood
THE SIXTH SENSE   35p
THE INFINITE HIVE   35p

Douglas Hunt
EXPLORING THE OCCULT   30p

June Johns
KING OF THE WITCHES (illus.)   25p

Eric Maple
THE DARK WORLD OF WITCHES
(illus.)   30p
THE REALM OF GHOSTS (illus.)   30p

Leon Petulengro
SECRETS OF ROMANY ASTROLOGY
   AND PALMISTRY   20p

Ira Levin

'At last I have got my wish. I am ridden by a book that plagues my mind and continues to squeeze my heart with fingers of bone. I swear that Rosemary's Baby is the most unnerving story I've read' – KENNETH ALLSOP

'. . . if you read this book in the dead of night, do not be surprised if you feel the urge to keep glancing behind you' – QUEEN

'a darkly brilliant tale of modern devilry that like James' Turn of the Screw, induces the reader to believe the unbelievable. I believed it and was altogether enthralled'

— TRUMAN CAPOTE

Science Fiction in Pan

These and other PAN Books are obtainable
from all booksellers and newsagents. If you
have any difficulty please send purchase price
plus 7p postage to PO Box 11, Falmouth,
Cornwall.
While every effort is made to keep prices low,
it is sometimes necessary to increase prices
at short notice. PAN Books reserve the right
to show new retail prices on covers which may
differ from those previously advertised in the
text or elsewhere.